By the same author:

Cover photo: Old Town Square, Krakow, Poland

ID 135365468 © **Patryk Kosmider** | **Dreamstime.com**

Cover design: Raymond McCullough, Precious Oil Productions Ltd.

Angel
on Guard

Gerry McCullough

Published by

Precious Oil
PUBLICATIONS
www.preciousoil.com/publications

ISBN 13: 978-1-7384365 0 7

ISBN 10:   1-7384365 0 0

First published **2023**

10a Listooder Road, Crossgar, Downpatrick, Northern Ireland BT30 9JE

Thanks to my husband, Raymond, for cover design, editing, proof-reading and general encouragement.

Chapter One

Angeline Murphy, Angel to her friends, devil to her enemies, ran lightly down the steps of the BBC building at the corner of Belfast's Ormeau Avenue, and turned the corner into Bedford Street. Her day's work in the BBC was finished, it would soon be Christmas, and Angel had booked two weeks off work to enjoy the festive season. She loved Christmas, and she was looking forward to seeing more of her friends and family, to watching some good films, and to eating and drinking to her own satisfaction.

It was getting late, but Angel intended to get in some last minute Christmas shopping before going home. She pulled her warm jacket, with its artificial fur collar, more closely around her, jammed the woolly hat further down on her head, and hurried along towards the city centre. She waited at the traffic crossing, then walked quickly over the road into Donegal Square West, and saw the Christmas lights shining everywhere. The City Hall was lit up as if by magic, and the stalls of the Christmas market glittered all around it.

'Please! Please help me!'

A soft voice in her ear made her turn her head.

A young woman, scantily dressed for such a cold winter's day, in a flimsy summer jacket and a very short cotton frock, was stretching out a hand towards her. She had long, straggling dark hair swept back from her forehead, and huge piteous dark brown eyes which seemed on the verge of shedding a flood of tears. It was clear that she was in trouble of some sort.

It was not in Angel's nature to turn her back on anyone in need.

'Yes?' she said.

'Please! I've nowhere to go. I need help.'

Angel made a quick decision. 'You're freezing. Come on, I'll get you a cup of coffee. In here.'

She led the girl into the nearest coffee shop – a *Clements* – and sat her down at a table for two in a corner where they could talk privately. All round them the loud, excited buzz of the conversation of other Christmas shoppers would drown out whatever the girl had to say to her.

'I'll go up and get the coffee from the counter, if you wait here,' Angel said. 'What would you like? Cappuccino? Latte? Espresso?'

The girl looked puzzled. 'Coffee,' she said eventually.

'Black or white?'

'Black.'

It seemed to Angel, standing at the counter, that the girl didn't know anything about the different types of coffee now available in the more up market coffee shops. Her voice had already told Angel that she wasn't local. Was she a mid European from a poor background? It seemed possible.

She set the two black coffees down on the table, together with a plate of muffins, and offered the girl a packet of sugar. The girl seized it gratefully, opened it, and stirred it into her cup. When Angel offered her more, she took two more and her face lit up. She waited politely for Angel to lift her own cup, then started to gulp the hot liquid down eagerly.

'As black as the devil, as hot as hell and as sweet as love – the proper way to drink coffee, they say.' Angel sipped her own hot cupful, and grinned. The girl looked puzzled, but said nothing and continued to drink her coffee.

'My name is Angeline, but my friends call me Angel for short,' Angel said. 'What's your own name?'

'Elena.'

'Hi, Elena. So, you asked me for help. What can I do?'

'I have nowhere to sleep tonight. Can you help me get somewhere?'

'First of all, have a muffin, while I think about that.' She handed the plate to Elena and encouraged the girl to take one. The name of her friend Mary Branagh, who ran a community on the upper Antrim Road, and who had helped friends of Angel's – and Angel herself – before this, came at once to mind, but before bringing this waif to Mary, it might be good to find out more about her.

'So, Elena, tell me about yourself. Where do you come from? And why have you nowhere to sleep?'

Elena hesitated, biting hungrily at her muffin. Then all at once she burst into speech. 'I come from Poland. I lived there until I was seventeen. We were very poor. We lived in the country, and my father worked on a farm, until he was killed in an accident with a tractor – when I was fifteen.

'My mother did some work there, too, when she could, but I have seven brothers and sisters, so she had little free time. She had to look after us, especially my littlest sister, who is not three yet, and the next oldest who are four and five. The others go to school, but my mother still has to cook for them, make them clothes – oh, you must know how much work is to bring up children. When I reach seventeen and pass my exams, I leave school at end of year and look for a job.'

She fell silent, and Angel saw that there were tears in her eyes.

Angel waited silently, smiling sympathetically. Presently Elena went on.

'A friend of mine, Magda, tell me there are good jobs in England and Ireland. She know a man who organise jobs for Polish girls who want to go there to work. Magda say she intend to go, and she give me this man's address and phone number. His name is Szczepan, and he lives in Krakow. I ring him, and he say he'll get a job for me. He sound nice. I told my mother about it, and I say I send her money regularly, and come home as often as I can.'

Angel was still silent, but found herself unable to smile any longer. It was only too clear what was coming.

'He is a wicked man!' Elena burst out. As she talked faster, and was clearly getting more upset by the memory of the things she

3

was sharing, the girl's English had begun to get a little worse. 'I go to Krakow by bus to meet him, and he pretend that he has jobs for Magda and me as waitresses here in Northern Ireland. He say because we both speak English it easy to get us jobs.'

'Yes, you speak English well,' Angel murmured.

'We both learn it at school.' Elena almost smiled for a moment. 'I thought I need to speak Irish to work here, but not. Everyone speaks English good.'

Angel couldn't help laughing, but stopped herself at once.

'So, what happened, Elena?' she asked, and saw the girl's face crumple.

'He gets man called Pete to take us to airport and put us on plane to London. Another man meet us there put us on plane to Belfast. Then man called Jason meet us here. There were no jobs in cafes. Instead, he took us to a house in the country where he brought men to us, for us to sleep with.' Elena's voice had sunk to a whisper. 'We have no money. We don't know where we are. It is dark when we arrive, and the country is strange to us. We are kept locked in our bedroom except when he come to fetch one of us to go to another bedroom where there is a man.'

'Us? You and Magda?'

'No, there are twenty of us. We sleep in a big room – a dorm, a dormitory, I think one of the girls call it. The windows are barred. We can't get out.'

'But you are out now.'

'Yes.'

Elena looked down into her empty cup.

'More coffee?' Angel suggested.

'Please. You are very kind.'

Angel took the cups to the counter for a refill. When she sat down again, placing Elena's cup in front of her, she remembered to offer the sugar. Elena took some eagerly.

'Muffin?' Angel asked.

'Please.'

'So, I have a friend who'll look after you for tonight, at least. We'll think about what to do after we've sorted that, okay? Drink your coffee and don't worry. You're going to be safe, Elena. Do you understand that?'

Elena smiled tremulously, and began to gulp her second cup of coffee. Angel allowed her to enjoy it in peace, without further questions. When the girl had finished, she said, 'Okay. Time to go.'

Elena got up stiffly. Angel realised that she was in pain.

'Are you sore?'

'Yes, when I sit for a while, or lie down, the soreness comes back.'

'Come on, my car's not far away, parked behind the BBC building. We'll go and see my friend. Her name's Mary. Mary Branagh. You'll like her.'

It occurred to her, as they walked the short distance to the car, that she was expecting Elena to trust her, and to trust Mary, too. For all Elena knew, they might be mixed up with the people who had imprisoned her. She smiled encouragingly at the girl, and hoped she wouldn't decide to run away. She would learn to trust them, over time, if she gave them the chance to help her.

As she unlocked her car and ushered Elena into the passenger seat, Angel could barely contain her anger. The brutes who had obviously beaten Elena up to get her cooperation and submission deserved anything Angel could do to them. She was determined to take action, to stop this horrific business and to punish the men who ran it. Quite how, she didn't know yet. But she would find a way.

Chapter Two

In the huge house on the outskirts of South Belfast, two men were talking. The current speaker was a big man, with wide shoulders – which he certainly needed to help him carry the enormous amount of weight spread over his body, especially round the stomach. His face just now was bright red with anger. His hair receded from a forehead corrugated with frustration, incredulity and horror.

He cursed freely, his speech interlarded with four letter words.

'Jason, you'd better have a good story,' he said amongst many other things. 'I want to know how this happened. The boss will want to know as well, see?'

His companion winced visibly. He was a slender good looking young man, dressed much more smartly than the other, in a grey pinstriped suit of the type worn by businessmen, with a yellow silk cravat tied round his throat and tucked into his open necked pale blue shirt.

'Bobby, I just don't know. It's a mystery.'

The two men looked down at the body lying between their feet, soaked in blood from a cruel gunshot wound in the head.

'And what am I supposed to do with this stiff?' broke out Bobby after a moment's silence. 'How am I going to get rid of it? This ain't the sort of guy who won't be missed. The polis'll be hunting round after him and if they find out he's been here, we'll be in big trouble – no matter where we dump him.'

He glared at Jason again. 'This is all your fault. And the girl's gone, you tell me? And all the rest of them? So what happens when she spills her story and points the cops here?'

'She doesn't know where she's been,' said Jason, trying to keep his cool. 'None of them do. She won't have a clue – won't be able to tell anyone where to look. And she won't want to go to the cops, anyway. This is murder, don't forget. She'll be scared silly.'

'Maybe,' Bobby conceded. 'Who knows? And we've lost all our merchandise. We'll need to get hold of a whole new cargo. We'll just have to hope for the best on that one. But the worst of it is this girl. If we could get her back, now, that might save any more trouble. But, hey, the main thing is this stiff. We need to get rid of the body, somehow.'

'Well, that's your type of thing, Bobby, not mine,' Jason murmured hopefully.

'Right now, it's yours as well,' Bobby told him forcefully. 'I'll need help to get him out to the car. Then we'll have to find somewhere to dump him out of sight, somewhere no one goes looking as a general rule. Any thoughts about that?'

Jason pondered. 'I might have.'

Bobby grabbed three plastic raincoats from the wardrobe and found two pairs of gloves. He handed a raincoat and one pair of gloves to Jason, instructing him, 'Put these on. We need to keep ourselves free of blood.' He put on the second raincoat and the gloves himself, then wrapped the third raincoat round the dead man, particularly the head, being careful as he did so to avoid getting any blood on himself. 'We'll clear up here after we've dumped him. Don't need to waste time right now.'

Together the two men lifted the body. They crept cautiously down the stairs, needing to avoid being seen. The girls had all run, leaving their dormitory empty, and Jason knew that there were no clients around right now. There were no live in servants and the cook and cleaners who came in daily were long gone. It should be safe enough. But still, they were careful.

When they left by the kitchen door and reached the Shogun 4x4 – which had been left parked at the rear of the house – Bobby opened the back door of the car. Together they prepared to hoist the body into the rear space. The plastic coat would be between the dead man and the seat. 'That should minimise marks on the upholstery,' Bobby grunted. 'Come on, now, heave. Let's get it inside before any nosy so and so comes poking into our business.'

The body was much heavier than Jason had expected, getting it down the stairs had been a nightmare, but with considerable difficulty he managed his share of the work, heaving it onto the back seat. A few minutes later they had it in the car with the door *safely closed and were driving as fast as they could – first out into the street at the front of the house, then turning off quickly, to reach winding country roads – heading for the place Jason had suggested.*

When they turned off presently into an even more private path, the four by four moved easily over the rough track. Jason directed Bobby through what he explained was the side entrance to a big empty demesne house. They drove on for some time, Jason giving directions. 'Pull up here,' he said at last.

They were in an overgrown patch, hidden from normal view by a clump of trees, none of them very tall, although high enough to give cover. Clearly they were of relatively new growth.

'This used to be the kitchen garden,' Jason said. 'I lived near here as a kid, and the house was empty even then. I used to come in here with my mates and play pretend games – cops and robbers, pirates, stuff like that. The house is closer than you might think. I think the servants used to come out to pick vegetables and to draw water from the well. Before my time – but the well's still here.'

Bobby looked at him.

'We can dump the body in the well,' Jason explained. 'We'll have to lift the cover off first. But with two of us, that shouldn't be too hard.'

'Not a bad idea,' Bobby said grudgingly.

'I'll go first and check exactly where the well is,' Jason offered. 'I remember it okay – but it was a while ago, I'd just better make sure I've got it right.'

He slid out of the passenger seat and disappeared into the darkness, leaving Bobby to the unpleasant company of the dead man and the loneliness of the empty house and grounds. After what seemed to Bobby an unnecessarily long time, Jason came back.

'Okay,' he said. 'We still have to get the cover off, but we might as well take the stiff along with us.'

Trying to stifle their groans – they were tough men, weren't they? – the two men lifted the body out of the car and stumbled off into the blackness of the night, Jason leading the way. Bobby had brought the torch he kept in the glove compartment of his car, but it was hard enough to manage it while still doing his share of carrying the dead man. After a while he switched it off and stuck it in his pocket, relying instead on the faint moonlight which shone down on the path through the kitchen garden.

'This is it,' Jason whispered presently. The car had already made plenty of noise, to say nothing of their stumbling progress towards the well, but somehow Jason felt safer whispering. 'Put him down, and let's get the lid off.'

They dumped the body beside the well, and Bobby looked at the heavy concrete lid with considerable apprehension.

'Okay,' he said. 'Let's get going.'

Together the two men each grasped one side of the lid and began to heave. Nothing happened.

'This is useless,' Bobby said.

'Tell you what,' Jason suggested, 'we should try sliding it sideways instead.'

Bobby was too winded to reply, but grunted in affirmation.

'Push to the right,' Jason said. 'My right and your left, that would be,' he added hastily.

They began to push. At first it seemed like more of the same – nothing happening. Then they felt something give, and suddenly the lid was beginning to slide across the top of the well.

'Don't let it go over the edge onto the ground,' Jason gasped. 'We'd never get it back up again. Let's just lift yer man now.'

They stopped pushing and left the heavy lid balanced precariously halfway across the top of the well, while they bent to pick up the dead body. As before, Jason took the head while Bobby lifted the legs. They had begun to swing the man head first over the edge of the well when a thought occurred to Jason.

'Shouldn't we get the raincoat off him? When they find him, maybe it could be identified?'

'Get a grip on your panties!' scoffed Bobby. 'It's Asda's best – they must sell hundreds of 'em all over the country, with our weather. 'Sides, what'll we do with it, all covered in blood? We'll have to dump it sometime. Might as well be here. The big idea is that nobody's

going to find the body, right? Why would anyone go poking in a well that isn't ever used?'

'Fair enough.' Jason continued to push and pull the body until it was in a position to slide down into the watery depths far below. The splash that followed seemed remote but still fearsome.

'Let's have a wee break,' suggested Bobby. 'Then we'll get thon lid back on and get the hell out of here.'

'Right.'

They sat side by side on the edge of the well and smoked quietly for the time necessary to finish a cigarette each. Then Jason stood up. 'Don't know about you, big man, but I'd like to get this over with. If you've had enough of a rest, let's get working on that lid.'

They threw the butts of their cigarettes down the well, and bent afresh to their task.

But before they could get the lid moved into place they began to hear cautious movements in the trees around them.

'What's that?'

'Dunno.'

'Let's get out of here.'

As they hurriedly turned to go, a shot sounded from nearby, then another one, then a whole barrage more.

The first shot caught Jason in the back. The second hit Bobby's chest. There was really no need for the next half dozen, but they were fired anyway, to make sure the job was completed.

Chapter Three

Mary's community house was halfway along the Antrim Road on the outskirts of Belfast. It was a reasonably big place. It could shelter the half dozen who lived there and went in and out to work – as teachers, nurses, even a supermarket checkout worker – and still have room to give refuge to people in need.

Angel drove up to it and parked inside the gate on the small tarmac area amid the flowerbeds and grass. The house looked bright and welcoming, with lights shining from the downstairs windows. Angel took Elena over to the door at the side of the house which was always kept unlocked until night time, and pushed it open. Warmth and light flooded out, together with an aroma of apple and cinnamon scented Christmas candles and coffee. And something else harder to pin down. A sense of peace, of comfort.

'Mary! Are you there?' called Angel, and a voice replied at once,

'In the quiet room. Come on through.'

Smiling reassuringly at Elena, Angel led her over to a door at the rear of the hall, and they went in. The room was lit only by candles, and soft music came from an iPod on one of the low tables beside a bible and a wooden cross.

'Here I am, looking for help again, Mary,' Angel said. 'This is Elena, who needs a bed for the night.' She grinned at the slim girl with the short curly fair hair who had sprung to her feet from the couch by the low table, reaching out her arms to hug the new arrivals in turn, and smiling a welcome.

'Come and sit down, both of you,' Mary Branagh said. She sat back down, patted the couch beside her and moved over to make room. Angel went to sit beside her, first pushing Elena in the direction of a soft armchair nearby across the table. There were more than a dozen other people in the room, most of them lying back on chairs and couches with closed eyes. 'We're in the middle of evening prayers, Angel. You can join in, or just sit and wait, whichever.'

She lifted the bible from the coffee table and, opening it at a bookmark, continued to read from Psalm 27, 'The Lord is my helper. Why should I be afraid? What can man do unto me?'

The newcomers sat quietly until the reading ended, followed by prayers from most of the people present.

As always in this place, Angel felt peace flooding through her. She didn't know how Elena was reacting, but a quick glance at the girl's face showed her that some, at least, of the anguish had faded away, leaving Elena looking more calm than Angel had yet seen her. It was a temporary change, she realised, but it must be doing the girl some good.

Presently the evening prayers came to an end, a number of people left, and Mary turned to her visitors.

'I'll find Elena a bed, certainly, but first how about some supper? We're just about to eat. Come through to the kitchen.'

'Sounds good,' Angel agreed enthusiastically, and they followed Mary back into the hall and across to a large room smelling pleasantly of food.

'You've met most of us before, Angel, but Elena, this is Susie, and Dave, and Johnny, and Tim, and Liam and Aoife. They live and work here. We have others who come for the prayer time, but don't live here, but they're all away home now. Come on, everyone, food.'

The kitchen was as warm as the quiet room, with a big farmhouse style table and chairs taking up a lot of space in the middle, and an Aga stove along one wall, where two huge saucepans were gently simmering.

'Find a seat,' Mary said, 'and I'll just check that supper's ready. My night to cook!'

'Just as well it isn't Johnny's, when we have guests,' murmured one of the girls, earning a ripple of laughter from the others, including Johnny.

'I'm getting much better!' he protested. 'You said you enjoyed my chilli last time it was my turn.'

Amid laughter and chatter, they settled down round the table, until Mary called, 'Okay, guys. Come and get it. Lift a plate from the pile here, all of you.'

Everyone responded, including Angel and Elena – after Angel had nudged the Polish girl and drawn her over to the rapidly forming queue. Mary, wrapped in a gaily coloured apron, was wielding a ladle and dishing out generous helpings of rice from one of the large saucepans, followed by chicken curry from the other.

'Dave, could you get the salad out of the fridge, pet? And Aoife, the bread is in the usual place.'

A bowl of salad appeared on the table, followed by salt and pepper, and a French loaf, as Dave and Aoife willingly forfeited their places in the queue to be of help.

Presently Angel and Elena found themselves sitting before savoury smelling plates of rice and curry, and being offered salad and bread.

Mary set out a jug of water with ice and lemon slices floating in it, and passed round glasses.

'Now,' she said briskly, 'let's give thanks. Thank you, dear father, for providing this meal. Dig in, everyone.'

The meal was a pleasant break for both Angel and Elena. Angel asked after Mary's boyfriend, Jonty, and was told he was on tour in the States with his band *Raving*, but due back in a couple of weeks.

'You must miss him, Mary.'

'I do. But that's what I get for having a rock star for a boyfri end.'

'So, any plans?'

'Yes, we're hoping to marry in the spring. You'll get a card, so be sure and be there, girl!'

'And where will you live? What will happen to the community?'

'Oh, Jonty will move in here and help to run it like the rest of us. We all have jobs, don't we? So what's the difference?'

'Fair enough,' Angel admitted. Why should it seem different? If Mary and Jonty didn't see it that way, why should she?

The relaxed, friendly chat went on as people ate, but only too soon it was time to clear up, and then time for Angel and Elena to sit down privately with Mary in the room reserved for relaxing and tell her Elena's story. No one else was there at the moment.

Mary, as Angel had expected, was both horrified and full of sympathy. 'I knew stuff like that was supposed to be happening – even in Belfast,' she said. 'People who come here often tell me things – that's natural. It seems to me that Elena should go to the police.'

But at the word police, which apparently was familiar to her, Elena at once burst into hysterical tears. 'No! No! Not the police!'

'But, Elena, you haven't done anything wrong,' Angel protested.

'They would send me home! And my mother would know all about it!'

To Angel, these didn't seem important enough reasons, and she was about to say so when she noticed Mary frowning her to silence.

'We understand, Elena,' she said soothingly. 'Sure, don't worry, we won't do anything you don't want. Right now, I think you should go to bed and have a good sleep. Time enough to decide things in the morning. Since this is Friday, I'll not be working and we'll have plenty of time. Meanwhile, darlin', you're safe here, so don't worry.'

She drew Elena out of the room, an arm comfortingly round her. 'Be back in a minute, Angel.'

When she returned presently, it was to report that Elena was safely tucked up in a warm comfortable bed in one of the spare rooms, and showed every sign of going straight off to sleep.

'So now, Angel, what are we going to do about this whole situation?'

'I know what I want to do,' Angel said forcefully. 'Stamp on this business until it's done for, for good, right?'

'Right,' agreed Mary.

'First and most important is to rescue those other girls and get them somewhere safe. The next is to find the people who've set it up, and see that they're stopped completely.'

'I agree absolutely. But have you any ideas on how to go about it?'

'I suppose we should start with Elena. She doesn't know where she was, but she managed to get into the centre of Belfast okay, so I think she might be able to retrace her way, some of it at least. I plan to make a start on that tomorrow.'

Angel stood up.

'But before I take myself off home, Mary, there's something I want to talk to you about. I've been working up to it for some time.'

'No problem, girl. Come into the prayer room and sit down again and I'll put the *Do Not Disturb* sign on the door.' She led the way into the room where they had prayed before supper, and went to hang up the sign. Then, returning she settled herself on the sofa beside Angel.

'So, tell me about it.'

Chapter Four

Angel leant back on the sofa and collected her thoughts. Although she had wanted for some time to talk to Mary about her problem, she now experienced a strong reluctance to go through the horrors of her past life with her husband Michael, now dead.

At last she brought herself to begin, speaking in a slow, hesitating manner very different from her usual style of conversation.

'You know my story, Mary. We've spoken about it before. How I married an attractive, even fascinating man – clever, good looking, well off – and lived to regret it bitterly.

'I met Michael in America, where I was working for a film studio. We settled in Belfast, and I expected to be really happy. But in a very short time Michael began to show his anger with me about every little thing, and then to beat me up. Each time, he would say afterwards how sorry he was, and I found myself forgiving him.

'At first I tried to fight back, physically, but it was no use. It would be different now. The first thing I did when I walked out on him was to take lessons in self defence. No man is ever going to be able to beat me up again. And no man has.

'Well, you know how I found out that Michael was unfaithful, and also a murdering brute. I wasn't the only one he'd hurt. I finally made up my mind to go. He came home just as I'd finished packing a suitcase, and I swung the case at him as he came up the stairs towards me and knocked him down. He fell down stairs and was unconscious for a few minutes and that gave me time to get out of the house, jump into my car, and drive away.

'I came to you, then, Mary, and you took me in and let me stay until I'd recovered enough to leave. I went on holiday to Greece, and almost ran into Michael there. He ended up dead – not because of anything I did – and it was as if a huge weight had rolled off my back. I swore that never again would I marry and allow another man to have the power over me Michael had had.

'I wonder now why I didn't leave him long before I did. But, you know, Mary, I had a built in respect for marriage. I hated to give up on it. But now I was free at last, I wasn't going back to that slavery.

'It's only recently that I've begun to think about my attitude and wonder if it's okay, or if I need to change it. But how? I hate the thought of marriage. There's a fear of it deep inside me. What can I do?

'You're a wise person, Mary. Tell me what I can do.'

Mary sat quietly for a moment, looking at Angel with a deeply sympathetic look. Finally she spoke.

'I think you know yourself, Angel.'

Angel rested her head in her hands. Presently she looked up, and her eyes fell on the bible lying open on the low table in the middle of the room. It was near enough to be read easily. The book was open at the Lord's Prayer, and Angel read, 'Forgive us … as we forgive everyone …'

Such familiar words, but their meaning sank into Angel's heart and mind as if for the first time. '… as we forgive everyone …'

'You mean,' she said slowly, 'that I should forgive Michael?'

Mary's answer was oblique. Instead of saying, 'Yes,' she said, 'As long as you continue to hold hatred for Michael in your heart, for that length of time you'll continue to live under a burden. Michael has gone. You are the one who suffers now for your unforgiveness, Angel.'

Angel thought about it. Yes, she was the one who was suffering. She was unable to commit herself to a new relationship as long as the bitterness she still felt for Michael dominated her thoughts on that subject.

Chapter 4

And she wanted to be able to commit, she realised now, and had wanted to ever since she had met Josh Smith and got to know him. She remembered the time in Corfu when she had thought Josh was dead. The pain she had experienced then had been real enough to show her what she felt for this man.

'Yes. I see that,' she said. She smiled wryly at her friend, sitting beside her offering sympathy, but refusing to lie, refusing to pretend that everything was all right, to let her off the hook. She experienced a rush of gratitude for Mary, and found herself praying inwardly, 'Thank you, Lord.'

'But I don't know if I can genuinely forgive him, even now,' she said. 'I forgave him so many times in the past, and he just went on beating me up.'

'Forgiveness doesn't mean believing that what you are forgiving was okay. What Michael did was very much NOT okay. It just means that you don't hold it against him any more. You have been forgiven for some bad things, I'm sure, Angel. If you accept that forgiveness, you must return it by forgiving others. In this case, Michael.'

Angel nodded. She understood what Mary had said, she knew it was true.

'All right, Mary. Will you pray with me, show me what to say?'

So the two girls sat side by side and Mary took Angel's hand, and they prayed together.

Presently Angel wiped the tears from her eyes and managed to smile.

'Mary, suddenly I feel so light.'

'Good,' said Mary briskly. 'You've achieved something important today, Angel, you've dealt with a grief which has been holding you back in your relationships with others. You'll see the difference now, I promise you.'

'I believe I really will.' Angel smiled again, then she stood up, and as Mary also rose to her feet the two girls hugged.

'I'll head back home now, Mary. Tell Elena I'll call for her after breakfast.'

'Well, just remember that tomorrow's Saturday. This crowd of hard working people sleep in and have a late breakfast on Saturday mornings, so don't you dare to come hammering on the door until after ten o'clock, girl!'

Chapter Five

Breakfast and prayers were over when Angel arrived back to pick up her waif.

Angel spoke privately to Mary first. 'I've been thinking, Mary. Elena is right in saying she won't be allowed to stay here, legally. She doesn't even have a ninety days visa for a tourist. I was wondering if you know anyone in Dublin – or anywhere else down south – who might give her a job and fix up somewhere for her to stay, and keep a friendly eye on her?'

'I'm sure I do, Angel. Let me think for a moment.' She stood, her eyes closed and her forehead creased in thought. Suddenly she opened her eyes again. 'The very people! Jenny and Johnny have just opened a bookshop cum café in Drogheda. I'm sure they could make room for Elena there. And they're both the kindest of people – the heart of the roll, as the saying is. I'll get in touch and see, but I'm sure you can take it as happening. When it's agreed, I'll drive Elena down, to avoid trouble with passports at the border, okay?'

'That's fantastic, Mary! You're a gem! Jenny and Johnny are the very people! Thanks so much. I think we'll wait to tell Elena until you hear back from Jenny and Johnny, though.'

After a further brief chat with Mary, Angel turned to the Polish girl, who had been helping with the washing up in the kitchen, and now came out to join them.

'So, Elena, you ended up at the City Hall, where we met. How did you get there? I mean, by bus or on foot? Or did you get a lift in a car?'

'I walked – a long way.'

'Good. We'll go back there and try to follow your route back.'

Elena followed Angel out to her car. She looked puzzled but docile. It seemed that she trusted Angel as a puppy might trust its new master.

Or, thought Angel, as a duckling might trust the human it had fastened upon as its new mother.

She parked in her usual work day space, near the BBC building, and they walked back to Donegall Square West, at the side of the City Hall.

'Which direction did you come from, before you spoke to me?' Angel asked.

'Up there.'

Elena pointed towards Howard Street.

'Right, we'll start there.'

Angel strode briskly off along Howard Street, with Elena trotting beside her.

'Did you come from the left or the right at the main road –Great Victoria Street?'

Elena pointed again, to their left. It was the direction which would take them eventually to Shaftsbury Square. She seemed sure enough of her way, so far. Angel felt encouraged. She had been afraid Elena would be lost after the first turn off. The girl seemed to have quite a good sense of direction.

Continuing along Great Victoria Street, they eventually reached Shaftesbury Square, and for the first time Elena seemed a little unsure. She looked at Angel helplessly.

'I came from one of those streets, but I'm not sure –'

She broke off. Angel considered her next move.

'Do you remember passing anything in particular, Elena? A restaurant, a supermarket, a church?'

Elena brightened up. 'Yes, a church, maybe. A big building that looked like a church. And before that, a very big old building, an important one, I think.'

'Okaay! The building like a church would be the *Crescent Arts Centre*, I should think. And the very big important building would be *Queen's University*, at a guess. Sure, we'll work on the idea that it was, and head that way, up Bradbury Place and along University Road. And you can tell me if you recognise the buildings.'

They crossed Shaftesbury Square and when they had walked up Bradbury Place and on into University Road, Elena exclaimed at once, 'Oh, yes! This is the church I saw. I wanted to go in and ask for help, but no one was there and the door was shut.'

'It's not actually a church, Elena. It used to be a girls' school, and now it's an Arts Centre. The next landmark you mentioned should be Queen's. This is it we're coming to now. Do you recognise it, or what?'

Elena's face made it clear that she did.

'It's the University,' Angel explained. 'Impressive, isn't it?'

But now where, was the next question – Malone Road or Stranmillis Road? University Road, when it had passed Queen's University, split into these two major roads. Would Elena remember which she had come down?

But somewhat to Angel's surprise, she did. She'd been walking on the same side as the university, passing the gates of a park just before she saw the buildings – 'Botanic Gardens,' Angel interjected – and just before that she had passed another large building – 'The Ulster Museum,'– and she knew she hadn't crossed the road.

'Okay, Stranmillis Road,' Angel said. 'We'll see how we get on, but I'm wondering if I should leave you in a coffee shop and go back for the car. If you came right along Stranmillis Road, it's a fair distance, and there may be more after that.'

They walked for another ten minutes, then Angel, noticing how tired Elena had begun to look, decided it was time she had a rest.

'Okay, kid, I'll leave you in the next coffee place with a cup and a sandwich, while I fetch the car. Don't move, right?'

Elena nodded. She allowed herself to be led into a clean bright café, one of the many along Stranmillis Road, and sat quietly at a corner table sipping the coffee Angel had bought her, while Angel hopped on a bus heading in the direction of the City Hall, and retrieved her car. Twenty minutes later, she pulled up outside the café, sounded the horn and signalled to Elena to come out.

'Can't stay here or I'll get a ticket. Jump in, and we'll move on as slowly as possible. Give you a chance to look around for things you maybe recognise.'

They drove on slowly, trying not to hold up the traffic behind them too much, and presently passed Ridgeway Street, the home of the *Lyric Theatre*. Not far ahead on the opposite side loomed the entrance to Stranmillis College, the teachers' training institution.

'Do you remember if you came across the river where the road bends round and down to it?' Angel asked. 'I suppose you must have.'

'Yes. Yes, water shining in the dark, the street lights shining on it!'

'Good.'

They turned down and drove past Governors Bridge – which was one way – Angel intending to circle over the next bridge and double back. It was beginning to get dark, and the street lights, with the Christmas decorations attached to each one, had lit up, making everything seem even darker. It was coming up to the shortest day in the year.

Angel looked round her, wondering if they could go much further. How much more would Elena remember? Her journey had been mostly, or possibly entirely, in the dark. How many more landmarks could she have noticed?

As they approached the Governors Bridge again from the other side, 'Stop!' said Elena suddenly.

Angel pulled over.

'I didn't come this way,' Elena said. 'It was back across the bridge. I didn't go over it.'

'Okay. We'll drive back over the bridge and turn left.'

'I walked along beside the water. I remember the lights shining on it. Before that I walked along a street, and before that again, along a path by the water.'

'The Lagan towpath. Okay, let's try going that way.'

She pulled out and drove back across the bridge, around the roundabout and into the nearby car park. She had often parked here on visits to the *Lyric Theatre*.

'Out we get.'

They left the car and crossed to the near end of Governor's Bridge, and Elena pointed out the way she had come, climbing up from the path down beside the river. They scrambled down, through the tunnel under the end of the bridge and began walking back along the way Elena remembered coming.

After a while the path petered out into a street and they started along it.

'I thought I might knock on one of these doors,' Elena said. 'But then I thought I hadn't got far enough away, so I kept going on.'

'So, you hadn't come far when you reached this street?'

'Oh, yes, quite far. About as far as we've come today. But not far enough. I was very afraid.'

They came out of the street and walked once more along the towpath. The lights shone on the river beside them. They walked on, covering, Angel reckoned, about a mile further.

'How did you get onto the towpath, Elena?'

'I came through wide fields, close to the big house where they kept us.'

'That would be the Lagan Meadows. But wasn't there a road to go by, instead of getting into the meadows?'

'Oh, yes, but they could have followed me by car if I'd gone that way. Magda said to get into the fields and keep out of sight until I was somewhere very safe, very public. That's why I kept on till I reached the crowds, the market, the big building in the centre of the city.'

'The City Hall.'

'Yes. And I was still afraid to speak to anyone, to ask for help. But then I saw you. And I saw that you had a kind face. So I spoke.'

'I'm so glad you did.' Angel gave Elena a brief hug. Then she said, 'Do you know, Elena, I'm beginning to think I've walked you far enough for today. We still have to get back, after all. It must be a couple of miles back to the car.'

They turned round and headed back.

Elena, who had walked quite a few miles yesterday, it appeared, was beginning to look worn, and Angel felt some compunction at having brought her so far.

'I tell you what, Elena, I'll give Mary a ring to say you won't be back for tea, and then we'll go for a meal somewhere nice, okay? Once we reach the car we won't do any more walking tonight. Later on, I'll drive us by that road you avoided back past the Lagan Meadows, and see if you can point out this big house to me. Don't worry, we won't leave the car. I'll drop you back to the community house and you can get another good night's sleep. Any exploring there is to be done, I'll do by myself later on.'

They made their way back to the car. Elena, in spite of obvious efforts, lagging noticeably. Angel called Mary, and then rang to book a table at one of her favourite restaurants. They drove back down the Stranmillis Road until they reached Bradbury Place.

'We should probably park down one of these side streets,' Angel decided. 'I'm going to take you to *Darcy's*. It's a place I love. I've often got parked just outside it, but at Christmas time I wouldn't like to count on it. Sorry, I promised you no more walking, didn't I? But it'll only be a few hundred yards.'

They had no trouble parking. It was early yet for eating. They strolled down Bradbury Place, past *Lavery's p*ub, and there was *Darcy's*, not far from the corner of Shaftesbury Square.

Chapter Six

Both girls enjoyed their meal, in the pleasant ambience of *Darcy's* restaurant, with its old fashioned tables and chairs and its friendly waiters and waitresses. As she enjoyed her own chicken with asparagus, Angel was pleased to see Elena eating her well cooked lamb shank enthusiastically. The girl needed as much nourishment as Angel could cram into her right now. It would be good to see her regaining her strength and her peace of mind.

Angel finished off her own meal and put down her knife and fork. After inquiring about Elena's age, and finding that she had turned eighteen a few months ago, she had ordered Elena a glass of white wine, and the same for herself, hoping this also would perk Elena up.

'Okay, pet, we'll make tracks now.'

Angel paid with her debit card, led Elena out of the restaurant, and turned left in the direction of her car. They had gone only a few steps when they were halted by a noisy crowd on the pavement right in front of them, spilling over onto the road, outside *Lavery's*. The focus of the crowd seemed to be a fight of some sort, and people were circling round the two combatants.

'Maybe we should cross over and get out of the way of this,' Angel suggested. She reached out to take Elena by the arm, but the girl had sprung forward.

'Magda! It's Magda!'

In the centre of the crowd a girl in her early twenties, a sturdily built girl with long blonde hair flying wildly round her and an attractive face full of anger, was tugging furiously to retain her hold on her shoulder bag, while a brutal looking man with wild sandy hair and a pale freckled face tried to pull it away from her. Angel could see the tattoos spread along his wrists and up onto his arms. Neither combatant would let go their grip.

Somehow or other the man's actions were forcing the girl to swing wildly round in a circle while he in his turn rotated violently, his face crunched up in fury. The girl's long blonde hair swung out crazily round her face, almost blinding her at times, but she hung on relentlessly to the bag.

Elena sprang forward and began to tug with useless rage at the man's arm, trying to unfasten his grip, but with the same arm he used his elbow to thrust her away, and his grip tightened on the straps of the bag as he continued to swirl the other girl in a dizzying circle.

Angel took out her mobile phone and rang the police, explained the situation and identified the place. Then she stepped forward, judged her moment carefully, and kicked the sandy haired man sharply in his solar plexis. With a huge groan he toppled over, but even then managed to retain his hold on the strap of the shoulder bag. As he fell, he dragged Magda, still holding tightly to her bag, down onto the pavement with him.

Angel was astonished at the strength which enabled the freckled man to retain his grip. Further action was required. She bent forward and, with her hand held steady and rigid, chopped the man's wrist hard. She hoped not to break it, but by now didn't really care if she did. The man yelled and his fingers dropped feebly from the strap he had been clinging to.

At the same moment, Madga struggled to her feet and still holding tightly to her shoulder bag took off down the street at speed, round the first corner and out of Angel's sight. In two minds as to whether or not to go after her, Angel heard the sound of a police car drawing up, and decided that she must remain with Elena.

The young Polish girl tugged frantically at her arm.

'The police! If they see me and ask for my name they'll say I must be sent home!' she whispered feverishly in Angel's ear.

'Okay,' Angel murmured back. 'No need for you to be involved. Walk away, back towards where we left the car. I'll follow you as soon as I can. Don't run. You don't want to be noticed.'

Then she proceeded to cope with the police she had summoned. There were two of them. The sergeant was first out of the car immediately followed by a constable who had been driving.

Angel identified the sergeant as the person to speak to. 'Great! You've got here really fast!' she said. 'I'm the one who rang you. This man attacked a young girl, and tried to steal her handbag. I'm afraid she's run away now, but there are plenty of witnesses here.'

She gave her name and address, arranged to come to the police station the next day to sign a statement, and watched in satisfaction as the brutal looking man was bundled into the police car and driven away. Time to go after Elena, now. Angel set off back to her car, hoping that Elena had reached it in safety.

She had parked the car down the first side street – a place darker than the main road and lit only by a few street lights. The car was in a space about halfway down on the right hand side. A dark figure loomed beside it, and by the light of the street lamp Angel was able to see as she came nearer that it was Elena. She breathed a sigh of relief and clicked her key to open the doors as she reached the girl.

'Come on, let's get in,' she said briskly. 'It's all over now. The police are gone.'

Elena got in obediently on the passenger's side.

'Now,' said Angel as she slipped into the driver's seat, 'I'm going to take you back to the community house and Mary will look after you tonight again, as I promised – while I go and investigate this house where you were kept. But first of all I want to hear a bit more from you about that incident tonight. That was your friend Magda, you said? So who was that man? And why did he want her handbag? He was very persistent about it. But he could hardly have expected that a girl like Magda would have much money in it.'

'Yes, that was Magda.' Elena stopped after her first few words and stared at Angel with frightened eyes.

'Okay. So who was the man? I think you know him, Elena. Don't pretend.'

'Yes. Yes, I know him.'

'From the house?'

Elena nodded unhappily. 'He was one of the guards.'

'Guards?'

'Yes, there were two of them. They kept an eye on us, made sure we didn't try anything. If we didn't do as we were told, they beat us up.'

Angel shuddered.

'Why would he have wanted Magda's handbag? I can see that he might have wanted to grab her and take her back. But why was he so keen to get her bag?'

'I don't know.' Elena sounded miserable.

'But maybe you can guess? And by the way, does this animal have a name?'

'Jason called him Marty. But the girls called him Brutus. It was a sort of joke, I think.'

'Suits him. But about the bag, Elena?'

'He thinks she has her gun in it. Maybe.'

'Gun?'

'Magda stole his gun from the other guard. Simon, but we called him Slimy.'

'Stole it?'

'Yes, she pretended to like him and she sort of rubbed up against him, and got the gun from his belt when he was busy taking hold of her.'

'Clever girl!' said Angel approvingly. 'So that was how you got out? She threatened him with his own gun?'

'We tied him up. She held the gun on him while the rest of us got his handcuffs and put them on him, and tied up his legs and tied him to a chair. Then Madga went off to explore, to see the best way out, she said.'

Elena broke off.

'Who had the gun?'

'Magda took it with her.'

'And?' Angel inquired.

'She came back and sent me to get out by the back door. She said to keep away from the main road and to cut across the fields.'

'So what did she and the other girls do? Didn't they all come with you?'

'Magda said there was something she wanted to do first to make things safer for them. To make it easier to escape without being followed. She told the other girls to keep watch on Slimy until she got back.'

'So you went out?'

'Yes. But as I was getting out of the back door, I heard a lot of shouting and I heard Brutus. He was running towards the dormitory, I think. He was firing his gun. At least I heard shots. I don't know what happened after that. I thought if I went back I couldn't be much use, but if I went on and escaped, I could get someone to help the other girls, maybe.'

'Looks as if Magda escaped, too, at any rate. But who knows about the others?'

Elena nodded.

'This Brutus must have come across her by accident, I guess. If he'd been following her, he'd have caught her yesterday, not tonight.'

'He might have been in the pub,' Elena suggested.

'Well, he's in a police cell now, I hope. And we should tell the police the whole story, now, Elena, and bring them in on it.'

Elena looked suddenly desperate. 'No! No! Not the police. Jason explained that to us early on. The police would send us all back to where we came from, because we weren't allowed to be in this country without a permit.' She gave a despairing sob.

'But, Elena, wouldn't you like to go back to your family?'

'Not if they were told what I've been doing. My mother would be so upset. I can't let that happen to her.'

It wasn't a suitable time to attempt to reason with the girl, Angel knew. Later, when Elena had recovered from her dreadful experience, she might, with Mary's help, persuade her that her mother need not know the details of what had happened. And perhaps that, even if she knew, she would be so glad to have Elena safely back, rescued from the traffickers, that she wouldn't blame her daughter for something she'd been unable to help.

'Okay, Elena,' Angel said. 'I'll take you back to Mary now, as I said I would. She'll look after you tonight, and for as long as necessary. And then,' she added with determination, 'I'm going to drive out towards this house where you were kept, and see if I can find out what's happening there now. And what I can do about it.'

Chapter Seven

Shortly after Angel was driving along the Malone Road, looking out for Delamore Park on her left. Looking up *Google Maps,* she had come to the conclusion that this was the street which best matched Elena's description of its whereabouts.

Reaching it, she turned into the broad street with its large houses set in spacious gardens, and wondered which was the one where Elena had been kept. She had managed to get a better description of the house from Elena before setting out, and knew that it was not close to the other houses, but was set further back from the road and at a distance from its nearest neighbours.

She had driven for some distance before she found something which seemed as if it might be the house she was looking for. Unlike most of the other houses it looked large enough to house the twenty girls Elena had spoken of, even if they were all in one big dormitory, and still have space for other bedrooms for the men who came there, and for the guards and the man in charge. It was worth checking out, anyway.

Angel drove past the house, looking for somewhere discreet to park, well out of sight of anyone who might be inside. She found a place where the trees gave her a good deal of protection, pulled up, and collected her torch, gun, and hoodie. For good measure she added a cosh which she had recently acquired, and a coil of rope which she wound round her waist in case she needed to climb in. Then, getting out of her car, she pulled on the hoodie and made sure that the hood, well forward over her head, concealed most of her face. Time to go.

Moving cautiously, she approached the house. Going boldly and openly in by the front gate and along the drive to the front door was not the best plan, she had already decided. Okay, it was very dark, but the street lights, few in number though they were, made it possible for any passerby, on foot or in a car, to see her. Not something to risk. Instead, she made her way round the fence that surrounded the property, looking for an easy way in.

The darkness and the surrounding trees continued to protect her. Presently she came to a gap where a couple of the fence planks had been pulled away. The gap left wasn't big. A heavy man might have found it a problem to get through it. But Angel, although strong and agile, was also slim and slender. She slid through the gap sideways without too much difficulty.

A quick flash of her torch showed her she was standing on grass. A wide lawn, dotted with trees and bushes. Easy territory to make her way through without being seen. Moving quietly from bush to bush, with occasional pauses to reconnoitre from behind the thicker tree trunks, she arrived in a tarmac surfaced area, to the rear of the house. There was a row of three garages, and parked in the open, near the back door – which probably opened into the kitchen – was a flashy looking BMW in bright scarlet. Angel approached it and tried its doors. No good. They were, naturally enough, securely locked. She could see nothing helpful through the windows.

The next move was to try the back door of the house. Angel had come equipped for a spot of breaking and entering, but her tools were not needed. The door was unlocked. Nor was it bolted on the inside, for when she tried the handle the door opened with no difficulty. Angel was not to know that Bobby and Jason, leaving by the back entrance for maximum privacy, had been too encumbered by the dead body they carried between them to do more than shut the door behind them.

The door, as she expected, led into a large kitchen, well furnished with modern equipment which shone white in the dark, dishwasher, tumble drier, washing machine, oven, microwave, extractor. Angel stood and listened for several minutes. She could choose to switch on the lights and see what she was exploring, or she could use brief flashes of her torch and hope to stay safe. It depended on whether the revolt and escape of some, if not all, of the girls had caused a mass exit of the men running the place, in fear of the arrival of the police.

There were no sounds from the rest of the house. Still, Angel decided to play it safe until she had explored further. She switched on her torch, and moved over to one of the doors on the far walls which must lead either into the other rooms or into the hall. Then she switched the torch off again before opening the first door, the one which was placed to one side of the kitchen.

She was looking into a living room. Light shone into it through the huge windows looking on the street and the street lights. There were soft rugs on the wooden floor, large comfortable armchairs and small coffee tables. A wide screen television with a DVD player beneath it took up a considerable part of one wall. No occupants, currently, she was glad to see.

A door was set into the wall on her left, parallel to the third door in the kitchen. Angel assumed that both doors led into the hallway. She might come back and search the living room and kitchen presently. But for now she wanted to see for herself what was upstairs.

Still moving lightly she opened the last door from the kitchen, and found herself, as expected, standing in a wide hall, with a flight of stairs opposite her. There were doors on the far side of the hall, clearly leading into a range of other downstairs rooms, but for the time being Angel did no more than peer quietly into each, ascertaining that no one was there. Then she headed off up the stairs.

There were two flights, each broken by a landing where the stairs turned round at right angles. At the top of the first flight, a corridor led off on both sides, with a number of doors placed side by side. Angel moved silently along until she reached the first door. It would be a bedroom, she expected. Taking hold of the door handle, she turned it as quietly as she could, pushed the door open a little, and looked in.

The room was dark inside. It was possible that someone was sleeping there, although it was still early for that. Angel turned on her torch and took a quick look. There was a bed, but no sign of anyone sleeping in it. She pushed the door further open, switched on the room light, and moved forward.

It was a large room, comfortable looking. A couple of big, soft armchairs were placed over by the window. There was a desk with a computer and DVD player. The bed, set against the right hand wall, was king size and had piles of luxurious multi-coloured pillows heaped at its head, besides a thick warm looking duvet with a cover in scarlet patterns of woven silk.

In the next bedroom along the corridor – a spacious, comfortable room like the one she had first explored – there was something more interesting. Angel, crossing the room, stopped. Looking down, she could see that there was a pool of blood on the floor. She knelt down to explore it further. It was mostly dried up, but still sticky in places. It seemed as if an attempt had been made to clear it up. But it hadn't been too successful. She looked round to see if there was anything else that would tell her what had happened.

Not far from the pool of blood a shell case was lying. Someone had been shot here.

The built in wardrobes had mirrors inset in their sliding doors. Angel approached the wardrobes and slid back the doors. There was room for a complete outfit, but in fact there was only one man's jacket hanging in the right hand side.

It was an expensive looking jacket, Angel noted. Part of a suit, she thought. Slipping it off the hanger, she laid it out on the bed and felt the pockets. The inside breast pocket held the most interesting stuff. There was a wallet and a separate card case. The card case held a number of credit cards. The wallet held a driver's licence and a rather thin wad of money – which looked as if it had been disturbed. The notes were crumpled and their edges were far from being tidily lined up.

It seemed possible that it belonged to whoever had been shot and that whoever shot him had helped themselves to some of his cash. The mystery was why they had not taken it all, and the credit cards, too, but Angel thought that possibly the shooter hadn't had time to do anything but grab a handful of notes and get away quickly.

The driver's licence, and the credit cards, told Angel that the jacket belonged to someone called Jackson Morrison. One of the visitors to the house, Angel thought – unless it was one of the men who ran it. She didn't know, offhand, which she would consider most guilty. It shouldn't be hard to track him down. The driver's licence gave her his address. When she had finished exploring the premises she would make it her business to check him out. Elena might recognise his name, or the photo on his licence.

Angel studied the photo carefully. The man looked about fifty. He had thick grey hair, a red face and the sort of craggy features which some people might consider handsome, but others would not – thick lips, small eyes set close together, and a pug nose. His double chin completed the picture. Angel found him repulsive.

Leaving the contents of Morrison's pockets for the police to find, Angel left the room and moved on along the corridor to explore further.

The next room gave her nothing. The furniture was similar to the first, but the wardrobe held nothing, and there was nothing to be seen lying around. As she opened the third door, Angel maintained her caution. She shone her torch around for a brief moment before entering and saw little but emptiness. She stretched out her hand to the light switch in order to see more clearly. Then she stopped, her hand still not touching the switch.

A noise had come to her ears. A noise like a saw, or an animal groaning or snuffling.

Angel realised abruptly that it was the sound of someone snoring. Across the room on the right hand side, there was someone sleeping in the king sized bed.

Chapter Eight

Angel froze.

Slowly she recovered, and felt in her pocket for the gun she had naturally brought with her. Then, moving as quietly as possible, she approached the bed. She pulled the gun out of her pocket and aimed it at the sleeping man. He had heard nothing. Angel grasped her torch in her other hand and shone it on the sleeper's face.

She saw a thick set unattractive man with a pudgy face and ginger hair straggling down over his forehead. As she watched, the light shining in his eyes woke the man, and he moved his head restlessly, trying to avoid the torchlight. He sat up suddenly. Angel spoke.

'Don't move.'

She turned the torch so that it shone on the gun in her right hand.

'You see this gun? I really don't want to shoot you. All I want is some answers.'

The man's mouth gaped open. 'Don't shoot! Don't shoot! I'll tell you anything you want!'

'Who owns this house?'

'I don't know! Please don't shoot me! It's the Boss, that's all I know! Jason knows – or Bobby.'

Angel recognised the name Jason as the man who had met Elena and her friend Magda at the airport. Bobby was a new one.

'Where are Jason and Bobby?'

'They haven't been around for a couple of days. I don't know where they are.'

The man's lips were trembling. Angel wasn't sure how much of his lack of knowledge was true. Was he more afraid of his boss than of her gun? Since she had no intention of actually shooting him, it was hard to be sure. In any case, shooting him would mean that there was no way of finding out anything he did know.

'What's your own name? Do you happen to know that?'

'Oh, yes! I'm Simon Montgomery.'

Angel remembered Elena's words, 'Slimy, the girls called him.' And it was his gun that Magda had stolen. That was helpful. If Simon had no gun, there was no chance of him suddenly producing it and starting to do some shooting himself.

'Okay, Simon. Start talking. What do you know about this racket? And there'd better be something, because I don't plan to waste my time on you otherwise. My gun hand's getting fed up with waiting and learning nothing.'

'The Boss works with a guy in Poland. Least, that's what I heard. This guy in Poland rounds up girls, flies them over here. He's not the one at the top, mind you. There's a bigger man in control. But honest, I don't know any of their names. It was Jason who got me into this. He said he could get me a job as a guard, easy work and good money. Ask no questions and you'll be told no lies, he said. The money was good, like he said. Suited me.'

'And how long ago was this? When did you start working here?'

'About three months or so.' Simon licked his lips nervously. 'I'm not doing anything wrong, missus. All I do is look after the girls.'

'And see they don't escape, and do as they're told, right?'

'Well – yeah, I suppose so.'

'I think you'll find the law considers that wrong enough to be going on with, Simon.'

But even as she spoke, Angel was reflecting that the law could do nothing without Elena's evidence, and at the moment Elena was afraid to give it. The last thing she wanted was to have the police brought into it. Angel would have to find another way.

'Are there any of the girls still here?' she asked. There had been no sound of anyone else in the house, but it was as well to ask.

'No, they all cleared off when Magda told them to. I dunno where any of them went.'

'Right. I'm going to have a look round now. But first of all, I'm going to tie you up and leave you here until I'm finished. Don't try anything silly. Get off the bed and lie facedown on the floor over here. Keep very still. Put your hands behind your back Stretch them up to me.'

This was the tricky part. If Simon decided to risk being shot while she was tying him up with one hand and keeping the gun aimed at him with the other, she'd be in trouble.

However, Simon seemed reluctant to take any risks. He got out of bed as instructed and stood there shivering in his T-shirt and boxers.

'Lie down like I told you.'

Simon lay on the carpet face down and put his hands behind his back.

Angel, who was deft with both hands, transferred the gun to her left hand and kept it steadily aimed at Simon's head, while with her right hand she unwound the rope she carried twisted round her waist, wound it round Simon's wrists, and used her teeth to secure a firm knot. Then she moved to his ankles and repeated the process with the other end of the rope.

Confident that Simon couldn't move, she completed the business by pushing a scarf into his mouth and tying another one round his head to keep it in place.

Her exploration of the house was necessarily fast. She didn't want to leave Simon on his own for long. Who knew how clever he might be at untying ropes?

So she left his room, moved along the corridor trying doors and examining the rooms which were uniformly empty.

She moved to the next floor up, the top one, and found the same absence of occupants. However, she discovered one interesting thing in her search. On the top story, one room stretched the width of the house and was clearly the girl's dormitory. It was bleakly simple, with no adornments or pleasant touches.

Angel felt it was worth her while to search it thoroughly in case there was anything left behind which would help her to identify any of the girls who had been imprisoned there, and in fact she found several objects which had been left behind in their hurried exit. There was a makeup set in a case, a bible, a nightdress stuffed under a pillow, and a purse with some loose cash. None of them seemed likely to lead to much, but Angel collected them and put them in her backpack.

An anonymous call to the police, reporting the blood, the empty house, and the driving licence, etc., of Mr Jackson Morrison ought to get some response. It seemed a possible way of exposing the owner of the house without bringing Elena into it.

To expose the people trafficking might be more difficult. The girls' dormitory should give the police some hint of it unless they were really thick, which Angel knew most policemen weren't. But it would be even better if she could track down some of the girls and get their evidence. Supposing some at least of them were less frightened of the police than Elena.

Time to leave. But what about Simon? Leaving him tied up wasn't an option. Supposing the police ignored her call and didn't bother to check out the house. He might remain there for days, helpless. No way would Angel do that.

And, in fact, it occurred to her, Simon would be a very useful witness if he was prepared to repeat to the police even the little he had told Angel. The ideal would be to untie him and remove his gag, but lock him in somewhere that had a key. None of the bedrooms seemed to have one, but the bathrooms were better equipped. Angel took the time to identify a bathroom along the corridor not far from Simon's room which had an actual key and could be locked from the outside. Then she went back to her captive.

'Okay, you, Simon – or Slimy – you've got a choice here.' She released him from the gag so that he could speak to her again. 'I can leave you tied up here until someone happens to come along and find you. This year, next year, sometime, or never. Or you can make a bargain with me.'

The man's eyes rolled in fear. His forehead was covered in sweat.

'Don't leave me like this!'

'I'm going to untie you. Don't try to run. I still have this gun, see?'

'No, no, I won't!'

'I'm going to lock you up securely. Then I'm going to phone the police. When they come, you're going to tell them all about this place. Just what you told me. Do you understand, Simon?'

'Yes, yes, I understand.'

'Don't mention me. You don't know me, and I'll be long gone, so there wouldn't be much to tell them about me, but I don't want you to mention me at all. If I find out afterwards that you've talked to them about me, then me and my little gun will come looking for you, get it?'

'No, I swear I won't!'

'Okay. I'll undo your legs first, then your arms. Stand up as soon as you can.'

It didn't take long for Angel to release him from the rope, which she wound about her waist again, keeping the gun steady on Simon as she did so. The man hadn't been tied up for very long. He soon recovered from the first stiffness.

Angel marched him at gunpoint along the corridor to the bathroom, pushed him in, and locked the door.

Angel on Guard – *Gerry McCullough*

Chapter Nine

The next thing was to get in touch with the police. It might not be the best move to use her mobile. Angel wasn't sure if the local police had the equipment to track down the location of a mobile phone call, but she intended to take no risks.

Instead she found the nearest street phone, and gave her message as quickly as she could, giving the address of the house first, and then mentioning the blood, the empty dormitory, Jackson Morrison, and the presence of a valuable witness locked in a bathroom.

She wasn't very happy with the response. There was quite a bit of unbelief in the voice which answered her and they kept insisting on knowing her name and whether she was still at the house.

'I'm not at the house,' Angel said firmly. 'And you'd better be there soon, if you don't want the witness to break out and do a runner before you get there.' She put the phone down.

It was true that she wasn't at the house right then, but she lost no time in getting back there. She wanted to keep watch, mainly to check that the police came, but also to make sure Simon didn't manage to escape. And to see if anyone else – any of the previous occupants of the house – came back.

It was a cold night for standing around. Angel chose a spot behind some shrubs in the front garden where she had a good view of the entrance. She was reasonably confident that Simon wouldn't be able to break out of the bathroom. He had no tools there to help him to tackle the door, and since he was in his bare feet, kicking it down probably wasn't an option. She wished the police would hurry up. Still, nothing for it but to wait.

After what seemed like an eternity but which her watch told her was about twenty minutes from her phone call, she heard a car skidding to a halt at the gates. A uniformed policeman got out of it and tested the gates, which were padlocked shut. He went back to the car and returned with what was probably a screwdriver, although Angel couldn't see clearly enough from her place of concealment to be quite sure. He worked at the gate for a while, then there was the clink of the padlock falling and the man called out, 'Okay, Billy.'

He pushed the gates wide and waited until the car had passed through them and pulled up to allow him to get back in. Then they drove on towards the house.

Angel moved forward quietly from behind the shrubs. She wanted to be sure about what happened next, and it was hard to hear anything from her position. As she came nearer to the now open front door, she could hear shouts and responsive bellows. The shouts were from the police, alerting each other as to their movements, and the bellows, she was sure, from Simon, demanding his release.

Abruptly Angel froze. Light was streaming from the open front door. By it she could see a figure straining forward, like herself, to see what was happening. At first it was impossible to tell who it was. But then, as the figure moved forward and its face bent into the light, she suddenly knew. It was Elena's friend, Magda.

Why had Magda come back? Was she looking for something? Had she planned to meet someone here? From the story Elena had told Angel, Magda was definitely not on the side of the people who ran the business. Or had Elena got it wrong?

But, no. Magda had organised the breakout, had made it possible for Elena and the other girls to escape. There was no way she would have done this if she had been on the side of Simon and his bosses. So why was she here?

Angel decided that she needed to know.

Slipping round behind Magda, she came up to her without being heard. Her arm went out and her hand clamped firmly over Magda's mouth, while her other hand pressed her gun into Madga's neck.

'Don't move, don't speak. Come with me.'

She drew Magda away from the house into the darkness.

Chapter 9

The best thing, she decided, was to take Magda well away from the house. In fact, to her car. She had parked it well out of sight of anyone in the house. Moving quietly and keeping a firm grip on Magda, she made her way out of the grounds, through the now wide open gate, and to the dark street where the car still sat unnoticed. It wasn't easy to get Magda inside without giving her an opportunity to get away, but Angel, using one hand to keep a good hold on Magda and the other to click open the passenger door of her car, managed to propel her inside. She slipped in by the rear door and clicked the locks shut. Pointing her gun at Magda, she said sharply, 'Look at me, Magda.'

Magda swivelled round. Her face expressed her amazement at being addressed by name.

'Who are you?'

'A friend of Elena.'

'What?'

'You heard me.'

'But Elena has no friends in this country.'

'I met her yesterday in the centre of town and bought her a coffee. She told me her story.'

'And you didn't turn her over to the cops?'

'Why would I do that?'

'If she told you what happened then you've gotta know we're in this country illegally, since Brexit.'

'So?'

'Well, are you just going to break the law?'

'I don't want to break the law if I can help it. But I've given Elena my word not to turn her over to the police. Elena has told me as much as she knows about this racket. But it's not a lot. I think you know a considerable amount more, Magda, and I mean to hear it from you. I'm planning to clear up this business and put the guys responsible behind bars.'

'If you really mean that –' Magda said slowly. Then she asked again, 'Who are you?'

This time Angel answered her fully.

'I'm called Angeline Murphy – Angel to my friends. I work at the BBC. And it makes me angry and sad to see this sort of thing going on in my home city. I intend to put a stop to it, see? So, are you going to help me, Magda?'

'Didn't I see you earlier tonight?' Magda asked, peering at Angel more closely.

'Yes, Elena and I saw the fight outside Lavery's. When Brutus tried to get your shoulder bag. Why was that, Magda? What was he looking for?'

'Who knows? He was drunk. Probably for the gun I took off him.'

Angel looked at her. She was pretty sure Magda was keeping something back. Perhaps after a while she would trust Angel enough to be more forthcoming.

'We need to talk. Is there somewhere we could go instead of sitting in this car getting cold? Somewhere you've been staying?' she asked.

'Yes. Good idea. I've been staying in a bed sitting room up the Lisburn Road,' Magda said. 'I saw the sign up offering rooms for rent when I got away from that house, so I took it in the meantime. While I work out what I'm doing myself.'

'Right.' Angel started the car and drove back in the direction of University Road, then turned down Fitzwilliam Street, beside what had been the old Students' Union building – now rebuilt. This soon brought them out on the Lisburn Road.

'Turn left,' Magda said. 'It's quite a long way up. You turn off at Tate's Avenue.'

'Oh, you're in The Village?'

'I've heard it called that,' Magda said.

Chapter 9

Angel drove on, passing the City Hospital on the right, then turned right into Tate's Avenue.

'Second on the left after the bridge,' Magda said.

Chapter Ten

The streets in The Village – as the area was known – consisted of terrace houses of the two up, two down type. Magda's room was the upstairs back in one of these houses, and when she led the way into it, the room struck Angel as small, scruffy and depressing. But she realised that Magda had hardly been in a position to pay for anything better. In fact, she wondered how Magda could pay for anything at all – unless it was Jackson Morrison's money that was paying, as seemed quite possible.

'Sit down,' Magda said, pointing to a choice between a hard wobbly looking chair, and the edge of the bed. Angel choose the bed, which at least was unlikely to break or fall over.

'I can make you a cup of coffee, if you like,' Magda offered, indicating a shelf at one side of the room where an electric kettle and two mugs sat beside a jar of instant coffee, one of powered milk, and a small pile of the type of sugar sachets you got in cafes. Near this was a small sink with two taps, marked hot and cold.

'Thanks, that would be nice.'

The atmosphere seemed to have changed since Angel, not many minutes ago, had held Magda up at gunpoint and threatened her. Somehow, the Polish girl was suddenly on top of things, and Angel was content to allow this position of affairs to continue until she had learnt more. Magda, she was certain, knew far more about what had been going on that Elena did.

She took the offered coffee when Magda had finished making it, and for a few minutes the two girls sat eyeing each other over the rims of their mugs, sipping thoughtfully. Magda was on the rickety chair, but seemed to be managing it without difficulty.

'So,' Angel said at last. 'Tell me more. What's your story? And do you have names for the guys who got you into this?'

'Some,' Magda said cautiously. 'I know the name of the guy in Krakow who persuaded me to come over here, on the promise of a decent job. And not just me, but my friend Elena. I don't mind being conned so much myself. I can handle my own problems when I have to. I've been around. But Elena's young and innocent. I hate to think that I let her in for this business. And, believe me, I'm going to make sure the people who conned us don't do the same thing to anyone else.'

'So, the name, Magda?'

'His name is Szczepan Kowalski. But he's only a go between. There's a big chief who tells him what to do, and who runs things here.'

'The guy who runs things here, that wouldn't be Jackson Morrison?'

'No, he's another one lower down the ladder. But how do you know about him?' Magda looked at Angel suspiciously.

'I found his jacket hanging in the wardrobe in one of the bedrooms in that house. There was a lot of blood about. It seemed likely some-one had killed him. I can't help wondering if it was you, Magda?'

'No!' Magda's eyes flashed in indignation. 'I don't go around killing people. Not that he wouldn't have deserved it. But I'd rather have got some information from him. It's bad news if he's really dead. I think he knew the name of the big boss. Actually, I took some of his money earlier on, when I was planning to escape. He was asleep then – but certainly not dead.'

So she'd been right about the money, when she'd suspected that Magda had taken it. Angel had no problem with that. Magda obviously needed money to help with her getaway, and with the release of all the other girls.

'You could probably have got away a lot sooner if you'd wanted to, right?'

'Yeah. But I didn't want to slip away by myself. I wanted to get everyone else safely out, too.'

'You speak very good English, Magda,' Angel found herself saying, her natural curiosity asserting itself. 'Much better than Elena. How come?'

'Oh, that's because I worked here for a couple of years, a while ago. I picked up plenty then. I thought it would be good to come back. Thought I could get a pretty good job – I have qualifications. But I'd overlooked the whole Brexit business. Now you're not in the EU any longer, people from other countries can't just come over here to work any more. But Elena has never been out of Poland until now, so her English is what she learnt at school. And pretty good for that, I think.'

'Oh, yes, it is, I didn't mean to be critical. Considering how little Polish I know, I'm in no position to criticise. But go on. You were telling me your story.'

'Szczepan arranged flights for us to London, and a guy called Tommy O'Leary met us, and got us transferred to Belfast International Airport. We were met there by Jason Crawford.'

Angel nodded. This was the story she'd heard from Elena, except that Magda had the full names of the men who had dealt with them.

'You can imagine the rest. When we got to the house in Delamore Park, we found out almost at once that we'd been taken in by a people trafficking gang. Like you said, I could have slipped out easily enough, but I wanted to help the other girls get away – especially Elena, which was harder. And' – her face suddenly grew grim – 'I wanted to check out the names and addresses of the people running the trade. Well, I got enough of them – wrote them in my notebook which I carried in my shoulder bag and never let out of my sight – and then I stole a gun from one of the guards, and the rest was easy.'

'Okay!' Angel said briskly. 'The next step is to chase down the leader. You say you have an address?'

'You bet I have. The guy who tried to grab my shoulder bag was trying for the notebook. I don't know how he knew about it, mind you. But he didn't get it – thanks to you, by the way. I should have thanked you earlier.'

Angel waved Magda's thanks away. 'Is it far? Outside Belfast or what?'

'No, it's on the outskirts. On the Golden Mile.'

'Near Holywood, then? Okay. Do you want to come with me? I'm going there now. It's dark enough to give me plenty of cover.'

Magda laughed. 'Do I want to come with you? Who is it who has the address? It's a question of, 'Do you want to come with me?'

'Right. So we're both going. Come on, then.'

Chapter Eleven

The so called Golden Mile lies just east of Belfast on the far side of the coastal town of Holywood, on the edge of Belfast Lough. Many of the wealthiest people around had their houses there. Magda, leaning back luxuriously in the passenger seat of Angel's car, gave directions.

'Turn up here. Yes, that's right. Drive for about half a mile. The house stands by itself in its own grounds. Yes, this is it. We'd better pull in and park behind those trees. We don't want him to see us coming.'

Angel obeyed. She parked behind a cluster of pine trees, admiring the beautifully landscaped place as she did so and the amazing view down to Belfast Lough, which lay shining in the moonlight and reflecting the many lights of the city.

'He?' she questioned. 'I don't believe you gave me this guy's name, Magda.'

'No.' Magda suddenly shivered. 'I've held back, because it's going to be hard for you to believe.' She hesitated for another moment, then plunged in. 'You'll have heard of him. He's one of your leading politicians – Liam Hawthorne.'

Angel gasped. The man was one of the few local politicians whom she admired. 'Magda! Are you sure?'

'Told you you wouldn't believe me,' Magda said gloomily. 'But it's true. He's the big boss.'

'It's not that I don't believe you. But – how do you know?'

'I told you I'd been gathering information for a while. I found an email from him on Jason's computer. It was password protected of course, but Jason, like the fool he is, had scribbled it down and kept it in his desk drawer. It was signed Hawthorne. And I over-heard a conversation between a couple of the customers – I hid in one of the bedrooms deliberately – mentioning his name, Hawthorne, and saying what a good guy he was that he put them in touch with that awful place. I don't think there's any doubt.'

Angel drew in a sharp breadth. 'If we want anyone else to believe us, we'll need solid proof. And here in this house of his is the most likely place to find it. I'm going in, Magda. You should stay in the car. I could probably talk my way out of it if I got caught, but you might find it harder. If you hear anything to make you think they've got me, run for it.'

'Run for it? What do you think I am? I'm coming in, too. Try to stop me.'

And in spite of Angel's attempts to argue her out of her decision, Magda followed Angel out of the car.

'Okay. This is where we have to keep absolutely quiet, you hear me, Magda.'

Magda nodded. 'I've done this sort of thing before.'

'Starting right now.'

Angel began to move cautiously across the rougher grass until she reached the wide spreading lawn, with its borders packed with flowers which cast their scents abroad in all directions. There she halted for a moment, beckoned Madga nearer, and indicated the patio doors around the west side of the huge building. Angel reflected that while the house where the girls had been imprisoned was certainly big, this politician's home was a mansion by comparison.

They ran along the edge of the lawn, shielded from visibility from the house by the large clumps of flowers and decorative grasses, and flattened themselves against the wall of the house. Angel had her picklocks with her, but hoped the no one had thought of locking the patio doors, which gave access to a sun room.

It would be the door from the sun room into the house which would be carefully locked at night. But with a bit of luck, it was still early enough for them to find even this inside door still unlocked.

Chapter 11

She felt the handle of the nearest patio door and turned it gently. The door gave.

'Yes!' Angel could not resist a triumphant whisper.

She pushed the door just wide enough for access, then slipped in, followed equally silently by Magda.

The inside door – which led, from what Angel could see through its glass, into a large, beautifully furnished living room – was not so easy. It had, indeed, been prudently locked. However, the upside of that was that probably the inhabitants of the house had gone to bed, which would make it much easier for the two girls to search it for evidence of the owner's connection to the people trafficking they knew he was involved in. The fact that there was no sign of any lights switched on confirmed her hope.

Angel produced her picklocks and went to work. Presently she heard a click and realised thankfully that she had managed to unlock the door. She pushed it open, and again the two intruders slipped quietly in.

Angel, deciding that unfortunately it was necessary to communicate with Magda – that was the trouble with having someone with you – said, in the lowest possible tone, 'We want to find his office and check his computer, okay?'

Magda nodded approvingly.

A quick look round showed them that the room they stood in had nothing to offer them. It was full of comfortable chairs, low tables, and vases of flowers, but nothing in the shape of desk drawers, filing cabinets, or computers. Angel crossed the wooden floor, keeping carefully to the huge soft rugs scattered about at random, with Magda close on her heels. There was a door in the far wall and when she opened it softly Angel saw that it led into a hallway lined with more doors. It was possible that one of these led to the politician's office. At the end of the hall, a flight of stairs ran upwards.

They moved along the hall, and Angel tried the first door on the right. It was unlocked. The girls slipped in and were pleased to find themselves in what was clearly an office, equipped with the most up to date technology.

On the large oak desk, polished to extremes, over beside the window, was a state of the art laptop. Angel went quickly across to it.

'Keep a look out, Magda,' she murmured. 'Let me know at once if you hear anyone.'

Magda, nodded, and took up a position by the door into the hall, holding the door almost shut, leaving a tiny crack through which she could hear anyone approaching. Angel set to work on the computer.

She saw at once that it was password protected, as most computers were now. No means of access to the files or even the email unless she could work out what the password was. Many people, she knew, foolishly kept a note of their password in their desk drawers, or even on the top of the desk. A quick hunt told her that Liam Hawthorne had not been quite so foolish.

The next possibility was to break, not the computer, but the man, as she had once been advised. The chances were that the password would be something that meant something to Hawthorne. His wife's name or her birthday, or his own. Or a favourite dog, or a son or daughter.

That was where, Angel realised, they had come unequipped with the necessary knowledge. She thought the wife's name was Lucinda. She seemed to remember reading it in a newspaper article. But as for birthdays, family names – or even less, family pets – her mind was a blank.

She took her phone from her pocket, logged in to the internet connection, and looked up Liam Hawthorne on *Google*. A moment later, she was clicking on various articles about the politician. She noted birthdays, his wife's name, Lucinda, and other details, and then went to work.

Twenty minutes later, it seemed she had tried everything possible. The password was clearly something less obvious. Angel sighed.

She was reluctant to give up, but it was hard to know what else she could do to find the password.

'Maybe we should just search for physical evidence, Magda,' she whispered. 'There might be notes in his secretary's room, d'you think? Or an address book. Or she might have a computer easier to break into.'

Magda nodded. The secretary's room would probably be next door to Hawthorne's own office. They went out into the hall again. The best options were the room directly opposite on the other side of the hall, or the next door along on the right. Angel was making up her mind to cross the hall first when both girls heard a sound. It seemed to come from up the flight of stairs. Angel moved quietly along the hall to the foot of the stairs and stood there listening. Magda came up alongside her and waited.

The sounds were louder now that the girls were nearer to their source. They could make out loud sobs, mixed with wails.

'Someone's in trouble,' Angel said. 'Could Hawthorne have some girls hidden here? Or just one?' She listened for a few moments longer, then made up her mind.

'Come on, Magda. We're going up to see.'

Chapter Twelve

The stairs were luxuriously covered in a thick carpet, soft and modern and brightly coloured. They led to a corridor which was a match for the hall they had just left, with another set of doors on each side of it, this time leading, Angel guessed, to bedrooms and bathrooms. They advanced towards the noise of sobbing. It was coming from the third door on the left.

Angel without hesitation gave a gentle knock on the door and then pushed it open. Someone was lying on the bed inside. Someone who sat up suddenly at the sound of their approach, and exclaimed, 'Oh!'

Angel and Magda found themselves looking at a beautiful woman with curly red gold hair, slim and attractively dressed, but with her make up devastated by the marks of tear tracks across her cheeks. Angel remembered reading an article a few years ago, at the time of Hawthorne's marriage, saying that Mrs Liam Hawthorne, the former Lucinda Kilpatrick, had been a well known model, who had come into modelling after winning various beauty contests. In spite of the tears, the woman certainly lived up the flattering remarks that the writer of the article had made about her.

'Oh!' she said again. 'Who are you?' Then her face brightened up all of a sudden. 'You're police, aren't you? Have you come with news of Liam? Have you found him?'

'Liam Hawthorne?'

'Yes – my husband. He's disappeared. I don't know what to do! But you can't be the police, or you'd know that already.' She came back to her first question. 'Who are you?'

'No, Lucinda, we aren't police. But we're looking for Liam Hawthorne, too. Maybe we can help you. When did he disappear?'

'He went off a week ago, after he got an email from Jason Crawford. I thought it was just on one of his business trips to Poland. But he always rings me when he's settled in at his Polish house, and when he didn't, I got worried. So I rang the house, and they said he hadn't arrived. In fact, they said they hadn't been expecting him – he hadn't let them know he was coming. So then I didn't know what to do.'

The woman looked at them, on the verge of tears again.

'Maybe we can help you,' Angel said slowly again. An idea had sprung into her head. A good idea? Or a very bad idea? She wasn't sure yet.

The woman went on, 'So I rang his partner Jason, and Jason said, 'Don't worry, Lucinda, I'll look into it for you.' He said not to bother the police with it yet, Liam wouldn't like the publicity if he'd only gone to see someone in a different town. So I didn't ring the police, but I've been getting more and more upset, and when I saw you I thought maybe Jason had decided to tell the police after all. But you aren't the police, are you?'

Angel made her mind up. 'No. We aren't the police. We're private. Your friend Jason hired us. He thought it would be better that way. He sent us round to talk to you for a start.' She knew this was a risky statement, one which Lucinda might easily see through any minute if Angel said the wrong thing, but it seemed worth the risk.

'What can you tell us about his business in Poland?'

'Oh, nothing really. Nothing. Liam never talked to me about his business. He knew business wasn't really my thing. It's so boring, isn't it?'

'Do you know the names of any of his business associates out there, then?'

'Well – there's Szczepan Kowalski, I suppose. He came to dinner here once, a year or so ago. I don't really know any others.'

'And do you have any contact details for this guy? Address, home or office? Phone number?'

'I expect it might be in Liam's address book,' Lucinda Hawthorne said doubtfully.

'And where would I find the address book?'

'Oh, it isn't a real one. It's just one of those online things. Liam kept so much stuff on his computer. I couldn't be bothered with all that, myself. I keep my address book in my bag. But I don't have those sort of addresses.'

Angel felt like groaning out loud. So near, and yet so far. Then something occurred to her.

'I'll need to get into his computer, then,' she said briskly, trying to make it sound as if it was the most natural thing in the world to break into someone's computer. 'You'd better give me the password.'

'Oh.' Lucinda looked doubtful. But not, Angel was glad to see, out of any feeling that she ought not to give away her husband's secrets. 'I'm not sure I can remember it, I'll have to think.'

She swung her legs down from the bed and sat up, leaning forward and taking up the position of someone who was thinking. It clearly didn't come easily to her.

'I'm not sure. I know he used my name at one time, because he expected me to be pleased about it, and I suppose I was in a sort of way. Then I think he changed it to his mother's name, which I have to say annoyed me. I never got on well with that woman – but don't tell him I said that! Especially since she died a year or two ago. I think he changed it again after that.'

Angel was surprised to realize that Lucinda still expected to find her husband alive – but indeed, so he might be.

'I think he wrote it on a post it and struck it inside the wardrobe door,' Lucinda said at last.

She rose from the bed with a graceful motion and crossed the room to the fitted wardrobes which stood along one wall. Sliding open the glass doors, she stuck her head inside and peered around. Then her hand went out, and she took something off the left hand side of the first of the inside compartments of the wardrobe.

'Here it is!' she declared triumphantly. 'I suddenly remembered that he'd stuck it there. Yes, he'd changed it again.' She looked at the word written on the post it in considerable surprise. 'What a funny password!' she said. 'What on earth does it mean?'

'Let me see.' Angel took the post it from Lucinda's outstretched hand and read it. Then she passed it to Magda. 'It's Polish, isn't it?' she asked.

'Yes.' Angel saw Magda shudder. 'Yes. Mrs Hawthorne, is this the name of your husband's business?'

'Oh. Why did you think that? No, I don't think it is. I can't remember it now.'

Magda spoke to Angel, drawing her aside and speaking quietly so that Lucinda Hawthorne couldn't hear much of what she said, or so she hoped. 'It's a horrible sort of pun. It means a prostitute, but it's a word not many people would use, if you see what I mean. He's referring to the girls he uses, as if they didn't have to be forced into the things he makes them do, as if they were only too willing.'

Angel shuddered in turn. 'I think we'd better have a look at this computer. See if we can find any addresses. Then,' she turned back to Lucinda, 'then I'd like to go out to Poland and see what we can find out there. Perhaps we can track your husband down, Lucinda.'

'Oh, that would be great!' Lucinda spoke eagerly. 'I'd be happy to pay your costs – flights, accommodation and so on. If only you can find Liam.'

Angel hesitated. There was no question that the money would be useful. She was sure Magda couldn't afford to pay for herself, and while Angel could cover her own costs, she couldn't manage Magda's expenses as well. And yet the Polish girl would be very useful to her – not least because, unlike Angel herself, she spoke the language. On the other hand, was it fair to take Lucinda's money and use it to send her husband to prison?

Then she glanced again at the password in her hand, and decided that the man who had run this business deserved everything he had coming to him. He had to be stopped. And Lucinda would be far better off without him.

'Good idea, Lucinda,' she said. 'Now, let's go down and get busy on this computer.'

Chapter Thirteen

They left Lucinda behind, once more lying down on the bed, though, Angel was glad to see, no longer weeping. She just hoped Lucinda wouldn't take it into her head to try ringing Jason again. If she managed to get hold of him this time and he spilled the beans, they would have to leave fast, and with no expense money.

They made their way quickly back to the office where they had found Liam Hawthorne's computer, and Angel sat down, opened it up, and typed in the password from the post it. She was glad it was in a language she didn't know and couldn't even pronounce. To her relief, the computer responded by opening a list of files designated by icons, including email and an address book.

Taking out the memory stick she had brought with her, she selected the address book and copied it, checking to see that was on the stick and could be opened and read.

Then she turned to the email folder, and scanned through the list. There were a few from the man Lucinda had mentioned – Szczepan Kowalski. She read through them. They mainly consisted of arrangements for Szczepan to book tickets for a number of girls, and get them over to London and then Belfast. Nothing she didn't already know about. She noticed that they were addressed to *Top Cat*.

There were other emails from the man Jason – the one Elena, Magda, and more recently, Lucinda – had all mentioned. His most recent email was just reporting that the girls they had expected had arrived. Again, there was no new information in any of them, except that they also were addressed to Top Cat.

Angel switched off the computer. She stood up.

'Okay, Magda,' she said. 'We'll go back upstairs and get Lucinda to transfer enough money to my account to cover our costs for a trip to Poland. Then we'd better get out of here, fast, before anyone arrives to blow the whistle on us. Okay?'

'Okay.'

Lucinda proved to be very accommodating. In a short time, the necessary money was transferred.

Safely back in the car, Angel drove swiftly to her own apartment.

'Now, first of all a cup of coffee,' she said briskly. 'Then, we should book the earliest flight and a hotel, and get moving.'

'Coffee keeps me awake at night,' Magda pointed out. 'But maybe you think we should stay awake and alert until we get to Poland?'

'That would be the idea.'

The coffee warmed them both up, and Angel led the way to her own laptop, and began to search for flights. 'This Kowalski guy has an address in Krakow,' she said, 'so we'll go for flights there. Do we need to go by London or Dublin?''

'No,' Magda said. 'There are direct flights from Belfast. I think they sent us by way of London to confuse us – to make it harder for us to tell where we were.'

'Yes, that's probably right. If there's something direct from Belfast, we'll get the first flight we can.'

'We'll need to pack – just a carry on bag would be quicker and easier.'

'So it would. I'll go by way of your room, so you can grab what you need, as soon as I've got us booked. We'll need a hire car, too.'

She sat down at her laptop and got to work.

'Okay, Magda,' she said presently. 'I've found a flight going tomorrow and there is a *Hilton Garden Inn* at the airport that can give us a room. Now I'm going to check that Lucinda's transferred money is safely in my account before I confirm the booking. While I'm doing that, do you think you can work out where this guy

Kowalski's address is? Somewhere in Krakow, but whereabouts? It would help to have at least a vague idea.'

'No problem. I can look it up on *Google Maps* if you lend me your iPad. I'm not familiar with Krakow, but if we get a car with SatNav, we can enter the address, even if I can't find it on the map.'

'Yeah, of course. I should have thought of that.'

The money was already in her account. Angel confirmed the various bookings, and hired a car which was equipped with SatNav.

Getting packed – both Angel and Magda – letting Mary and Elena know what was happening, and reaching *Belfast International Airport* in time to check in and work their way through Security at the extremely early hour required by the authorities, took all the time they had. There was no question of sleep that night. And she wouldn't be able to go to the police station to make a statement about Brutus and his attack on Magda. Well, that couldn't be helped.

Angel, who never found it possible to sleep on planes, spent the flight questioning Magda – who didn't want to sleep either – about Poland, in particular Krakow, one of the main cities.

Krakow was a much larger city than Angel had expected, according to Magda, full of impressive buildings which Magda described at length – such as the beautiful St Mary's Basilica, and the Old Town, with its huge square surrounded by the remains of the old mediaeval city. Angel knew she would enjoy seeing it, but realised regretfully that she couldn't spend time there sightseeing. She needed to track down the men who were running this despicable people trafficking business.

'We have two leads, as far I've been thinking, Magda,' she said presently. 'First of all, the name and address of his own house that we got from Hawthorne's computer. But secondly, there's the guy who arranged for you and Elena to go to London with a promise of jobs when you got to Belfast. We have an address for him, but I'm hoping you might have his mobile number?'

'Oh, sure, no problem there,' Madga assured her. 'Szczepan Kowalski. I have all his contact details on my phone. But I don't think he's anything but a gofer – at the foot of the ladder.'

'Fair enough,' Angel agreed, 'but we should probably look into him at some point. Hawthorne's own house first, then. Let's hope the SatNav can take us straight to the address we have.'

'Yep – but I sure hope we're going to the hotel for a rest first,' Magda said.

'Okay, that would be best,' agreed Angel.

Arriving at Krakow Airport, they went first to the car hire desk and collected their car, then drove to the *Hilton Garden Inn* – only a few hundred yards away – where they were able to park before going in.

'Let's go down and eat first,' suggested Angel. 'Unless you want to rest? I could go on down on my own if you'd rather wait.'

'I think I will,' agreed Magda thankfully, collapsing onto one of the twin beds in their pleasant room. 'See you later.'

Chapter Fourteen

The hotel dining room was buzzing – full of excited tourists. A rock band had just arrived, staying at the *Hilton* to prepare for their gig that evening. Angel was delighted to see Sandy McDowell, whom she had met through her friends Fitz, Jonty, Mars, and the rest – the members of Fitz's band, *Raving*. Angel waved across the room, and Sandy, giving a shriek of delight, came rushing across the room to hug her enthusiastically.

'Come and sit with us!' Sandy invited her. 'It's great to see you again, Angel!'

'Us?' Angel asked.

'*Rock On* – I'm their lead singer now, did you know?'

'Wow! Congrats, sweetheart!' Angel said warmly. 'I noticed the posters saying they were playing here tonight.'

Rock On, an up and coming band, had impressed her when she'd interviewed them for her Arts programme a while ago. Sandy was doing well to have been chosen as their lead singer.

'What happened to Tommy McBride?' she asked. 'He was lead when last I was in touch. Did he leave the band?'

'Oh, no, he hasn't left us,' Sandy assured her. 'I don't know where the band would be without him. No, he decided to concentrate on playing guitar, writing the songs – or most of them – and arranging gigs. He says that keeps him more than busy enough. Here –' she dragged Angel by the hand over to a noisy table where half a dozen people were eating, drinking, and joking – 'Tommy, you remember Angel Murphy, don't you?'

Tommy, a huge, overweight but nevertheless amazingly attractive young man, surged to his feet and hugged Angel until she wriggled free, laughing and protesting.

'Tommy, you'll squeeze me to death!'

'Angel, darlin', what a marvellous surprise! Are you staying over-night? You gotta come and hear us – I'll get you a free ticket. You're looking as beautiful as ever! Come and sit down.'

Sitting among the band members with Tommy on one side and Sandy on the other, Angel joined happily in the laughter and jokes. The band – aware that they would be playing in a few hours – were keyed up, energised and terrified, keeping themselves from fear by their jokes, on an adrenalin high.

'You're right in the middle of McDonald's now, Angel,' Robin the drummer told her, trying to look serious.

'What do you mean?' Angel asked.

'Well, Tommy's nickname for ages has been Big Mac,' Robin told her. Angel realised that she should have remembered that. 'And now that we have Sandy McDowell singing lead, she has to be Little Mac, of course.'

Angel couldn't stop laughing. After the horrors of the last week, starting with the cold and shivering Elena, then hearing her story, and the continually upsetting facts that had emerged at the house where the girls had been kept, and from Magda, it was wonderful to escape from misery into fun. But she was a still determined to put an end to Liam Hawthorne's dreadful trafficking.

'So, you're coming to the gig tonight, aren't you Angel?' Bobby persuaded her. 'And, I tell you what, we've been invited to an after gig party by Liam Hawthorne. He has a huge house out here – runs a business as well as being a politician. It'll be great – heaps of food and booze – you must come.'

'Liam Hawthorne?' Angel repeated slowly. 'Yes, why not, Bobby. Only one thing. I have a friend travelling with me, a Polish girl. I can't very well leave her in the hotel on her own.'

'No problemo! I'll get a ticket for her as well, and one more at the party won't matter.'

'Great!' said Angel briskly. 'Her name's Magda. She'll be delighted.'

Chapter 14

Heading back to her room after a marvellous lunch, with Liam's promise to send tickets for her and Magda to the hotel reception desk, Angel found the Polish girl still sleeping, and decided that a short rest would be a good idea for herself.

Getting up from the twin bed a couple of hours later, she showered and dressed, putting on a gold satin tunic which came to mid thigh and threading a gold ribbon through her soft fair hair. It was only when she dropped her hairbrush with a loud bang on the dressing table that Magda finally opened her eyes and sat up.

'You're dressed to kill, Angel,' she said sleepily.

'You're so right, Magda,' giggled Angel. 'I'm all set to kill Liam Hawthorne tonight.'

Magda looked puzzled, and Angel explained.

'So, we'll go to *Rock On*'s gig, and then to Hawthorne's party,' she concluded, 'and if we can't work out some way to take that fiend down tonight, we don't deserve this opportunity.'

'Wow!' Madga said enthusiastically. 'Talk about luck!'

'You'd better get changed, and then we'll go down and eat something. You haven't eaten since whatever meal you had yesterday – I don't want you collapsing just when I need you,' Angel scolded.

Madga obediently showered and dressed in a clinging scarlet top of almost see through chiffon, and a short cream skirt, while Angel withdrew to the balcony to give her some privacy, and surveyed the planes flying in and out of the airport next door. Then they went down to the hotel dining room. The menu – as well as more usual dishes – had a number of Polish specialities, and on Magda's recommendation, they both had *kotlet schabowy* – or schnitzel.

'That was great, Magda,' Angel said, laying down her knife and fork, 'but I don't think I can finish it.'

'No problem,' said Magda. Swopping plates with Angel, she happily devoured the rest of the meal. 'We don't want the chef to feel hurt and insulted,' she joked.

Having eaten every bite, she then went on to the Baked Cheese-cake, another Polish speciality, and insisted on Angel trying a bite, 'Just to see what you're missing.'

'Yum,' agreed Angel. 'I must definitely have this another time.'

Then, picking up their tickets for the gig at the reception desk, they went out to the hired car.

'It's just as well we got one with SatNav,' Angel said, 'for I couldn't follow the desk clerk's instructions on how to get to the pub where they're performing. Oh, I was forgetting, probably you followed every word, Magda, and would know your way round Krakow in any case.'

'I certainly understood the clerk,' Madga agreed. 'And I know the venue, *The Flying Machine*. It's one of the most popular pubs in the city. They set up gigs regularly, but only the best. Your friends *Rock On* must be good.'

'Oh, they are,' Angel assured her. 'Haven't you heard of them?'

'I haven't got out much for the last while,' Madga said. Then seeing Angel's dismayed face – how could she have forgotten what Magda had been going through for the past months? – she added hastily, 'but it would be just as well to put the address in the SatNav. I've never driven there, and I might take you the wrong way down one way streets.'

With the help of the SatNav, they arrived safely at *The Flying Machine*, a large new looking building flashing neon lights and posters advertising *Rock On*, with crowds of people pushing their way in at the entrance.

Inside, the venue was huge, with tables scattered all round, a stage crammed with sound equipment at one end, and huge speakers on the walls. Most people were pushing their way to the front, intending to dance. Angel was glad to be able to grab a table for herself and Magda not too far back.

'Keep our seats, Magda, and I'll push up to the bar and get us something to drink.'

Coming back some time later having reached the end of a long queue, she handed Magda a bottle of lager, and, opening her own, clinked it against Magda's.

'Here's to us and to *Rock On.*'

Before they had been settled down for long, several other people had joined them, filling the remaining chairs and then dragging two more seats from other tables to accommodate the rest of their party. Looking round the crowded room, Angel was glad to see that dress seemed to vary. Jeans were the most popular for both sexes, but many of the girls wore short skirts like their own, in bright exciting colours.

The sound of chatter filled the room, and Angel and Magda could hardly hear each other speaking. Then the MC announced *Rock On*, and the band ran onstage, waving and calling out to their audience. A roar of delight filled the room, with whistles, clapping hands, and stamping feet.

The band burst into their first number, and Angel – who had heard them before and thought well of them – realised that since then they had improved a thousand fold.

'Wow!' murmured Magda into her ear. 'You were right. They're amazing.'

The rest of the audience clearly thought so too. The cheering, stamping and clapping continued between every song. Angel, getting well into the music, was suddenly horrified to feel a hot, heavy hand creeping up her thigh under her skirt. Jerking back, she glared at the fat, unpleasant looking man sitting next to her. 'Stop that!' she hissed at him.

The man, however, ignoring her angry look, kept his hand on her thigh and continued to move it upwards. Angel reflected that it was a good thing she had changed out of her trainers to go out for the evening and was wearing her highest, sharpest stilettos. Lifting her foot she brought the heel down sharply on the foot rubbing against hers.

A sharp yell from the owner of the injured foot almost drowned out the band for a second, and the fat man jerked back as far as he could get, taking his hand with him.

'Keep away, unless you want more of that!' Angel said furiously.

Magda and those near enough to have taken in what was going on, were laughing. It took Angel a few moments to recover her temper, then reluctantly she laughed too. The fat man stood up, and took himself off, limping, to stand at the back with others unable to find a seat.

The band played on, and nothing else happened to spoil the gig for Angel, who was enjoying herself hugely. Her only wish was that Josh, her boyfriend, was with her. Josh worked with *Interpol*, and was currently up to his neck in a case whose details he had been unable to share with Angel because it was confidential.

It occurred to Angel that she should text him and ask if he knew anything about Liam Hawthorne. He might well have some *Interpol* info about Hawthorne which could help them in their determination to expose him for the villain he was.

Chapter Fifteen

The gig came to an end. Angel and Magda kept their seats and allowed most of the audience to leave before them. Angel wondered where to go backstage to find the band, who had promised to take them to the post gig party. It was very possible that there would be bouncers who would prevent them getting to *Rock On*. But she needn't have worried. Looking about her, she saw Sandy coming towards her, beaming with pleasure at such a successful gig.

'Angel! I'm so glad you came!'

'Wouldn't have missed it, Sandy. You were all great! I nearly died when your drummer ripped off his sweaty T shirt and hurled it into the audience. They certainly loved you, and so did we.'

'Aw, thanks, sweetie,' Sandy blushed. 'Hi. You're Magda?' she added, trying to change the subject. But it didn't work. Magda's praise was as enthusiastic as Angel's.

'Angel told me how good you are, but now I know for myself,' she ended. 'You guys are right up at the top!'

'So, are you both coming to this party with us?' Sandy asked hastily.

'Looking forward to it,' Angel assured her.

'Great. There should be a great spread – the guy's seriously rich and generous with it. Tommy and the rest should be along any minute. I got first go with the shower. You wouldn't believe the amount of sweat you build up at a gig,' she explained.

Just then Tommy – otherwise Big Mac – appeared, closely followed by Robin and the other two band members.

'Great to see you, Angel. And you, Magda. Aw, stop it,' as the girls repeated their praise of the gig, 'What we want to do now is sort out transport. You've got you own car? Well, probably best if Sandy takes Magda in the Minibus with the other three, and I go with you, Angel, in your car, to make sure you get there safely. Okay?'

Angel exchanged a glance with Magda, making sure she was happy with this arrangement, then nodded smilingly to Tommy. 'That sounds good, Tommy. Lead the way.'

The way took them to the outskirts of Krakow, to an area full of woodland and huge houses set in enormous grounds, where each house was so far back from the main road that it was difficult to see it. Driving through locked iron gates which opened when Tommy spoke into the *Ansaphone* set in one of the pillars, Angel found herself in a lovely garden where flowerbeds lined with numbers of flowers ran along each side of the long drive. As they drove in, lights came on to guide their way, and Angel could see – as well as smell – camellias, hellebore, all the flowers she loved.

The money for this must have come from the sale of those helpless girls hijacked with promises of good jobs and imprisoned in that hateful house back home in Belfast, Angel supposed. Suddenly the delicious smell of the flowers made her feel sick.

Driving on, they reached the gravel semi circle in front of the house, where numerous cars were already parked. Angel found room over to the left hand side, got out, followed by Tommy, and locked the car. Behind the huge gates it was probably safe enough from theft, but Angel was taking no chances on being left without a way of escape from this dreadful man, Liam Hawthorne.

Looking up at the snow covered house – which was blazing with light – she realised that the doors were wide open, with the sound of voices and music pealing out cheerfully. A large, red faced man whose blond hair fell over his left eye, was standing in the doorway, welcoming newcomers.

'It's the Big Mac himself!' he shouted at Tommy as he and Angel mounted the steps. 'And who's your lovely lady friend?' He beamed at Angel. His soft Irish voice reminded her strikingly of Belfast. She couldn't help thinking that, although this was obviously the party host, and therefore had to be Liam Hawthorne, he didn't either sound or look like the brute he must be.

'This is Angel Murphy, Liam,' Tommy said. 'You must have seen her on television back home.' He ushered Angel in past Hawthorne, who slapped his forehead melodramatically.

'Of course!' he roared. 'I should have recognised you at once, Angel. Come right on in and let me get you a drink.' Leaving the doors wide open, he rushed into the huge hall and on into the room on the right where drinks and a buffet meal were spread out in profusion. 'I can recommend the special cocktail created for tonight, in honour of out great local band, *Rock On*. I'm calling it Irish Mix – Irish whiskey, Bailey's Cream, and a few other secret ingredients. You'll love it darlin'.'

Without waiting for Angel's consent, he poured her a green coloured drink from an enormous cocktail shaker and thrust it into her hand, encouraging her to try it.

Angel took a cautious sip. It was good, but probably pretty strong. Angel intended to stay on the alert tonight. Drinking cocktails this size wasn't the best way to start.

The room was packed, and she could hear loud voices, shrieks and yells coming from another room across the hall. She was looking round for any sign of Magda or Sandy when a very attractive and beautifully dressed woman – probably older than Angel but looking quite young – tapped Hawthorne on the shoulder. 'Great to see you again, Liam,' she murmured, leaning close to his ear. 'Are you staying in Krakow for long?'

'Stella!' Hawthorne boomed. 'So glad you could come. Here, let me get you a cocktail.'

He turned slightly away from Angel to pour Stella a drink, and Angel took the opportunity to slip away. A quick glance around the room told her that Magda wasn't here. She must be in the room across the hall, unless she was upstairs – or unless there were even more rooms on the ground floor. Angel set out to look for her.

She intended to spend some time talking to Hawthorne later in the evening, but just now he was so busy welcoming guests that she didn't think it was the right time. Meanwhile, possibly she and Magda could do a bit of exploring, and see if they could find any evidence that Hawthorne was involved in people trafficking.

The room on the left of the hall was even larger that the one she had been in. There was another table full of food and drink, and Sandy, with Tommy and Robin, was standing at it, each helping themselves to the nourishment they badly needed after throwing themselves so energetically into the gig.

'Hi,' Angel greeted them. 'Any idea where my friend Magda is?'

'Oh, she met a friend – a local businessman, I think – and went off upstairs with him.' Sandy winked. 'The party's spread over the whole house, so she won't be lonely up there. I think that's mostly where people are dancing.'

Angel raised an eyebrow. 'Well, I suppose she knows what she's doing.'

'Oh, I guess she does – she seemed pretty happy to see him.'

Angel wasn't so sure. Could Magda have met the guy who'd entrapped her and then Elena? It seemed only too possible. Was she carrying out a bit of detective work on her own?

Slipping away from her company for the second time, Angel made for the stairs. Magda might be fine, but it would do no harm to check her out.

Music was pouring down from one of the upstairs rooms, getting louder as Angel approached it. She noticed that there were two rooms in use, one large and full of people and loud music, the other smaller and with dimmer lights, quieter music, and fewer people.

There was no sign of Magda in the bigger room. Turning away, Angel saw some people coming out of the small room and going back downstairs, probably for another drink. She moved over to the doorway and peered in.

There was only one couple left in there now. Angel recognised Magda's red skirt. She was dancing with a large heavy looking man whose back was to Angel so that she could only see his dark hair, hanging over the open collar of his shirt.

Magda seemed okay. Angel was about to go quietly away when she heard Magda scream. What was going on?

Chapter Sixteen

Then she saw that the man's hand was now clapped over Magda's mouth, and realised that he was twisting one of her arms up behind her back. Magda's foot was kicking him furiously.

Even as Angel saw what was going on, Magda, trying to kick harder, overbalanced. Suddenly she was on the floor, with the dark haired man, laughing viciously, on top of her. He was ripping off her chiffon top, and saying something in Polish which sounded both gloating and triumphant. Madga was still struggling, but ineffectively.

Angel, not pausing to think, rushed forward, grabbing up a heavy looking vase from a low table just inside the door.

Crash!

The vase broke over the man's head, showering him with water and lilies. He collapsed on top of Magda, groaning in pain.

It took both the girls all their strength to push him to one side so that Magda could escape from under him.

'Wow! Thanks so much!' said Magda breathlessly. 'I really thought I was for it that time.'

'What happened?'

'My own stupid fault. That's Szczepan Kowalski, who got me and Elena involved in this business in the first place. When he turned up at the party, I thought I could make up to him and get him to give out some info about Hawthorne and whoever else is involved. Get him to turn King's Evidence, maybe. More fool me. All he wanted was sex, and when he saw I wasn't putting out, he just decided to take me by force. Thank heavens you came along.'

'It was a good idea, Magda. But this Szczepan is obviously tougher than you hoped. Let's leave him to recover by himself and go back downstairs. Safety in numbers.'

Back in the larger of the downstairs rooms, they were hailed straightaway by Tommy.

'Come and meet some people, girls.'

He began introducing them to a number of men, and in a very short time they were both dancing with Tommy's friends. Angel was laughing at a clever remark made by her partner – one of the band, by name Eddie Peterson – when she noticed that someone had come up behind her. An arm crept round her waist.

'Hi, Angel,' whispered a familiar voice. 'Can I cut in?'

Angel stiffened. A thrill shot up and down her spine and her legs felt curiously weak. She twisted her head round to see the speaker.

'Josh!'

'Josh it is.'

'Josh, what are you doing here?'

'Probably the same thing as you, Angel.'

For a moment Angel leaned back into Josh's warm embrace, rejoicing in the sheer pleasure of having him near her again. Then she recollected herself, and said, smilingly, to Eddie, 'Eddie, this is my friend Josh. Josh, this is Eddie. Eddie, I hope you won't think we're really rude, but if you don't mind, I need to talk to Josh. Okay?'

Eddie put on a fierce expression. 'Fight me for her!' Then he laughed, and said, 'Okay, okay. But I'm hoping to see you later, Angel.'

Josh took Angel's hand and led her through the crowded dance floor and out through the open patio doors into the garden. The fresh night air embraced them in welcome, as they made their way over to a darker corner behind some rhododendron bushes. Stopping there, Josh took Angel in his arms and kissed her thoroughly.

Chapter 16

The kiss went on for some time. Finally Angel, shaken, pulled reluctantly away.

'Oh, Josh, it's so good to see you.'

'Yip.'

'But what are you doing here, really?'

'Tracking the traffickers. People trafficking, I mean.'

'Snap.'

'*Interpol* have been aware for some time of a gang based here in Poland, but until recently we haven't been able to get enough information about them, let alone evidence.'

'So what's changed?'

'A girl came to her local police and told them she'd almost been abducted, but had managed to get away, and she knew the plan had been to take her to another country and use her to make money.'

'And she was able to tell you the names of people involved?'

'That's it, Angel. The local police got in touch with us in *Interpol*, since it was an international business, and that's why I'm here – following up her info.'

'Well, Josh, it so happens that I'm probably following up a trail to the same people as you. Starting from the other end. Would Szczepan Kowalski be one of the names you were given?'

'Wow! Yes, that's the recruiter guy. How come, Angel? Where did you pick that name up?'

'It's a long story. I met this girl – Elena – in Belfast city centre one evening, and she'd just escaped from a big house up past the Lagan Meadows, where she'd been kept with a crowd of girls, lured there under false pretences – promises of jobs, and so on. She told me it was this Szczepan Kowalski who got her involved, here in Krakow.

Her friend Magda, the one who organised the breakout, helped me investigate at the Belfast end, and then flew out here with me to follow up things. You need to talk to her, she can help you. Incientally, this Szczepan guy is here tonight.'

'I know. That's why I'm here.' Josh looked at her. 'Angel, as usual you're being a great help. Really amazing. Thanks, babe.'

'Just the Murphy service,' Angel grinned. 'Oh, Josh. I've really missed you.'

'Me, too, Angel. Isn't it time we did something about this?'

He took her in his arms again, and time passed with neither of them aware of it.

They were interrupted by a loud voice calling, 'Angel! Angel Murphy! Are you out there?'

It was Tommy McBride.

'Over here, Tommy!' Angel called.

Tommy could be heard approaching through the bushes. Angel and Josh drew apart.

'Sorry to interrupt something, sweetheart,' Tommy apologised, laughing, 'but it's time to go.'

Angel glanced at her watch and saw with amazement that it was after two o'clock.

'We need our beauty sleep, another gig happening tomorrow, in Warsaw, up north, and we have to drive there and get set up and do the sound check. So an early start, right?'

'Tommy, I'm so sorry if I've kept you,' Angel said.

'No problem, Angel. But the bus has gone, and I'm depending on you for a lift.'

'Yes, of course,' Angel said hurriedly. 'I suppose Magda went in the bus?'

'I suppose so.' Tommy didn't seem too worried.

'Josh, looks like things aren't going to work out tonight. Can you come round tomorrow? I'm in the airport *Hilton Garden Inn*.'

Josh put his arm round her shoulder and gave her a quick hug. 'See you tomorrow, then, honey.'

The drive back to the hotel seemed very long. By the time they arrived, at nearly half past two, Angel was only too ready to sleep. Thanking Tommy for a great evening, she took the lift up to her room and went in quietly, quite prepared to see Magda already fast asleep on her bed. But the room was empty.

Angel sat down on her own bed, puzzled. Had Magda gone to the bar with some of the band for a last drink? But surely the bar would be closed down by now? She picked up the information booklet from the desk and skimmed through it. Yes, the times were there in black and white. The bar closed at two o'clock.

Then, perhaps a last drink in someone's room?

Angel picked up the phone and rang Magda's number. The phone rang and rang, but there was no answer. Next she tried Tommy's room number.

'Hi. It's the nuisance again. Tommy, Magda isn't in our room. Could you check with some of the others to see if she's with them – maybe having a last drink? I'm getting worried. You're sure she came back on the bus?'

'Okay, Angel, don't worry, I'll check. But I'm sure it's okay.'

'Thanks, Tommy.'

Putting down the phone, Angel sat down to wait for news of her friend.

It was five minutes later when Tommy rang back.

'Listen, Angel, Magda isn't with any of the others. They all went straight to their own rooms, like good little band members, and started in to get a good night's sleep. But, see, no one remembers her being on the bus. I suppose they thought she'd be with you. Sorry. Really careless of them. She must still be at Liam's house. Do you want me to ring and check?'

'No, don't do that, Tommy. Tell you what, I'll drive back and pick her up. She'll be needing a lift – and wondering where I've got to. Okay, thanks for your help. Sorry to bother you.'

She put down the phone in spite of Tommy's protests. The night had been getting chilly when they came back to the hotel. Angel slipped on a warm jacket, and headed back downstairs to find her car and drive back to Liam Hawthorne's, worry growing in her as she went.

Chapter Seventeen

To her dismay, the house was dark and quiet. She parked and walked round, looking for a light anywhere. At the back premises, she noticed light shining from one of the windows, and approached it cautiously.

Looking in, she could see Liam Hawthorne standing with his back to her, putting a spoonful of what seemed to be instant coffee, judging from the jar sitting on the worktop beside him, into a mug, and waiting for the electric kettle to boil. He bent down to take a carton of milk from the fridge, poured some into his mug, and went on waiting. Presently the kettle boiled, and he poured the boiling water into his mug. With a sigh of satisfaction, he sipped, then turned away from the worktop. He was facing Angel now.

Before he had turned completely round, Angel knocked hastily on the window.

Hawthorne both saw and heard her, and jumped in shock, almost spilling his coffee. He came quickly round to the back door, not far from the window, and called, 'Who is it? What do you want?' Then, as he focussed on her, 'Is that you, Angel Murphy? Is something the matter? Did you leave your handbag behind – or what?'

'Not my handbag – my friend,' said Angel crisply. 'My friend Magda. She hasn't turned up at the hotel. Is she still here?'

'No, no, I'm sorry, she's long gone, like everyone else. You were among the last to leave, Angel.'

'You're sure she's gone? Did you see her leave?'

'No I didn't see her. But probably, don't you think, she got a lift with someone. Or – er – went home with him, maybe? People do, after parties, don't they?'

'Magda wouldn't have gone off without telling me.'

'Oh, I don't know. She seemed to be getting very friendly with Szczepan. You know, Szczepan Kowalski, you met him, didn't you. Szczepan seemed very smitten. He told me he'd met your Magda before.'

'Szczepan is the last person she'd have gone off with – unless she'd had a roofie. Could we have a look around? She might have passed out and be lying somewhere.'

'Well,' said Liam reasonably, 'if you really think it's worth it, we can have a bit of a hunt. But I think my caterers would have noticed her, and told me, when they were clearing up, don't you?'

Angel had to admit that this seemed likely, but she wasn't going without looking round. Seeing she was determined, Hawthorne shrugged apathetically, and began to lead her around the house.

Angel followed him determinedly. She wasn't quite sure what she expected to find, if anything, but she knew it when she saw it – Madga's shoulder bag, kicked half hidden under an armchair in one of the upper rooms.

She pounced on it immediately. 'Her bag! She wouldn't have gone without it!'

'Maybe she dropped it earlier, and couldn't find it when she was leaving?' offered Hawthorne.

Angel wasn't listening to him. She had opened the handbag and was searching through it for anything that would help.

Liam Hawthorne stood watching her, swaying gently, his big red face redder than ever, his blond hair falling over his forehead. Angel realised that he was more than slightly drunk. It was no use expecting him to be of any help. Especially if – as she and Magda had suspected – he was the brains of the people trafficking gang himself. She straightened up.

'I'll take this and give it back to her when I find her,' she announced. 'Do you have an address for this Szczepan character, Liam?'

Chapter 17

'Oh, but if your friend Magda went home with him, she wouldn't want you to come bursting in!' Liam Hawthorne objected. 'And certainly Szczepan wouldn't.'

'I don't really care what Szczepan wants. The address?'

'I don't really know. He has a flat somewhere here in Krakow. And a house out in the country. But I don't have exact addresses for them. I usually just ring him, or he rings me, if we want to meet up.'

'That'll do.'

Hawthorne produced his phone. 'I'll text it to you.'

Angel produced her phone in turn, and the text message with Szczepan Kowalski's number appeared quickly.

'Okay, thanks, Liam. I'll head on, now.'

Making her way downstairs and outside to her car, it occurred to Angel that the sensible thing to do would be to phone Josh, and get him to go with her. It was quite likely, she realised, that Josh would have Szczepan Kowalski's address – or even both of them.

She settled herself in the car, and rang him.

'Josh?'

'Angel, babe.'

'Josh, Magda has disappeared. I think Szczepan Kowalski has grabbed her.'

Josh whistled.

'Bad news.'

'Can you come with me to find her?'

'Sure thing, Angel. Where are you?'

'Back at Liam Hawthorne's. But Hawthorne says Kowalski has a flat in the city. Do you have the address?'

'I have. I'll text it to you.'

A moment later the address appeared on Angel's phone.

'Can you find it?'

'Well, I have SatNav, so probably.'

'Tell you what, head back to your hotel and I'll meet you in the car park there, okay?'

'Okay. See you.'

Angel drove back along the by now very familiar road to the hotel. Sure enough, as she pulled into the car park, there was Josh waving at her.

'C'mon, get into my car,' he said. 'No point in taking two cars – and I know the city better. We'll start by heading for Kowalski's apartment, and while we drive you can fill me in on what's been happening.'

'Well,' began Angel, settling herself into the passenger seat of Josh's hired car, 'I couldn't find Magda when I was leaving Hawthorne's house, so I assumed she'd gone back in the band bus – she'd come in it. But when I got to the hotel, no sign of her, and the band hadn't brought her back after all. I went back to inquire at Hawthorne's. Liam Hawthorne thought she'd left with Szczepan. End of info.'

'But why would she do that?'

'She wouldn't. Unless,' a sudden thought struck Angel, 'she was still trying to get some info from him. But after what happened earlier, I don't think that's likely. Magda's brave, but she's not a fool.'

'So, what happened earlier?'

'Didn't I tell you? She thought if she cosied up to Szczepan she might be able to get him to open up and get some real evidence against Liam Hawthorne. But it ended up with him trying to rape her. I just got there in time. Not that she wasn't putting up a good fight herself.'

'Liam Hawthorne?'

'Yes, we're pretty sure he's Mister Big in the people trafficking thing.'

'That's not the line *Interpol* have been following.'

'Well, we based it on things Magda learnt while she was a prisoner in the house where they kept the people they'd taken. And we followed it up by breaking into his house in Belfast and questoning his wife.'

'Wow, Angel, you're some chick!'

'Well, so are we nearly at this guy's apartment, Josh?'

'Nearly there. I think I'll park as near as I can get to it. This time of night, there'll be plenty of space.'

Josh was right. There was room for him to park at the kerb, almost in front of Kowalski's apartment. There was a car just in front of it which they decided must be his own.

'So what's the next move, Angel?'

'Hammer at the door and bust in if he doesn't open it?'

'Yeah, well.'

'Why not? If that's his car, he's there.'

'But maybe Magda isn't.'

'True.'

'How about ringing her? See if she's able to answer.'

'Great! – it was the first thing I did, of course, but there was no answer. Maybe it'll be different this time.'

Angel took out her phone and rang the number Magda had given her.

The phone rang – and rang. But Magda didn't answer.

'So,' said Angel. 'How about it, Josh? Will we knock politely and then come away? Or will we beat the door in?'

'How about a combination? Knock fairly politely. And if no one answers, we can use brute force.'

'I'm for that. Let's go.'

They hopped out of the car, and were starting for the door, when suddenly it opened part way. There were two figures coming out.

'Quick,' Josh murmured.

They backed towards the car and slipped out of sight behind it. Angel could see round the nearside window. One of the figures was Szczepan. The other was Magda.

Chapter Eighteen

Angel watched anxiously. There seemed to be something strange about Magda. She was propped against Szczepan, and hardly seemed able to move her legs and feet. Szczepan was half carrying her, half dragging her along towards his car. Angel moved forward instinctively to intervene, but Josh's hand gripping her arm painfully halted her.

Whispering in her ear, he said, 'No. We'll follow them.'

Angel understood that Josh wanted to find out what Szczepan was up to, but her own feeling was that she wanted to rescue Magda before anything serious happened to her. She decided that she would have to trust Josh on this. She had asked for his help. No use doing that and then rejecting his advice.

They continued to watch silently as the man dragged the helpless girl to his car, opened the passenger door, and bundled her in. He ran round to the driver's side and jumped in. The engine roared.

Under cover of the noise, Josh said very quietly, 'Now.'

Moving quickly and cautiously, Josh and Angel slipped into their own car. They gave Szczepan Kowalski a minute of two to get away, then Josh pulled out after him, keeping a safe distance. Angel understood that Josh didn't want the man to realise he was being followed.

There was very little traffic on the roads so late at night. All the same the going was tricky enough. The drivers who were still around might all have been drinking, for they were swerving all over the road, and Josh needed all his skill to keep Szczepan Kowalski's car in sight without having an accident. She could only be glad – although aware that she was an excellent driver herself – that her own skills were not being put to the test tonight.

It was some time before they began to leave the built up area behind them and reach open country. There were fewer cars around now. They were heading in the opposite direction from Hawthorne's house, Angel noted.

The car in front pulled off to the right, and suddenly they had left the good straight roads and were driving through country lanes, winding and potholed. From fewer cars they were down to none, and were far too obvious to someone checking in their rear view mirror.

Josh slowed down to allow Szczepan Kowalski to get further ahead. It was important that he should not see their car following him. Keeping as far away and as slow as possible round the many bends, speeding up only when Kowalski was drawing too far ahead, Josh followed him until they reached a turnoff which took them within sight of high iron gates. Kowalski slowed to a halt and sounded his horn.

Presently someone opened the gates from inside, and the car pulled forward.

'Now what?'

'Now I think we get out and see if we can slip through those gates, or what.'

Josh parked well away from the gates – out of sight of anyone inside them – and he and Angel got out of the car and crept forward, concealed by the heavy bushes which lined both sides of the road.

The gates, when they reached them, were clearly impossible. They were shut and not only locked but bolted on the inside, as Angel could easily see. Moreover the bolt looked both big and strong.

'Well, we can't open them, Josh.'

'Climb over?'

'Yeah, possibly. But isn't someone close by inside?'

'The guy who let Kowalski in?'

'Correct.'

'You could be right.'

'So, let's walk round the edge of the property and see if we can find an easier place to climb.'

'Agreed.'

They set off round the grounds, walking at first towards their right – away from where they had parked the car – along a sturdy and fairly high wooden fence.

'This looks quite possible,' said Josh. 'But we should get further away from the gate and from whoever is on watch.'

They progressed onwards, finally coming to a point where the fence, and presumably the grounds, turned sharply left. Some yards further, the fence became lower and easier to climb.

'Good,' said Josh briskly. 'Let's try here. You'll need to hitch that skirt up. Not that there's much of it to start with.'

Angel looked down at her short golden tunic.

'I wore it for dancing, not for climbing fences.'

'Oh, I'm not complaining.'

He stopped where a sturdy oak tree with extending branches almost touched the edge of the fence.

'This looks possible.'

'Okay.'

'I'll go first, and then give you a hand up if you need it.'

Angel made a face at him. 'I think I can manage without help, dear Josh, thank you so much!'

'I guess you can, sweetie!'

In a short time they sat side by side, straddling the top of the fence, and gazed down into the grounds of the house.

'Not too high,' Josh said. 'We should be able to lower ourselves down and then drop, without breaking any bones.'

'No problem.'

'I'll go first, then I can catch you as you come down.'

'No way! I can lower myself, thanks.'

It occurred to Angel that recently Josh had become rather over protective. It was since he'd started hinting at marriage, wasn't it? It needed to be firmly stamped on, before it got worse.

Josh shrugged and turned to lower himself down. At the same time, Angel swung one leg back over the fence, so that she was sitting with her back to the house. Then she slid forward onto her tummy and taking a firm grip on the edge of the fence, lowered herself carefully to the full length of her arms. Then she let go, and landed nicely balanced beside Josh, who had preceded her by no more than a second. They smiled at each other.

'Now for the house,' Josh said quietly.

Angel nodded. They made their way as silently as possible through the bushes and undergrowth which spread from the foot of the fence across the area until it stopped at the edge of a grassy lawn. They halted to survey their surroundings.

Angel stiffened suddenly. Fierce barking had broken out not far away. There was a thunder of feet, and a moment later two huge dogs had arrived and were leaping at them. They were Alsatians, fawn coloured with eyes that gleamed in the darkness, and snapping teeth.

It took Angel a moment to pull herself together. Then she crouched down beside the first dog and began to stroke its back, murmuring endearments quietly into its ears. The dog slowly responded, no longer barking, but instead licking Angel's face tentatively.

Josh stood stock still, watching Angel in amazement, as she reached out one hand to stroke the other dog.

'Wow!' he said softly. 'I didn't know you were a dog whisperer, Angel.'

'Just a matter of not being afraid and treating them kindly.'

'Do you think they'll let us go on towards the house?'

'Sure they will, won't you, darlin's?'

She stood up as she spoke, a hand still caressing each dog.

'Come on, boy.'

Josh wasn't sure if her words were addressed to him or to the first or second dog, but all three of them obeyed her.

They moved quietly across the lawn, the people and the dogs.

'This might be the tricky bit. It depends if they've been trained to prevent people from breaking in.'

'Probably, don't you think?'

'Well, it would be a lot of trouble. More likely they're just trained to bark and scare off intruders.'

'Well, we'll soon see.'

They were nearing the house by now. A high wall, flowerbeds along its foot except for the wide patio doors just to their left. Angel and Josh approached the windows cautiously.

'I think if we try to break into these doors, smash the glass for instance, the dogs would be bound to bark, I'm afraid,' Angel said.

'Agreed.'

'So ...?'

'Let's see if I can pick the lock,' Josh said.

Josh took a good look through the unlighted windows. He saw no sign of anyone in the room behind them.

'See if you can keep those dogs away from me, honey. Preferably so they don't realize what I'm doing.' He produced a set of picklocks from the pocket of his jeans.

Angel moved a little further from Josh and the windows, taking the dogs with her, and began to stroke them and to murmur in their ears again, and the dogs fawned round her, eager for more affection. She couldn't help thinking that their owner must never have bothered to show them much love.

'Done,' came Josh's voice quietly only a few minutes later. Turning around, she saw that he had opened the lock and pushed one of the patio doors slightly open.

'Okay, do you think we can go in without the company of the animal kingdom?'

'We can try. But better have them with us than barking outside and attracting attention, right?'

'True enough.'

Josh slipped noiselessly through the narrow gap he had made in the doors, and Angel spoke firmly to her two friends.'

'Okay, boys, I want you to stay out here, okay. Stay!'

The dogs obediently sat down and looked at her, tongues flopping happily from their open mouths. Angel slipped through the doors after Josh.

'All's well so far,' she breathed. 'Let's see now if we can find Magda.'

'Right,' said Josh, and they set off to search the house.

Chapter Nineteen

They took the ground floor first, by silent consent keeping together.

The patio doors led into a sunroom, full of exotic plants and some trees. It took up considerable space. They wound their way through it, and opened the door at the end, into a huge living room. The living room was furnished in a modern style which was not in keeping with the house. The house looked as if it had been there for several hundred years. The furniture looked as if it had come out of last month's *Home & Garden* – or something similar that was popular in Poland.

There was no one there.

They looked round carefully, but before long Angel tapped Josh on the arm and said in a low voice, 'Nothing here. Let's move on.'

There were two doors. One led to a smaller, more cosy room with soft sofas and a widescreen television on one wall. Windows looked out towards the drive they had seen through the iron gate they had considered too hard to climb. There was nothing for them there.

The second door led into a hallway with other doors off it and a staircase climbing to the next storey.

'Up?' Josh suggested.

'Yes.'

They went to the staircase, treading lightly. The house was silent. It was as if there was no one there, although both Angel and Josh knew at least two people – Szczepan and Magda – were there somewhere.

The stairs reached a landing and divided into two branches, veering off to left and right. They could see two corridors above them with what might be bedrooms or bathrooms leading off them, or possibly more living space. The stairs continued upwards at the far end of each of the corridors.

'Some size of a house,' Angel thought. She kept silent. It reminded her of an Edwardian country house she had once seen while sightseeing in England. So many rooms, such elaborate decoration and furnishings.

They paused on the landing to make decisions, then Josh silently pointed to the right hand staircase, raising his eyebrows questioningly, and Angel nodded agreement. They went up the stairs, and paused again at the top.

It seemed appropriate to work their way through the various rooms lining the corridor, moving from the extreme right towards the extreme left. There was no one in the first room they tried. It was a bedroom, furnished luxuriously with walls painted pale green, a four poster bed with brocade curtains in a dark green and blue pattern, and three comfortable chairs in matching brocade covers with a number of soft cushions in blue and green of various shades.

There was a desk with a computer against one wall, and a door which led into an ensuite bathroom with a deep bath set into the floor in an ivory shade matching the washbasin, bidet, lavatory and framed mirror. The ceiling in both bedroom and bathroom were mirrored. It would be possible to watch oneself in a number of activities.

'Yuk,' was Angel's reaction.

'Oh, I don't know.'

'Typical male attitude.'

'Anyway, nothing here. Let's move on.'

They moved on.

There were five more bedrooms, similarly furnished, each with its ensuite bathroom, and in between the bedrooms there were two large living rooms, comfortably furnished.

Josh and Angel examined them all, with no results. They reached the left hand end of the corridor and stood at the foot of the stairs for a moment, thinking.

'Looks like they're on upstairs.'

'And,' Angel added, 'seems as if no one else is here. Unless there are other people upstairs as well.'

'And if there are, we'll need to be pretty careful.'

'Yes.'

They moved onto the first stair. As they did so, they both stiffened, and halted.

A gunshot sounded from a room directly above.

Josh pulled his gun out of his belt holster. He and Angel raced on up the stairs. In Angel's mind the fear took hold that someone must have shot Magda. Keeping quiet seemed pointless now.

'Magda! Magda!' she shouted.

'Yes?' a voice responded from the room they were about to reach. They came up to it and Josh flung the door open. They burst in, Josh with his gun pointed before him.

Magda was standing in the middle of the room, a gun hanging from one hand. At her feet was a huddled figure, blood streaming from his leg. A quick look told Angel that it was Szczepan.

'Magda! What happened?'

Magda stared at her silently. She was clearly in shock.

Josh spoke quietly.

'Magda, you don't know me, but I'm a friend of Angel's. Would you like to put down the gun?'

'Yes.' Magda set the gun down on a nearby wall cabinet.

'Come and sit down,' Angel said to her. She took Magda's arm and led her to a chair, noticing in passing that it was of a lower quality than the chairs in the rooms on each storey below. It was a hard kitchen type chair. The bed, against the far wall, was a single, hard looking bed with a thin coverlet and one thin pillow. A maid's room, Angel thought.

Josh picked up Magda's gun from the cabinet where she had placed it and stuck it in his pocket – first checking that the safety catch was back on.

'Is he dead?' Magda asked, shuddering.

'No. But he needs to have that leg bandaged, and then he needs to see a doctor. Otherwise he may well bleed to death.' He looked round him, and picked up a thin, ragged towel from the washbasin against the other wall, folded it, and pressed it on Szczepan's leg. The pillowcase – ripped along one side and rolled into a tight strip – served to tie the folded towel in place. Josh made it as tight as possible.

'We don't want him dying on us,' he said. 'Two reasons. It would make it worse for you, Magda. And I want to ask him some questions.'

'So, Magda,' Angel said again, 'what happened?'

'I'm not sure,' Magda said. 'I think I was drugged. The last thing I remember was being at the party, you had gone outside with your friend Josh – hi, Josh – and someone gave me a glass of wine. I can't remember who, but it wasn't Szczepan. If it had been him, I wouldn't have taken it, of course. I set it down for a moment while I was dancing with one of the guys from the band – Johnny, I think his name was – and then I picked up my glass and drank the wine. I felt the need of some fresh air, so I went outside.

'That's the last thing I remember until I found myself in this room, with Szczepan. He had a gun, and he told me to get undressed and lie down on the bed. There was no way I was going to do that, of course – gun or no gun. I pretended to – starting to undo my top – and I turned slightly away from him to do it, and he came over towards me, letting his aim with the gun drop down a bit.

'I waited for my chance and when the gun wasn't pointing straight at me and Szczepan was staring at what was beginning to show as I undid my top, I lashed out with my right heel and kicked him in the stomach. He staggered back and I grabbed for the gun as he started to drop it, and then I pointed it at him and told him to get back. He kept on coming, so I fired. I wouldn't have minded if I had killed him, but it only got his leg – I suppose you're right, Josh, it was just as well. But anyhow, we've won.'

She shuddered violently.

'You did well, Magda,' Angel said. 'You're right, we've won. And it's all okay, now. We'll get you safely out of here, and report an accident anonymously to the local police.'

'Well, you've not quite got that right, Angel,' Josh said. 'Don't forget, I'm here officially working with the local police. I'll ring them, certainly, but I'll tell them what happened. There's nothing for Magda to worry about. Szczepan is going to jail for quite a long time for kidnapping her, and since it was self defence, no one will blame her in the least for wounding him. At the same time, we need to get this guy to a doctor as soon as we can. An anonymous call, where they may not bother to respond straight away, won't work. I want him to survive, so I can question him, right?'

'Okay, Josh. I have to agree. But, Magda, don't worry, you'll be quite all right, as Josh says.'

Magda looked doubtful, but said nothing.

'C'mon, let's get Szczepan picked up, so's we can head downstairs.'

'Wait!' Angel said quickly. 'What's that?'

They all heard it. Footsteps on the stairs, coming up fast, making no attempt to keep from making noise. A triumphant grin spread over Szczepan Kowalski's face.

'Hah!' he crowed. 'Now who's winning?'

A moment later, the door of the room burst open. Two men, heavily armed with sawn off shotguns, burst into the room.

Chapter Twenty

'Drop the gun,' the first one told Josh. He was a thickset, barrel bodied man, his cheeks red with broken veins. He was wearing a tee shirt and jeans and a striped woolly hat pulled down over his ears. Apparently he spoke English, and knew that they – apart from Magda – were not Polish.

The second one was taller but skinnier, with gaunt cheeks. He was dressed like the first one, but without the striped woolly hat.

Josh set his gun down carefully on the cabinet.

'Put it on the floor, and kick it over here,' ordered Woolly Hat. Josh did so.

'Pick it up, Shuggie.'

The skinny guy picked it up and tucked it into the pocket of his jeans.

'Shuggie should be careful with that,' observed Josh casually. 'It's cocked and could go off any minute. Shuggie's legs – and stuff – could be in danger.'

Shuggie hurriedly took the gun out of his jeans' pocket and put on the safety catch.

'Good move, Shuggie.'

'Shut up,' ordered Woolly Hat. He kept his sawn off shotgun pointed menacingly at Josh. Shuggie's job seemed to be to cover Angel and Magda.

'Pat him down, Shuggie,' Woolly Hat ordered.

The second gun, the one Magda had taken from Szczepan, was still in Josh's pocket. Shuggie triumphantly discovered it and passed it to the other man, who nodded thanks as he took it.

Something apparently occurred to Woolly Hat. 'Hey, where are the dogs, Shuggie? I told you to bring up the dogs.'

'I don't like the dogs, Shorty,' Shuggie said, speaking for the first time. He had a high pitched, whiney, voice. 'You know I don't like the dogs. The dogs are your business.'

'I told you to bring them,' Shorty repeated. 'They'll help put a scare into these characters. Go and get them now!'

Shuggie backed slowly out of the room. That left Shorty on his own – Shorty and the sawn off shot gun. Probably enough to do the job, Angel considered. It would not be the wisest of moves to try to tackle him while it was pointed at them all, and especially at Josh.

'Now,' Shorty said. 'I don't know who you are, mister, but I don't reckon we need you. We've come for the girl. And, hey, I see we have a bonus, a twofer, two girls for the price of one. So when we leave here as soon as Shuggie comes back with the dogs, you can come too – until we find a good place to shoot you and dump you. Understand?'

'If you plan to shoot me anyway,' Josh observed, 'what's to stop me going for you now, grabbing the gun, and shooting both you and then Shuggie when he comes back? So maybe I get shot, but if I don't do anything, I'm going to be dead anyway, you say.'

Shorty looked a little uneasy. It may have been occurring to him that it would have been better not to be quite so forthcoming about his intentions. Then his face cleared, as he heard the sound of barking and footsteps, Shuggie and the dogs approaching on the stairs.

'So, whereabouts in Belfast do you and Shuggie come from, Shorty?' Josh asked conversationally. 'I think I could almost place you by the accent. East Belfast, is it?'

'Shut up,' said Shorty – he seemed to have little in the way of variety in his responses. Relief flooded his face as the door opened again. The two dogs came in, followed cautiously by Shuggie and the other sawn off shotgun.

Angel held out one hand to them.

The dogs bounded across the room, recognised Angel's scent as she offered her hand, and leapt up enthusiastically to lick her face. Angel knelt down to them for easier communication.

'Hey!' protested Shorty. 'What's going on?'

'Get him, boy!' Angel whispered softly. The first dog whirled around and made for Shorty. Shorty stepped back and collided with Shuggie. Shuggie had retreated from the dogs as soon as he came into the room and had been trying to keep out of their way behind Shorty, so he was perfectly placed for the collision. Shuggie in turn staggered back, dropping the gun and pulling Shorty with him as he fell over the second dog.

By now the two dogs were growling menacingly and jumping around both men. Magda, on the alert, grabbed Shuggie's shotgun. Shorty didn't let go of his, but when Shuggie pulled him over his aim wavered and suddenly he was pointing the gun in the air.

Angel sprang to her feet and took hold of it. Shorty – recovering himself – held onto it. But Josh wasn't slow to join in the struggle. It took only a few moments for him and Angel between them to gain control of the gun. Angel, relinquishing it to Josh, knelt down by Shuggie and retrieved Josh's own gun from Shuggie's pocket. Magda, still holding Shuggie's sawn off shotgun, took Szczepan's gun from Shorty's other pocket.

All four guns were now no longer in the possession of the gunmen.

Szczepan Kowalski, still nursing his bandaged leg on the floor, looked horror stricken. 'You clumsy fools!' he ejaculated in Polish. Both Josh and Angel understood enough basic Polish to follow this.

'At least we didn't get shot!' growled Shorty. 'You're the one who got us into this mess.'

'You didn't get shot – yet.' Josh's comment caused a sudden silence among the three men.

'It's time,' he went on pleasantly, 'for you guys to share a little information, okay? Like, who exactly are you working for? Is it someone from Poland or someone from Belfast? Whoever it is seems to use a mixture of useless thugs from both places.'

'Who are you calling useless –?' began Shorty, then, seeing the expression in Josh's eyes, he stopped talking.

'Why, you and Shuggie, of course, Shorty. And your mate Szczepan here. The three who are likely to get shot if you don't answer my questions.'

'Don't shoot us! Don't shoot us!' Shuggie gasped desperately.

'Shut it, you fool!' Shorty ordered him. 'He won't do it.'

Josh pointed the shotgun at Shorty. 'No?' he inquired softly. Shorty quivered. Suddenly he wasn't so sure.

'What do you want to know?' This was Shuggie.

'Weren't you listening? I want your boss's name, Shuggie.'

'It's Hawthorne,' Shuggie gasped out.

'Okay.' Josh took out his mobile phone and dialled a number one handed from his top ten list, still holding the shotgun pointed at Shorty.

He said, 'Hi.' Then he began a conversation in Polish which Angel couldn't follow.

'The police will be here in a matter of minutes,' he remarked to Angel. 'Meanwhile I reckon we should tie these guys up. Magda, you might have a look round for something to use. You'll probably need to go downstairs. We'll keep them covered till you get back.'

It didn't take Magda long to come back with a hank of clothes line and a sharp knife. She and Angel cut lengths of the rope and tied the men – first Shorty, then Shuggie. Szczepan seemed unlikely to give any trouble. He was looking pale and helpless, crouched on the floor nursing his leg.

Then it was just a matter of waiting for the short while it took for Josh's colleagues in the police to arrive, hustle the men downstairs, and put them into the waiting police cars. Szczepan was taken separately to an ambulance, with a double police escort. The shotguns were taken as evidence, together with a glass sitting on the cabinet which had held the drug Szczepan had planned to use on Magda.

'So. What did we learn from that?'

'Nothing new, Josh. We already knew Hawthorne was the boss.'

'Well, we guessed it. Now we have it straight from the junior thug's mouth.'

'That would be Shuggie.'

'Yeah.'

'We know he has guys working for him here in Poland as well as in Belfast,' Magda said.

'Didn't we know that already?' Angel asked her.

'I suppose we did.'

'Will Hawthorne be arrested?' Magda asked Josh.

'No. The word of a villain like Shuggie wouldn't be enough to convict him.'

'I guess not.'

'So,' Angel said, 'we need to catch him in the act. That is, actually with some of his victims, at the place where he keeps them prisoner.'

'When it was me and Elena,' Magda said, 'he didn't keep us anywhere. He used Szczepan to send us straight off to London, where that guy Tommy met us and put us on the plane to Belfast. It was Jason who met us there. Hawthorne never appeared.'

'But things are different, now,' Josh reminded her. 'He doesn't have Szczepan. He may have to get involved at a hands on level himself. Let's hope so anyway.'

He yawned suddenly. 'I reckon it's time we all got some rest. Let's go. I'll drop you two at your hotel, go on to mine, and pick you up in the morning.'

'Not too early!' Angel said.

'Right.'

Angel on Guard – *Gerry McCullough*

Chapter Twenty One

The drive out to Liam Hawthorne's house felt really familiar to Angel, as she sat beside Josh in his car late the next morning. But this was the first time she had driven here in daylight. Magda had elected to stay in bed for a while longer, recovering.

It was a fine, sunny day. On either side of the road there were trees which still held some leaves, the light sending a shining shower of spangles through the leaves onto the road, giving Angel and Josh alternate shade and sunshine.

'So, what's the plan, Josh?' Angel asked eventually.

'None, really. I thought we could park somewhere and watch to see if Liam comes out and goes somewhere suspicious.'

'Suspicious?'

'Yeah.'

'Like, not the supermarket or the nearest pub?'

'Got it.'

'And if he goes to a house or something where he has a lot of girls stashed, we jump out and threaten him with our guns, until he confesses?'

'That would be it. And we release the girls and get their statements.'

'And if he just goes for lunch in an up market restaurant with a friend?'

'Then maybe we follow the friend, see where that leads us.'

'Wow, that's some plan.'

'You got a better one?'

'I haven't got one as good.'

They parked behind a clump of trees by Hawthorne's front gate, and waited. After they had waited some time, Angel said, 'Supposing he goes for dinner with this friend you're imagining, rather than for lunch?'

'That would be a pain.'

They waited for a while longer. Then the gate swung open, and a large dark green Mercedes edged its way out. They could see that it was being driven by Liam Hawthorne, looking cool and casual, with one hand on the wheel and his other arm draped along the back of the passenger seat.

'Okay,' Josh murmured. He took off the handbrake and began to follow the Mercedes, keeping at a safe distance.

But Liam Hawthorne wasn't looking for a following car. He continued to drive casually, and Angel could have sworn he was singing to himself. They couldn't hear him from the distance Josh was keeping, but she thought she could see his lips moving in the mirror.

They were heading back to Krakow. Angel knew the route by heart by now.

Then, just before they reached the city, the Mercedes turned off.

'Another country house?' speculated Josh. 'Somewhere he keeps the girls?'

But before long, it became clear that Hawthorne was headed for the airport. There were signs saying 'Airport' at every turn off. As they neared the approach road and left the small country roads behind them, the traffic became heavier and it was easier for Josh to keep nearer to the Mercedes without being obvious, dodging behind other cars without losing track of his quarry.

When they reached the airport, Liam Hawthorne headed for the short term parking area, and pulled into a vacant space. Josh was able to park not too far away, where he could see what Hawthorne's next step might be.

At first Hawthorne sat in the car, looking at his watch at regular intervals. Then he got out and strolled over to the airport buildings.

Chapter 21

'Come on,' Josh said, getting out of the car.

'Wait a moment,' Angel objected. 'Shouldn't we wait here, to follow him when he comes back? Or at least one of us?'

'And suppose he flies off somewhere and we don't know where?'

'So, one goes and one stays.'

'I'd rather we didn't separate,' was all Josh said, giving no reason. He opened the door for Angel to get out, locked the car, and began walking.

After a minute, he explained. 'It's just a feeling I have, Angel. I don't want him to come back, and whichever of us stayed has to drive off and leave the other one. The one who was left wouldn't have a clue where to go to catch up.'

'Haven't you heard of mobile phones?' Angel asked sweetly.

Josh laughed. 'Got me there, honey. Well, put it that I think it's more fun when we're together, okay?'

Angel laughed in turn. 'That's certainly true, darlin'. Okay, we'll both go.'

Hawthorne was nearing the airport buildings by now.

'Hey!' Angel said. 'He's not going to Departures. So much for him flying off somewhere.'

'He's heading over to Arrivals,' Josh said. 'Must be meeting somebody.'

'An accomplice? Or just a friend, or an innocent business acquaintance?'

'Well, we'll see in another few minutes, if we don't lose him.'

They moved cautiously after Hawthorne, trying to keep out of his sight as much as possible. To their relief, he showed no signs of looking behind him for a possible follower. He halted at the luggage carousel and stood watching the new arrivals coming from the direction of the Customs bureau. Presently a red haired, well dressed woman of about forty came hurrying from that direction, and Hawthorne moved towards her with his arms outstretched.

Angel stiffened, and tugged at Josh's arm as the two met and hugged.

'Josh! It's Lucinda!'

'Lucinda?'

'Liam Hawthorne's wife!'

'Wow!'

'She knows me, she'll recognise me. I need to keep out of her sight. Here, give me the keys, I'll race back to the car while they're collecting her luggage. You can keep on watching them both.'

Angel grabbed the keys Josh held out to her, turned, and ran. She clicked to unlock the car, and dived in. Once safely inside, she considered how best to disguise herself from Lucinda's passing view if she came within range. She had sunglasses in her handbag, in spite of the time of year, because the sun had been glaring down on them for the past two days. She put them on. A large hat, to pull down over her face and hide it, would have helped. But she had no hat, large or otherwise.

She looked round hopefully. Yes! Josh had a baseball cap lying on the back seat. Angel, who knew nothing about baseball, didn't recognise the team from the colours, which were red and black on a white background. That didn't matter. Leaning over, she possessed herself of the cap and put it on. It was slightly too large, which was all to the good. She adjusted it in the rearview mirror, pulling the peak down over her face, and slumped down in the seat to add to her semi invisibility. For the first time, she had a moment to think.

What was Lucinda Hawthorne doing over here? She had said – if Angel remembered it rightly – that she never came out to Poland because she had nothing to do with her husband's business, and didn't even know what it was about. She'd also said that she didn't know where Liam was, and that when she rang the house she'd been told that he wasn't there and wasn't expected. Someone was lying. Or had she rung again and found that Liam Hawthorne had now arrived?

Something must have changed her mind to send her here. Had the police found something in the house in Delamore Park to lead them to Liam Hawthorne, and called with Lucinda? Had she come over to warn him – after all, he was her husband. No matter what he'd been up to, she probably felt a need to protect him?

Angel wondered.

Meanwhile Josh, hovering as far out of sight as he could, continued to watch the husband and wife.

They did nothing particularly interesting.

Firstly, they waited for Lucinda's luggage, a small pink spotted case with wheels, to come round on the carousel. Then Liam retrieved it, took the handle to wheel it in one hand and took Lucinda's hand in the other. Instead of going out by the exit, he led her and the suitcase to the nearby lift, went up a floor, and found a free table at the first floor bar.

Josh risked entering the same lift rather than lose them, and risked also taking a nearby table, after getting himself a beer. His hearing was sharp. He could manage to pick up at least some of what they were saying.

None of it seemed very important at first. There was the usual discussion of what they would like to drink, after which Liam headed up to the bar and came back presently with what looked like a beer and a glass of white wine – while Lucinda put in the time by viewing her face in a small mirror from her handbag and doing a few repairs to her makeup and hair. Then, when he had distributed the drinks, Liam inquired about her flight, which seemed to have been fine.

After that, Liam said, loudly enough for Josh to hear, 'But you shouldn't have come over, sweetheart. There was no need.'

Angel would have been gratified by the accuracy of her guess if she had heard Lucinda's answer, 'But, darlin' that policeman I told you about was asking all sorts of questions about you! I was terrified!'

'Nothing to be worried about,' Liam replied gruffly. 'Something about that house on Delamore Park, you said? But you know it's rented out, I never go near it, the rental agents handle everything to do with it – you should just have sent the police to them.'

'Oh. I didn't think of that.' Lucinda sounded very forlorn.

'Never mind,' Liam comforted her. 'It's nice to see you anyway. Finish up your drink and I'll take you home – well, my home out here! – and you can have a shower and a rest, and then I'll take you out on the town, show you some of the sights before it gets too dark, and eat out and dance somewhere good, okay?'

'That sounds lovely, darlin'. A shower would be great.' Lucinda swallowed the remnants of her wine, while Liam gulped down the last of his beer, and they stood up. Josh stayed put until they had left the bar and were heading for the lift. Then, leaving his unfinished beer, he strolled casually after them, and went downstairs, while the Hawthornes, encumbered by Lucinda's luggage, waited for the lift.

Chapter Twenty Two

Josh reached the car park before them and slid into the driver's seat beside Angel.

'Wow! Is that you inside that cap, sweetie?'

'No, it's the bogey man come to get ya.' Angel pretended to lunge towards him with her hands curled into claws, but Josh was too quick for her, grabbing her wrists in time to stop her.

'Okay, cut it out, Angel honey! I want you to tell me how come you know Lucinda Hawthorne, and how she comes into this. I listened to their conversation, and it sounded innocent enough. They're heading back to Hawthorne's house, now – right, here they come. Duck down again. You can tell me about it while I'm driving. We'll just check that they go where Hawthorne said, and then we'll go and get ourselves something to eat before we take it up again, okay?'

'Sounds good. You might want to check in with your mates in the local police and see if they've got anything more out of Shuggie and Shorty – not to mention Szczepan.'

'We'll do that, too.'

They saw the Hawthornes safely inside with no problems, then Josh turned the car towards the city.

'So, Angel, where does Lucinda Hawthorne come into this? How come she knows you?'

'When Magda and I went round to Hawthorne's house – on the other side of Holywood – she was there. To cut a long story short, she offered to pay us to come out here and check if he was okay. She thought I was a Private Eye, right, and I didn't disillusion her. That's about it. She didn't know anything about her husband's business or what he did out here, but she gave us the password to his computer and let us look at it in case it might be helpful.'

'Talk about helpful, she was – very!'

'We found his address book on his computer. I had a quick read through it and I copied it onto a memory stick, and took it away. Come to think of it, with the rush to catch a plane I haven't found time for a more thorough look at it yet. I don't have my laptop with me, and although I could have borrowed one at the hotel, it might not have been very private.'

'Have you got it there? If you'll trust me with it, I'll borrow a computer at the cop shop and see if there's anything important in it.'

'Great idea.' Thankfully, Angel handed over the memory stick to Josh, and leaned back to relax and enjoy the drive.

Angel knew this particular road well by now, but she was still unfamiliar with the rest of the city of Krakow, and the restaurant where Josh took her for lunch was a pleasant surprise.

Set in the old mediaeval town – *Stare Miasto* – behind the Main Market Square, it was beautifully restored, like most of the buildings surrounding it.

'*The Old Town Restaurant and Wine Bar,*' Josh said, ushering Angel in. 'Come and sit down, honey.'

The tables and seats were modern and comfortable. The walls were lined with attractive pictures of Krakow. Angel found herself sitting beneath one of the Main Market Square, with an old but very expensive looking car – a Bentley perhaps – driving across its wide expanse.

'So what do you recommend, Josh?' she asked. 'Remember I'm not familiar with Polish food and menus.'

'I think you could do worse than the *Zarek* soup, honey. It comes in a big hollowed out bowl of bread, the top sliced off and used as a lid, and the bread scooped out, to leave plenty of space to be filled with the soup. Warming, interesting, and yum yum.'

Chapter 22

And the soup, a meal in itself, was all Josh had said of it, when it came.

They were sitting at the window looking out on the Old City, and were already half way through their meal, when Angel suddenly remembered Magda, whom she had left peacefully sleeping in the hotel.

'Heavens, she'll be wondering what's happened to me! – Magda, I mean!' she exclaimed.

'Give her a ring,' suggested Josh practically.

'Right.' Angel took out her phone, and a few minutes afterwards heard a sleepy voice which sounded as if it owner had just emerged from the depths of sleep. 'Yeah?'

'Oh, sorry if I woke you up, Magda. I thought you might be starting to worry about where I'd gone. Go back to sleep, if you want to. I'll come round presently.'

'No, I'm awake now anyway. I need to shower and dress and get breakfast. See you when I see you.'

When their meal was over, Josh dropped Angel back to the hotel to fill Magda in about what had happened since they left her, and he himself went to contact his police friends.

Angel found Magda up and dressed and just starting into a large continental breakfast in the hotel restaurant – croissants, cheese, sliced meats, and fruit. Angel, after the meal she had just enjoyed with Josh, shuddered at the sight of Magda's piled plate, but decided that a cup of coffee would be a welcome idea. Fetching herself one, she sat down by Magda and told her about following Liam Hawthorne, and about the arrival of Lucinda. Magda expressed surprise.

'I thought she sent us out because she didn't want to come herself? Something must have happened to change her mind.'

'The police happened. They came around, asking questions, and I reckon Lucinda didn't know what to say to them and was scared of saying the wrong thing. So she hopped a plane to dump it in hubby's lap. The helpless little woman – I thought they disappeared when Queen Victoria died.'

'Oh, well,' Magda said tolerantly, 'Everyone can't be super-women like you and me, Angel.' They giggled together like – Angel realised – a couple of schoolgirls.

'So, are you going to get in touch with her?' Magda asked presently.

'I hadn't thought of it. But I suppose maybe we should. I don't want to let her know we were following her husband, in case she lets it out to him accidentally. So how would we know she's over here, then?'

'Could we bump into her accidentally on purpose?'

'That would be a good idea if we could manage it. But it would take some planning. Her husband is taking her out to see around the town this afternoon. Maybe we could follow them and bump into her somewhere. But I'd rather avoid him – he knows us both – and I suppose he knows about Szczepan grabbing you, and about me and Josh rescuing you, and getting his men arrested.'

'How would he know that?'

'Oh, I don't know – probably he has sources of information inside the police, don't you think? Or just his own spies. Well, let's drive out to his house when you're sure you've finished eating.'

'I'm finished now.'

'Sure? Don't want another few slices of meat or a couple more croissants?'

'Ha, ha. Come on. Let's go. We don't want to miss them.'

'She was taking a shower and a rest, and changing. I don't think she'd have been ready before now.'

The two girls went out to Angel's car and Angel drove out from the hotel car park, and along the road she was so familiar with by now.

She pulled up in the secluded spot in the shelter of trees where Josh had parked that morning while they waited to follow Hawthorne to the airport. They were just about in time.

Chapter 22

They had no sooner settled themselves than Hawthorne's car – the dark green Mercedes easily recognisable to Angel now – came sliding quietly out of the gates, and turned towards Krakow.

Angel pulled out after it, keeping – as Josh had done – as far back as she could while not losing sight of the Hawthornes. She was beginning to think that tailing people was not the most exciting part of catching criminals. In fact, it was extremely boring. But it did produce results – sometimes.

They drove on after the Hawthornes, until the big car pulled up in front of the *Wawel Royal Castle* – the residence of the kings of Poland for centuries, now an Art Museum – and one of the chief tourist attractions of Krakow.

Liam and his wife both got out and stood looking up the wide stone ramp leading to the building, and making comments. Angel parked round the nearest corner, and she and Magda got out and cautiously made their way closer to their targets. Then they had a stroke of luck. They heard a mobile ring.

Clearly it was Liam Hawthorne's mobile, for he took it out of his pocket and listened. Then he switched it off again, and they could just make out his words. 'Lucinda, I'm sorry, but I need to go and meet this fella. Sure, if I buy you a ticket you could go in and explore this place, see the paintings and look at the great view of the Vistula River, and get yourself a cup of coffee or a glass of wine when you've finished at this wee café bar over here. If I'm not back by then, wait for me. I'll be as quick as I can.'

He went over to the entrance and came back a moment later with a ticket. Then he gave Lucinda a quick kiss on the cheek, got back in the car, and drove off, waving one hand out of the car window.

'Wow! What an opportunity! Come on, Magda! Let's catch her up.'

Angel darted up the access ramp where Lucinda had just gone – Magda following – catching up with her as she reached the plaza at the top. She caught hold of Lucinda's arm, 'Hey, hang on a minute!'

Lucinda's jaw dropped as she turned around and gazed at Angel in confusion.

'Angel Murphy! What are you doing here?'

Chapter Twenty Three

'You sent us here, Lucinda, have you forgotten?'

'No, of course, I haven't forgotten. But I meant, it's such a surprise to bump into you like this.'

'Small world,' Angel said flippantly. 'As Bertie Wooster says, 'I've never known a smaller!' But the big question is, Lucinda, what are you doing here? You seemed all set to wait at home until we had found out about your husband for you, when we last spoke.'

'Oh, it was so terrible! The police called and were awful. They seemed to think I was guilty of all sorts of things. Well, not me, maybe, but Liam, my husband. They said two dead bodies had been found near that house in Delamore Park that Liam owns. They'd been shot. They were lying beside an old well, and when the police looked into the well they found another body there, and it was a man who'd been shot, too. They'd been killed less than a week ago.

I explained to them that Liam couldn't have had anything to do with it, because he'd been in Poland for several weeks, but they didn't seem to believe me – so what could I do except fly out here on the next plane to tell Liam to look out. Even though I know he couldn't have done it, they seem to think he might have men working for him who were around there, and who could have done it on his orders. I really don't believe that, but I had to warn him, didn't I?'

'I suppose you had, as a good wife,' Angel agreed. 'But when exactly did your husband leave for Poland, Lucinda? Can you remember?'

'Yes, because I put it in my diary. 'Liam left for Poland tonight. I wish he would stay at home more. I hope he'll be back in time for my birthday.' It was on December the first. My birthday is next week, on December twentieth.'

'You should remind him,' Angel said absently. 'I always start mentioning that my birthday is coming up soon, about a fortnight before the date. Not that I have a husband to remind, any more. Just friends.'

Magda broke in. 'Do they know who the three men are?'

'Yes, they've identified them. And it's all very well for Liam to tell me the house is rented out and he knows nothing about the people who have it, that it's all done through renting agents. But how can that be true when two of them worked for him? People I'd met through him.'

'And their names?' Angel asked patiently.

'One of them was Jason Crawford. I mentioned him to you, didn't I? A really nice guy. I liked him a lot. The other was a bit rough. I think Liam used him as a sort of bodyguard – being in politics Liam's had all the usual threats, of course, so he thought he needed someone looking out for him. The guy's name was Bobby Boyle. His and Jason's fingerprints were in the system from the times they'd been arrested – I didn't know Liam employed people like that!' Lucinda seemed about to burst into tears, so Angel spoke quickly in an effort to prevent this.

'And the third one?'

'The one who was down the well. They think Jason and Bobby put him there. He was Jackson Morrison, and he was a business acquaintance of Liam. They got his DNA from the blood donors' records, I think the police Inspector said. What was he doing there? And why should it be anything to do with Liam's house, even if it was nearby?'

'I expect they found traces of matching blood for this guy Morrison at the house,' suggested Magda. 'There'd be bound to be some, even if they tried to clear it up, if that's where he was shot. I happen to know that both Jason and Bobby Boyle were frequently in that house. Although I don't intend to tell the police that. But they deserved everything they got.' Her mouth tightened grimly.

'Oh, no, you mustn't tell the police anything about all this! Liam would be in such trouble if they found out. Please, promise me you won't tell!'

'No problem,' Magda said at once. Angel said nothing. She had every intention of telling Josh as soon as she saw him, and he would no doubt pass it on to the local cops.

'I certainly won't tell this Belfast inspector anything,' she said after a short pause. 'I'm hardly likely to see him, am I?'

Lucinda seemed content with this, not taking in the omissions in Angel's promise.

'Now,' she said, 'let's go and sit down somewhere – over at that café place. We can get some coffee and talk. I want to know everything you've found out.' She took Angel's arm and began to lead the girls towards the attractive, lively café Liam had mentioned to her earlier.

Angel went along with it – after all, Lucinda had paid their fares and expenses, and had every right to expect a report.

Lucinda pulled out a chair and sat down. 'I love these warm, friendly little cafes, don't you?' she said chattily. 'So continental! Such a pity it can't be open air, but it would freeze us all in this winter weather. Liam said this was a nice place. He's meeting me here as soon as he can get back.'

Angel, who had been about to follow Lucinda's example and was halfway to sitting down, hurriedly sprang up again. 'No way! If your husband is meeting you here, we can't risk him coming along and seeing us talking together. You wanted to keep it a secret from him that you'd employed people to look into what he was doing, didn't you? That's why we've been keeping away from you while he was with you, why we waited to speak to you until he was gone.'

'Oh.' Lucinda's face fell. 'So what can we do?'

'We'll meet up later on.'

'But he wants to take me out later, for a nice dinner and dancing.'

'Well, sorry, Lucinda, but I think you'll have to give it a miss – if you want to hear what we've found out. After your meal, tell him you've got a headache and don't feel up to dancing – after the flight and everything. He'll take you home, of course. Go up to bed, and after you've given it a reasonable time, sneak out. He might even have gone back out himself. That would make it easier.'

'But how can I get anywhere to meet you? I don't have my car over here. I've been relying on Liam to drive me around.'

'Give me a ring as soon as you're safely out of the gates, and we'll pick you up, okay?'

'Okay,' Lucinda agreed, but Angel thought she sounded dubious. She sat for a moment, biting her lower lip. 'I don't like the idea of lying to Liam,' she explained. 'But, yes, all right, I'll do it. Give me your number.'

Angel texted her number to Lucinda's phone, then she and Magda gathered themselves hastily together and hurried back to the car where it was parked round the nearby corner.

'So much for our high strategy,' Magda commented as she settled herself in the passenger seat and fastened her seatbelt. 'What next?'

'I think I'd better get in touch with Josh,' Angel decided. 'He may have got some useful info from his police pals.'

She put a safe distance between herself and the café where Lucinda sat waiting for her husband, then pulled in and parked. After thinking about it, she decided not to ring Josh, but simply to text him. 'He probably wouldn't want to talk to me in front of his police friends. Certainly he couldn't pass info on to me. Texting would be better. He can text me back, or ring if he's somewhere private enough.'

'And then?'

'Depending on what he says, we might have a better idea of what to do next, right?'

The message sent, there was no waiting gap. Josh came straight back to her.

'Meet me in *Rynek Glowny* – the Main Market Square. Twenty mins. Love and kisses.'

'It's a bit of a big, busy meeting place,' Magda commented. 'Will you see him easily, do you think?'

'I will. I'd know Josh anywhere,' Angel said firmly. Then she felt herself blushing.

'Maybe I should take myself off?' Magda asked slyly.

'No way. You and I are in this together, Magda. I need your language skills, apart from anything else. And I don't want you wandering round on your own. Liam Hawthorne might try to grab you again, or put one of his other men on to do it, who knows? Assuming he still has some other men, that is.'

They drove to a street near to the square, Magda giving directions. They were early, so they found an empty table at the window of another café with a good view over the square, and ordered the coffee they had missed out on when Lucinda casually remarked that Liam Hawthorne might show up at any moment. They could see the market building which covered the centre of the square and consisted of numerous shops and some cafes – attractive and ancient looking. To one corner of the square they could see a huge church with two enormous towers – which Magda identified for Angel as St Mary's Basilica.

Magda sipped her coffee slowly. 'If it wasn't winter, and so cold,' she said presently, 'this would be an open air café, like in other continental countries. Just like Lucinda would have liked.'

To Angel, she seemed rather uncomfortable.

'Angel,' she said after another pause, 'there's something I should probably tell you. But not if you're going to pass it on to your *Interpol* friend, Josh.'

'Magda, you'd better think twice about it, then. Because I tell you straight, Josh and I don't work like that. We share everything we know with each other. Started off like that and have kept to it ever since.'

'Are you going to marry him?' Magda asked abruptly. 'It sounds like a married relationship.'

'I don't know. My first marriage left me burnt. He was a vicious, violent brute. I managed to forgive him – with Mary's help – but I'm still not sure I'm brave enough to risk a repeat.'

'If you know Josh well enough, you could be confident he isn't the same type – so no repeat. You must have some idea if you want to or not.'

'To tell you the truth, he hasn't asked me yet.' Angel turned a laughing face to Magda. 'I'll decide when he does. Mind you, he's come pretty near to it more than once, but we always seem to get interrupted.'

'That means you *are* going to.' Magda sat quietly thinking for a moment or two. Then she said, 'I think I won't tell you this right now, Angel. I need to think a bit more about it.'

'Up to you,' Angel said lightly. 'I think I need more sugar in this coffee. It's quite bitter. Reach over the sugar bowl from that table behind you, darlin'. Ah! That's better.'

Magda turned away to replace the sugar container she'd borrowed from the next table, and at the same moment Angel let out a pleased cry. 'Josh!'

Josh, looking around him, had appeared at the far corner of the square. Angel sprang to her feet and waved. 'Over here, Josh!'

Josh waved back, and began to make his way towards them. He was accompanied by a short, sturdy looking man, dark haired and with piercing blue eyes.

'Who's that with him?' Magda whispered in frightened tones.

'Dunno. One of his police friends, probably.'

'I can tell you one thing about him. That's the man who was with Szczepan Kowalski the first time I met him.'

Chapter Twenty Four

'Does he know you?'

'Maybe. Maybe not. I didn't meet him, not to speak to. He left before Szczepan came over to me. But I'm quite sure it's the same guy.'

'Okay. We'll say nothing about him to Josh until we find out how the land lies – if he's working with Josh or if he's just a casual acquaintance Josh happened to bump into on his way here. If it's that, Josh will say goodbye to him as he comes over.'

But far from saying goodbye and getting rid of the dark haired man, Josh put one hand on his arm as they approached the table where Angel and Magda sat, and led him up to be introduced.

'Angel, Magda, this is my good friend Pete Gillespie. He's been working on the same stuff as me for some time now. He may have some info that will help us.'

Magda was sitting staring at Gillespie. Realising this she dropped her eyes and picked up her coffee cup, pretending to drink, trying to conceal her face as much as possible.

'So, nice to meet you, Pete,' Angel said smoothly. 'Are you joining us for coffee, both of you?'

'Sure thing,' Josh said, pulling out a chair for Pete and one for himself and waving one of the waiters over. 'What'll it be, Pete? Coffee?'

'Latte, Josh. Ta.'

'And cappuccino for me. How about yourselves, girls? Refills?'

'Great,' Angel answered for both of them. 'Cappuchinos. But, listen, Magda and I need to check if this place has a ladies' room at the back, okay. We won't be long. Go ahead and order for us, thanks.'

She bundled Magda to her feet and across the inside of the café towards the back. 'We need a chance to talk,' she whispered to Magda as they made their escape. 'Can you ask one of the staff for directions?'

Magda spoke in Polish to a waitress hurrying past with cups of coffee for someone, got a quick response and a pointing finger, and turned back to Angel.

'Down there,' she said briefly, and took Angel across the room and down a flight of stairs to a clean, well equipped room with cubicles, wash basins, and mirrors. It seemed empty. The cubicle doors were all ajar.

'So, quickly,' Angel said. 'Do you want to duck out before this guy Pete starts remembering you, or would you rather face him out, tell Josh about seeing him with Szczepan, and see what happens?'

'What do you think?'

'I think you should stay here while I go back and get hold of Josh on his own. I'll tell him, and let him play it from there. Besides, I want to talk privately to Josh, see what he's found out and tell him what we've learned from Lucinda. Does that suit you?'

'Yeah, that sounds about right. But you won't be able to keep Josh away from the guy for long – I think you'll have to leave the exchange of info until later. Just tell him about his mate Pete, and say you need to talk privately, at more length, when he's got rid of Pete Gillespie, okay?'

'Okay.' Angel hugged Magda briefly and made her way back to the window table.

Standing carefully where she could see – and be seen by –Josh, and out of sight of Pete Gillespie – who was sitting with his back to her – she beckoned to Josh, at the same time putting one finger of her other hand to her lips in a request for silence. Josh, a well experienced *Interpol* agent, gave nothing away, but stood up in a leisurely manner, and Angel could see him telling his friend something, but could not make out the words. A moment later, Josh had joined her and drawn her back well out of Gillespie's line of sight.

He slipped his arm round Angel and kissed her lightly. 'Was this why you called me over?' he asked, grinning.

'Not entirely,' Angel said, smiling back. 'Josh, that man you brought with you. When Magda first talked to Szczepan, that man was with him, and left just before Szczepan came over to her. She's quite sure. She doesn't know whether he recognised her or not, but the chances are he didn't. She doesn't trust him, and I must say, neither do I.

There're lots of things I want to tell you about what we've learned, and lots I want to hear from you about what you've got from Szczepan, and from Shorty and Shuggie – the three S's – and any other sources your cop friends have, but not in front of this guy who hangs out with Szczepan.'

'Fair enough. I've not known Pete long enough to trust him one hundred per cent, myself. Inspector Josip Buczek, a guy I've known for yonks, introduced us, and he seemed to trust Pete completely. He told me he was 'a good guy, with a lot of info.''

'So?'

'So, I think I'll go along with you and Magda for the time being. Go back and tell her to nip away out of sight, and wait for you in another café – there's no shortage of them. You can ring her when Pete's gone. When you've done that, come back and I'll get Pete to share some things with you that he's told me. Then we'll excuse ourselves, say we need to catch up on our love life, right, honey? And so we do!'

He gave Angel a final hug, then drifted back to the table, while Angel went to find Magda in the ladies' room.

When she came back almost immediately, she smiled at Pete and sat down. 'Sorry to be so long, guys. But my friend isn't feeling too well. She's got a taxi back to our hotel, and just wants to lie down quietly. I'll check in with her later, but right now she'd rather be left alone. So, Pete, Josh says you've got lots to tell us?'

'Some, anyway, Angel,' Pete smiled. 'Josh has probably heard most of it already, from Inspector Buczek, I've been keeping him up to date, and I believe he's passed my info on to Josh regularly. But let's assume he knows nothing about what I've been doing, and I'll tell you both.'

The waiter arrived with the coffees, a small plate for each of them, and a large plate with a selection of attractive looking pastries.

Josh thanked him, and explained to us, 'I had to cancel Magda's coffee, and I thought we might all enjoy a pastry, why not? So I ordered these at the same time.'

Apparently he had used this as an excuse for leaving Pete for a few minutes. He didn't explain how he knew Magda wouldn't be returning to drink her coffee, and Angel just hoped Pete wouldn't notice this. However, a moment later it was explained.

'Yeah, you were right in thinking she didn't look well, and might have to go and lie down, Josh,' Pete commented.

'Well, Angel, to begin. I've been working on this people trafficking thing for nearly a year now, and one of the first people I identified as mixed up in it was this guy Szczepan Kowalski – whom you and Josh have just brought in. You have clear evidence against him for the first time. I won't go into how I first found out he was involved – it came from a girl he'd tried to hook in, who had more sense and said no to his offer – but she didn't want to give evidence against him, though she didn't mind telling me. So I can't tell you her name without breaking a promise.

'Anyway, I got close to Szczepan, and managed to get into his email without his knowledge, and I made a note of his main contact. This was a guy who went under a pseudonym – *Top Cat* in English – and I couldn't trace him back. But two things were clear. One, that he was the boss. And second, that he was operating from Northern Ireland.'

Angel, as she listened to Pete, was becoming more and more convinced that Magda had jumped to the wrong conclusion. Just because she'd seen Pete with Szczepan, it didn't mean they were working together. According to himself, Pete had spent a lot of time with Szczepan once he'd managed to get Szczepan to accept him. Probably when Magda had seen them together, Pete had been trying to get closer to Szczepan and get more information from him.

'Another useful thing I found out from hanging out with Szczepan,' Pete went on, 'was that the gang has a headquarters here in the city where they sometimes keep the girls before sending them off to their final destination. It's near the Old City, behind St Michael's Church, down by the river. Not all the girls go there, of course. Most of them go directly to the airport and Szczepan sees them onto the plane, going to Belfast via London. But there are some who are going to the Middle East. They've been starting up a new market there, with customers in Saudi Arabia and such places – or so I think. I have to admit I've no real evidence of that, yet.'

'What you need is an undercover agent, a girl, naturally, who'd be willing to let herself be taken along there and could pick up the evidence for you,' Angel put in. She was getting very interested.

'I don't think we have anyone on the staff who'd be very happy about doing that,' Josh said drily.

'Well,' said Angel, 'what about me? I'd be glad to volunteer.'

Chapter Twenty Five

'No way!' said Josh sharply.

'Why not? I could do a good job, I'm sure. And, of course, you and the other good guys would come bursting in and rescue me at the right moment.'

'It's no joke, Angel,' Josh said severely. 'You'd be taking a horrible risk.'

'I don't see that, Josh,' Angel said. 'The worst that could happen to me would be the sort of thing that's already happened to Magda and Elena. What's so special about me that I can't be allowed to risk it? In any case, I'd make very sure it didn't happen. I'm not a child. I know how to look after myself.'

Josh was scowling at her by now. 'Don't be too sure of that. You don't have all the cards, honey. Just listen to me. These are evil men.'

Although he called her honey, his voice was angry. Angel ignored him. Instead she stood up, smiled at both men, and said with ice in her voice, 'Well, give it a bit of thought. I must go now.'

'I thought you and I were going to take time for a chat together, when Pete had finished sharing?' Josh still sounded annoyed.

'Maybe later. I need to check on Magda, see if she's okay. Nice to meet you, Pete. Be seeing you, Josh.'

She headed off across the square towards the side street where she'd parked her car. Before she left the square, she was aware of running footsteps behind her, and swung round. But it was only Josh. He caught up with her and seized her by the arm. She immediately pulled away from him, and glared into his face.

'Angel. Please don't rush off like that. Listen, honey, I'm sorry I upset you. I know you can look after yourself. But if you tried anything like you were suggesting, I'd go out of my mind with worry.'

'Josh, I've had my fill of a man who wanted to control my life, and didn't care how he went about it. I don't want another one.'

'You won't get one, I promise you, sweetheart. Angel, this isn't the best time to say it, but you must know I love you. I want to spend the rest of my life with you. But I don't intend to control you. I suppose it looked that way, just now. Hey, I'm sorry, honey.'

Angel stood stock still, gazing at him. So it had come. She'd known for some time that Josh was waiting for the right moment to say this sort of thing to her. And she still didn't know how she wanted to answer him.

'Josh, are you asking me to marry you?' she said at last.

Josh looked surprised. 'Sure, I suppose it amounts to that. I certainly picked my moment, didn't I? In the middle of the first major row we've had, in the centre of crowds of tourists and other people. Come over here away from the worst of it, and let's talk.' He took her arm again, and led her gently to the edge of the square and into a quiet street where they could sit under a tree.

'Well, honey? How do you feel about it?'

Angel looked at him, saying nothing. She saw the anxiety in his eyes, and felt moved. There was no doubt in her mind that she loved Josh, but – in spite of the time she had spent talking and praying with her friend Mary, when she had finally, after severe struggles, managed to forgive Michael, her dead husband – there was still a great reluctance to trust another man as she had once trusted Michael. She had loved Michael, at the time when she had married him. That had proved to be the worst mistake of her life. Now she had to decide if she was going to jump off the cliff again – with no safety net.

'I tell you what, Josh,' she said at last, smiling at him to take away any sting from the words, 'I can't answer you straight away. I need some time to think about it – to decide. Do you mind?'

'I understand, honey. You went through a tough time in your first marriage. I swear to you that I won't be giving you a repetition of that. But I can see why you need time to think. Take whatever time you need. Just don't keep me waiting till my ninetieth birthday, right?'

Angel laughed. In a flood of relief, she remembered that she could always laugh with Josh. 'Before then, darlin'. In fact, before mine, too.'

Josh took her in his arms and they kissed. A long, satisfying kiss.

'Now,' he said briskly, as he released her, 'down to business. Tell me everything you and Magda have learned, and then I'll tell you what we got from the three villains, Szczepan, Shorty and Shuggie – the three S's. We ought to have a name for them. The Marx Brothers, or something like that.'

'Not the Marx Brothers – I like them, especially Groucho!' Angel protested. 'How about The Three Bears?'

'Good idea. The Three Bears – but Goldilocks stole their porridge.' He tweaked Angel's fair hair, and laughed.

'And intends to steal their buns as well!' Angel laughed back. 'Well, here goes.' And she proceeded to tell him about how she and Magda had tailed Lucinda and Liam, and what Lucinda had told them about the three dead men, the inspector who had called on her, and her hurried flight to warn her husband.

'H'mm,' Josh said. 'Yes, there's some new stuff there. Who's been shooting right, left and centre? And why? It sounds like someone who was against the people trafficking, don't you think? Or maybe more than one person?"

'Possibly. Anyway, Josh, it's your turn, now. What did you learn that we didn't already know?'

Josh took a moment to sort out his thoughts. Then he began.

'Szczepan said nothing new. His boss's name is Hawthorne. That's about it. The only new things we learnt about him and his role in the gang came through Pete Gillespie, who did a good job in getting close to him. You've already heard that. This headquarters in the city is the most important thing. If we keep an eye on that, we may be able to catch Liam Hawthorne going in and out, and overhear what he says to his staff. We'll try to get in to bug it, if possible. There can't be too many of the gang there, now that we've caught a few, so that makes a quiet break in a lot easier to arrange. The bug would give us some evidence, I should think.

'Shorty was even less communicative. He's the sort of tough guy who keeps his mouth shut and says nothing, no matter what you offer or threaten. A Belfast 'wee hard man.' We did our best, but got silence and more silence.

'Shuggie is a different matter. He was only too eager to talk – trying to get a deal for himself. The trouble, there, was that he didn't know very much. The one thing we did get was that according to Shuggie, an important customer from the Middle East is sending his representative over to talk to the boss and set up an arrangement to have a number of girls brought over there, soon now. Shuggie thought the Rep was due tomorrow night, but I'm not sure how much weight to put on his info. He might know, or he might be only guessing, and possibly guessing wrong.

'That's about it, Angel. We'll try to get a bug set up on the premises tonight, and keep a good watch on the place, starting straightaway. Josip will handle all that, of course. You and I should probably concentrate on the Hawthornes. See what he's up to.'

'I almost forgot to tell you, I'm meeting Lucinda tonight for further talk. The way I put it, it's so I can report to her about what Magda and I have been doing. But actually, it's to try to get more info out of her about Liam. She must know more than she's told us – or I should think so, anyway.'

'Good. That might well be useful,' Josh agreed. 'Do you want me there?'

'I'd love to have you there, darlin', but how am I to explain you to Lucinda? She's dead against cops of any sort knowing anything about her husband. She's paying me because she thinks I'm a Private Eye, and won't pass anything on to the authorities. I reckon *Interpol* counts very much as the authorities!'

'Couldn't you say nothing about my job, and pass me off as your boyfriend who's turned up unexpectedly, and is keen to help?'

'Possibly.' Angel sounded as doubtful as she felt. Then her face cleared. She laughed, and said, 'Okay, then, why not? I don't see how she could know who you are, do you? We pick her up together and take it from there.'

'Great.'

'And now, Josh, I really do need to go and catch up with Magda. I've left her hanging for far too long. See you later, darlin'. I'll give you a ring.'

Chapter Twenty Six

When Josh had left her to go back to his own car, Angel rang Magda's mobile and was answered almost immediately.

Magda gave her directions to the café where she was waiting to hear from Angel.

'I'll wait for you outside,' she offered. 'Then you can't miss me. But don't be too long, I don't want to freeze to death while I'm waiting.'

It didn't take long for Angel to find the cafe where Magda was waiting and they walked back the short distance to her car.

'What now?' the Polish girl wanted to know.

'First of all,' Angel said, 'I suggest we go back to the hotel and have a rest and then a good meal, before we head out to get Lucinda. We need to make sure we have everything we might need, as well, before we leave. And I need to fill you in on what I've learnt since you left.'

So as she drove back to the hotel, she told Magda about Pete Gillespie's story, and explained that she'd reckoned it sounded reasonable, but had still waited until she got Josh alone before sharing information with him.

'The most important two things we've learned are first of all about this headquarters in the city, and secondly about this customer from the Middle East and his representative who's coming over any time now to make arrangements.'

'I'm still not too convinced about this Gillepsie man,' Magda said. 'But as long as we don't tell him anything, I suppose it doesn't matter. But don't start trusting him, Angel or next thing you know you might find yourself grabbed, like Szczepan with me.'

'Fair enough. I won't trust him to that extent. But I think we can trust what he said about the headquarters.'

'Did he say exactly where it is?'

'Yes, but it didn't mean much to me. Near the Old City, behind St Michael's Church, down by the river. I expect you would know where to find it.'

'Yeah, no problem there. So, are we going to check it out?'

'Later tonight, I hope. That's my idea, anyway. Oh, by the way, Josh is coming with us to meet Lucinda. He offered and seemed keen, and I thought it couldn't do any harm. He'll be an extra gun, at the very least. It's a pain that you can't take guns on an aeroplane since 9/11. Have you still got that gun you took off Szczepan?'

Magda looked at her in surprise. 'How did you know?'

'Well, I was there! I saw you take it, and I noticed you didn't hand it over when Josh and I turned in the sawn off shotguns. I don't know why Josh didn't notice – but maybe he did, and thought we'd be better off keeping it.'

'Okay. I suppose I should have known you'd see through me. I have it in my shoulder bag, here.' She produced the gun, and Angel said hastily, 'Put it away, for heaven's sake! We're driving in the middle of the city. Do you want a cop to see us and stop us and take it off us?'

Magda, smiling, slipped the gun back into her bag.

'And while I think of it, can you shoot, Magda?'

'Oh, yes, I can shoot all right.'

'Because, unless you're very expert, you should probably give it over to me and let me handle any shooting we need – or don't need, I hope and trust!'

'If you like,' said Magda indifferently. 'I don't like guns. I'm only too happy to hand it over.' She fished in her bag and took the gun out again. Angel looked carefully all round, but there seemed to be no one – either pedestrian or car – near enough to see in detail what she was holding.

'Keep it down low,' Angel ordered. 'Set it on the floor behind my foot. Okay. Is it loaded, by the way?'

'I suppose so. I didn't check.'

'You've been carrying around a gun which might be loaded without checking? Is the safety catch on?'

'I didn't look.'

'Unbelievable.'

Angel drove until she reached a quiet street, then pulled in. Reaching down, she took hold of the gun carefully, and checked it, her head low enough to see while keeping the gun below the level of the windows.

'Okay,' she announced presently. 'It's loaded, but the safety catch is on.' She slipped the gun into her own bag and sat up again.

'Now, back to the hotel. I hope you've nothing more like that to spring on me, Magda.'

They reached the hotel, and before doing anything else Angel announced that she needed a shower. Magda lay down on top of her bed while Angel showered and changed into dark clothes suitable for the evening ahead. Coming out of the bathroom, she saw that Magda was either asleep or nearly so. Before checking, Angel switched on the hairdryer supplied by the hotel, and quickly dried her hair.

'Magda,' she said softly when she had finished.

The girl seemed to be deeply asleep. Angel thought she could hardly do better than to follow her example. She lay down on top of her own bed, and closed her eyes.

It was nearly two hours later that she woke up again, and by then Magda had clearly woken already, for the sound of the shower was coming from the bathroom. Coming out wrapped in one of the hotel's white, fleecy bathrobes, Magda gave her hair a rub and switched on the drier.

Angel sat up on her bed and spoke over the noise.

'Time we were making a few plans, and then eating. Don't forget, we have to get out to the Hawthornes' place in time, and I don't suppose it will be more than an hour or two, now, before they get back themselves.'

'Okay.' Her hair dry, Magda switched off the drier and sat down on her bed.

'We both need to dress in dark clothes – jeans and trainers we can move about in quickly. Have you got things like that, Magda? Dark trainers, in particular? I can lend you a warm sweater in a dark colour – we'll need warm sweaters, it'll be cold later on, I should think. If it's not, we can leave them in the car.'

'I have dark trainers, dark green, as it happens,' Magda told her. 'But I'd need to borrow a dark sweater, thanks.'

Good,' Angel said in satisfaction. 'Then, I always like to take some rope on these little excursions, and my instruments for opening locks in case we happen to need them.' She moved around the room, gathering up the things she'd mentioned. Magda, in turn, began to get herself dressed in appropriate clothes.

'So, what are our plans?' Angel asked. 'We want to check out the headquarters later on, and we'll have to decide if we leave Lucinda home first, or if we take her with us.'

'Take her back first,' said Magda promptly. 'She'd be nothing but a nuisance if we brought her.'

'That's probably so. Still, we'll take the things I suggested in any case. We don't want to waste time having to come back to the hotel for them when we've finished with her. Another thing, how much should we tell her?'

'I think we can tell her about Szczepan, and how he tried to snatch me back, and how we caught him and Shorty and Shuggie.'

'The Three Bears.'

'What?'

'Oh, just what Josh and I have been calling them.'

'We shouldn't tell her about the headquarters, I think.'

Chapter 26

'No, I think you're right there. And we mustn't let on that Josh is anything official, okay?'

'Okay.'

'Right, that seems to be everything sorted, as far as we can for now. So,' said Angel in a determined voice, 'now for something even more important. Food!'

'Food!' agreed Magda, and the two girls, dressed by now in suitable clothes for their night activities – although not, it had to be said, in clothes suitable for a meal in the dining room of a flashy hotel – headed down in the lift to replenish their strength.

Chapter Twenty Seven

Rested and well fed, they were ready to go. But first, Angel rang Josh, and agreed with him that he would take his own car and meet them a mile before the destination. The two girls took Angel's hired car out of the city and along the road to the Hawthornes' country house, and stopped at the place arranged.

It had been dark for some time, and neither car was easy to spot beneath the overhanging branches of the trees, even though by now they had few covering leaves. Josh got out of his car and came over to them.

'I suggest that we all three share one car, Angel. I can leave mine here, and we can take yours, if you like, or vice versa.'

'We'll take mine. Hop in the back.'

Josh opened the rear passenger door and slipped in. 'So, what's the plan?'

Angel was pleased to see that Josh seemed to have no intention of taking over what had, after all, been her idea.

'We can wait here until we see Hawthorne's car pass us on his way to the house. Then I think we should go after him, leaving a reasonable gap for safety, and wait for Lucinda to appear. Okay?'

'Sounds good,' agreed Magda, and Josh said, 'Okay, honey.'

'If Hawthorne comes out again, intending to go back to the city, it would be a good idea to follow him,' Magda suggested.

'That's true,' Angel said. 'Perhaps we should rethink this. We could keep both cars in action, and one could meet Lucinda and one follow Liam.'

'You'll need to meet Lucinda,' Magda said quickly. 'So I should follow the man. You get into Josh's car with him, Angel, and let me take this one.'

'How good a driver are you?'

'I can drive. Do you want me to give you a test run?'

'No, no,' Angel said hastily. 'I'm sure you can drive fine. Okay, then.' She had detected a note in Magda's voice of annoyance at Angel's repeated questioning of her ability – first to shoot, and now to drive.

'We shouldn't change over just yet,' Josh said. 'It would be a pity if Hawthorne came along just as we were all moving about. Once he's past us will be time enough.'

'So, Josh, did you speak to your Inspector friend and arrange for him to bug the headquarters place?'

'I spoke to him, yes, honey. But I don't know if he's managed it yet or not.'

'I suppose he'd have to get someone inside to do it,' Magda put in.

'Something like that,' Josh agreed. He was listening intently. 'I think that might be Hawthorne's car coming now. We should all duck down, just in case.'

They could all hear it now, the noise of a powerful engine coming closer. Instinctively, they all followed Josh's suggestion and ducked low inside the car.

Angel managed to keep one eye above the window ledge, just enough to catch a glimpse of the car and its occupants. She could see Lucinda, looking tired and stressed, and Liam Hawthorne, his gaze fixed straight ahead on the road. Then they were past.

Josh and Angel got out of Angel's car, and into Josh's. Angel had decided that Magda would need their gun more than she would herself. But she didn't want to argue about it with Josh. Instead, she set the gun down quietly on the driver's seat as she got out, and winked at Magda as she came to change places.

Chapter 27

They waited for ten minutes to see if Liam Hawthorne was going back to town for an evening out. Presently came the sound of his car, moving fast. A minute or two later, they saw it whizzing past them, and shortly after that Magda pulled out in Angel's hired car and followed him.

She was driving very competently, Angel noted, and keeping to a safe distance back. It was unlikely that Hawthorne would notice her.

'Cool,' said Josh. 'So, we head up to the house now?'

'That's right.'

Josh was driving – since it was his car – but Angel decided that there was no reason why that should be a problem.

'We don't need to get up to the door,' she told Josh. 'Even if Liam Hawthorne left the gate open, it would be too obvious. There must be some staff around who'd notice us. I arranged with Lucinda that she would slip out and meet us outside the gate.'

'Good.'

They didn't have to wait long. Pulling up in the shelter of the trees where they had waited that morning, they stayed in the car until they saw Lucinda creeping cautiously out of the gate to stand looking round.

Angel got out of the car and went over to her. 'Hi, Lucinda. You made it, then? No problems?'

'Angel, you're here, then. No, I changed from my evening gear into jeans and a dark sweater – only took a minute – and here I am. I hated deceiving Liam. But in fact, he seemed quite keen to drop the plans for dancing. He said he'd had some appointments himself for the evening and might as well pick up on them, now. He went off straightaway, when he'd seen me in.'

'That's great,' Angel approved. 'Makes it safer for you. My friend Josh came with me, by the way. He was meant to be seeing me this evening, and when I phoned to put him off, he sounded so disappointed that I thought he might as well come. You'll like him. You can trust him as much as me.'

That was certainly true, but how much could Lucinda trust her? She had every intention of handing Liam over to the police as soon as she had the evidence against him.

Lucinda looked rather doubtful, but when Josh got out of the car and came over, it didn't take long for him to charm her into being delighted with him.

'We should get into the car,' Angel said. 'It's too cold to stand around talking outside. I wouldn't be surprised if it started to snow.'

'Yes, let's do that,' Lucinda agreed with a shiver.

They got in, Josh in the driver's seat with Angel beside him, and Lucinda in the back. Angel twisted round to speak to her over the back of her seat.

'So, Lucinda, I said I'd give you my report on what Magda and I have been doing since we flew in here.' Angel proceeded to tell Lucinda how they had come to the Hawthorne house with friends for a party, how Szczepan Kowalski had grabbed Magda, drugged her, and taken her by way of his city apartment to his country house, how she had followed him, freed Magda, and had handed him over, with two other gang members, to the local police.

'Your husband wasn't involved at all, except for giving the party,' she assured Lucinda. 'I said nothing to the police about him.'

She carefully omitted all mention of Josh's role in the proceedings, for fear it might slip out that he had connections with Inspector Buczek, or even with *Interpol*.

Lucinda's eyes grew bigger as the story unfolded. At the end of it, she said, 'How awful for Magda! And for you, too, Angel. You were both in such danger. I don't know how you managed to come out of it alive – and to capture those three terrible men.'

'Oh, I've done things like that before,' Angel said easily. She ignored a nudge from Josh – who appeared to think this was very funny – and stretched across unobtrusively to nip him on the leg, below Lucinda's range of vision.

'Ouch!' said Josh. 'Sorry, a bit of cramp.'

'So, Lucinda, your turn,' Angel said hastily. 'Did Liam say anything tonight that helps us?'

'Not really. Angel, I'm sure he has nothing to do with this awful stuff and those terrible men. He's not that sort of person. I wondered what his business over here was, because he never told me about it, but, then, why should he? I'm not a business person, I couldn't have got involved in it in any helpful way, if he'd told me things.'

'So, he said nothing about it tonight. Not even who he was going to meet, or where, or what the meeting was about?'

'He said he had to go to an old building behind St Michael's church,' Lucinda said. 'I think maybe he's working on buying up old buildings and renovating them. The property market has been booming again for a while now. It would be just like Liam to jump on it, while he can. He likes to make money, as long as it doesn't interfere with his politics. And now, while Stormont isn't sitting, he has lots of free time on his hands.'

Angel said nothing. The place Liam was making for sounded very like the headquarters Pete Gillespie had reported on and Shuggie had also spoken of.

Chapter Twenty Eight

'Did he intend to stay out long, did he say?' she asked after a minute.

'No, but I suppose it depends. If he was meeting business friends, they may have decided to go on for a drink somewhere after they'd finished inspecting the property – if that's what they were doing.'

They talked for a while longer, but Lucinda seemed to have nothing definite to add, and Angel, although she could have said plenty about Liam Hawthorne's guilt, didn't intend to lose Lucinda's trust and support at this stage. She might yet be a lot more useful.

'Well, Lucinda,' she said finally, 'I suppose we should let you get back to the house before anyone notices you aren't in your room. Are any of the staff likely to go there, to check if you're okay, or something like that?'

'No, none of them know me well enough to feel they should bother to be as helpful as that. It's the first time I've been out here, like I said. I don't think they'd come to my room. If one of them did, and asked about it, I'd just tell them I felt like some fresh air and went for a walk in the garden.'

'That's a bright idea,' Angel nodded. 'We'll call it a day, then – unless you want to ask anything, Josh?'

Josh smiled his most charming smile at Lucinda, winning a friendly response. 'Mrs Hawthorne –'

'Oh, call me Lucinda, please, Josh!'

'Lucinda, then. I don't want to hurt you or make you angry, but your husband seems to leave you alone far too much of the time. Did it ever occur to you, just as a possibility, that he might have a girlfriend?'

Lucinda bit her lip and lowered her eyes.

'I only ask,' Josh said, 'because that's so often the case when a husband spends a lot of time away from home. Mind you, looking at you, it's hard to believe a man would be fool enough to cheat on you, but most men are fools, aren't they?' He smiled at her again, allowing his admiration to show in his eyes.

Lucinda burst into tears. Angel hastily leaned over to pat her hand and Josh produced a large, clean handkerchief and thrust it at her. After considerable gasping and blowing, Lucinda managed to shut down the tears at last and began to mop her face with the hanky, blowing her nose fiercely in conclusion.

'Yes, it occurred to me,' she said. 'I found a text he'd sent me by mistake, addressed to someone called Aleksandra. I didn't ask him about it. I didn't want to lose him – more fool me! I wondered if he might be going to see her tonight. I didn't mention it to you and Magda when you came out here, Angel, because I didn't want it to be true, but I thought you might find out something about her when you were looking into his business. But you haven't mentioned it so far. There wasn't anyone called Aleksandra at that party you and Magda went to, was there?'

'No. Liam wasn't with anyone in particular, that I saw. He danced with various different girls, but didn't seem all that interested in any of them. And when I went back afterwards to find Magda, he was on his own, no sign of any woman around.'

Lucinda looked relieved. 'Then maybe I misunderstood the text. Oh, I do hope so.'

'You should go back to bed now, Lucinda, and have a good sleep. You need it after the flight and the emotional upheaval you've been through. Josh and Magda and I will all keep an eye out for any sign of another woman in Liam's life, okay? But I really don't think you need to worry about Liam having a girl friend.'

Lucinda nodded obediently and got out of the car. She looked relieved as she waved goodbye to them and made her way though the gates with all the grace of her previous career as a model still evident in her walk.

'Are you thinking what I'm thinking, Josh?'

'I expect so. This Aleksandra isn't a girl friend. She's a prospective victim of the people trafficking racket. Or else a partner, working with him in it.'

'Got it.'

Josh started up the car and reversed out onto the road, heading back to Krakow. 'Time we went after Hawthorne and Magda. Do you think you should text her to check if Hawthorne's heading where he told Lucinda he was going?'

'Yeah, definitely.'

Angel opened her phone and began texting busily.

Before long her phoned pinged and Magda's answer came back. 'Seems to be heading in the right direction for the HQ.'

'Okay,' Josh said. He was driving as fast as was realistic on the country road. As soon as they came to the turn off to the main carriageway, he put his foot on the accelerator and upped the speed. 'I'd like to catch up with Magda before she gets too close to Hawthorne,' he said.

'That would be wise.' Angel thought for a moment and then said, 'Not that I don't trust Magda, right? But my impression of her, in the short time I've known her, is that she doesn't mind taking risks. I don't want to find that she's doing something daft by the time we catch up with her, like holding Liam Hawthorne up with the gun she has with her. Or even shooting him.'

'She has a gun?'

'Yes, the one she took off Szczepan. She didn't hand it in.'

'Wow! Hawthorne is too dangerous a man for Magda to try that on her own. Well,' he added grimly, 'I have a gun, too. But we'd better make sure we get there in time.'

'I couldn't agree more.'

Josh stepped even more firmly on the accelerator.

'I think,' he said after a few minutes, 'I might know a shortcut to this HQ place. Pete pointed it out to me on a map of the city this afternoon, after you and I separated. If I can remember it properly, it might make a big difference to our time getting there. On the other hand, if I get it wrong –! Do you agree that we should try it?'

Angel nodded. 'Go for it.' She felt a tingle of happiness that Josh was taking her opinion on board, not simply making the decision himself. This sort of thing promised well for any future they might have together. She bit her lip, and switched her thoughts back to business.

'If that's where he's heading, it more or less proves that he's involved in the people trafficking, don't you think?' she said. 'Up to now, we only have people's word for it. Lucinda, Magda, Shuggie and Szczepan. If we can catch him there, that's more like evidence.'

They drove as fast as they could down the side road Josh had chosen. The night had grown colder and the sky, already dark, was growing darker. Angel shivered even in the heated car, and looked expectantly for the first snowflake, but so far the snow was holding off.

Suddenly there was a bang and the car skidded to a halt. The front tyre on the driver's side had blown.

'That's the trouble with these side roads,' Josh said, getting out to inspect the damage. 'Potholes – or, in this case, a lump of metal in the middle of the road. How it got there, who knows?' He crouched down for a closer look. 'Yes, probably part of a wrecked car, left lying about when they took the rest of the car away. I'm going to have to change the wheel, Angel. Sorry.'

Chapter Twenty Nine

He went to the boot and took out the jack and the spare tyre.

'Anything I can do to help?' Angel inquired.

'Best thing you can do is take my torch and stand behind the car to warn any approaching motorists to keep clear. I'll turn on the flashers, but it will do no harm to have the torch as well.'

'Okay.'

Angel took the torch and positioned herself where cars coming could see her in good time to stop, while Josh set to work.

He worked quickly and neatly, jacking up the car, undoing the wheel nuts, and taking off the damaged wheel. He lifted it into the boot and soon had the spare wheel in place. Standing up, he brushed his hands together, squirted on some hand wash, and wiped them with the towel he kept for things like this.

'Okay, honey,' he told Angel.

They got back in the car, and set off again, this time moving more cautiously.

'More haste, less speed,' Josh said ruefully. 'We'd have been better to stick to the main road. Instead of saving time, we've wasted about ten minutes or more. Never mind. Nothing we can do about it now. There are the lights of the city, and we should be approaching it quite near to the area we're heading for.'

'Well, that's still good,' Angel said cheerfully. 'We might not be too far behind Magda, then. We'll just have to trust she keeps her head and stays in the background.'

They could see the river, and further on a scattering of old looking houses, among which they hoped to find the gang's headquarters as described by Pete Gillespie. Angel began looking out for St. Michael's church.

Poland is a country of many churches, so that it would be easy to pick the wrong one. But quite soon Angel saw what must be St Michael's. There was a sign, in Polish, which made it harder for her to be sure, but didn't that word look like a Polish version of Michael?

'Isn't that it, Josh?' she ventured.

'Where? Yeah, must be! Good girl. I think we'd better park out of sight of the area where the headquarters is supposed to be, and get out. We can carry out a reconnaissance, see if we can find Magda, or Hawthorne. Preferably Magda first.'

'Okay.'

Angel slipped out of the passenger door, closing it gently behind her, and she and Josh met round behind the car.

'I'd like us to stay together,' Josh said. 'If we separate it will be hard to contact each other, supposing we find one of them, without making some giveaway sound.'

Angel agreed.

'Let's head towards the back of the church first, and check out the buildings there,' she suggested, and Josh said, 'Okay, babe,' and took the lead in the direction she had pointed out.

There were very few lights. The buildings – as they came around to the rear of St Michael's church and approached a number of squat, rather dilapidated houses and some industrial sized places – were mostly in darkness, and the street lights were few and far between. Angel was tempted to suggest using the torch, but realised that it would be of little help, and would most likely give their position away to anyone on watch.

Moving quietly towards the old buildings, Angel thought she heard a noise coming from the nearest one, one of the larger, industrial sized places. Someone inside there? Or the white noise of machinery left running overnight, a heater or alternatively a fridge keeping a store of frozen goods from being ruined. A flake of snow fell on her nose and made her jerk back and look up.

The threatened snow had finally begun to fall, at first in scattered flakes, but then as it settled in, in thicker and thicker bursts.

'We'd better get inside somewhere,' Josh said. 'This place looks like a possibility for the HQ. Might just as well try it, as any of the other buildings. We can't just hang around out in the snow. Let's see if we can get in without being seen.'

'Okay.'

They went closer to the building and walked along it, searching for a vulnerable door or window, and found themselves feeling along a huge wooden door with iron bars across its width, meant to allow access for vehicles. It was securely fastened, but set into it was a smaller door meant for people. It wasn't immediately obvious if it could be opened with any ease. Josh shone his torch on it for a fleeting moment, shielding its light with his other hand, and Angel saw that the door had a simple lock. She knew she herself could open the lock without much difficulty, and guessed that Josh was thinking the same.

'Could you shine the torch on this lock for me, honey?' he asked. 'I needn't tell you to shield it as much as possible with your hand, but although I might get the lock opened in the dark, a little light on the subject would help.'

He handed the torch to Angel, who took it and shielded it with one hand before switching it back on. Josh bent over the lock, planning to work on it quickly with the tool he had taken from his pocket.

But first he tried the door cautiously and it began to move inwards.

'Hey! It's not locked.'

'Okay,' he said. 'You can switch it off now, babe – oh, you've already done that. Great. Let's go in.'

The snow was beginning to lie now, and its light brightened up the night. It was much easier to see around them than it had been earlier while it still hung in dark heavy clouds above them. But the cold hadn't lessened, nor was it likely to until morning brought the sunlight.

'Let's go,' Josh said.

Taking one of Angel's hands, he led the way cautiously inside.

As they advanced across the wide open floor, where a couple of large vans were parked, Angel became aware again of the white noise. Definitely a machine, she decided, not a person. That was a bit of a relief.

But were they in the right building? And if so, was it here that Liam Hawthorne had been heading? Why was there no sign or either Hawthorne or Magda?

It was unlikely that she and Josh had got here first. The breakdown and the need to change the tyre had robbed them of any advantage in time they might have gained by using Josh's shortcut.

The answer might be that this wasn't the headquarters. There was no real evidence that it was.

They moved on round the building in the darkness, with occasional flashes from Josh's torch and a growing brightness through the small windows set high in the walls as the snow lit up the outside world. They found nothing.

There were the two vans they had already noticed, and at the back of the wide space where they were parked was a small area with a wooden half wall separating it off from the rest of the floor space, with a rickety table and chair, and an ancient computer. Angel, remembering the state of the art hardware in Liam Hawthorne's house in Belfast, as well as the technology in his house outside Krakow, found it impossible to believe that his gang's headquarters had nothing better than this. Josh was coming to the same conclusion.

'Got it wrong this time, honey,' he whispered. 'We'd better get out and try some of the other buildings.'

Chapter 29

Just then, footsteps sounded. They seemed to be coming from overhead. There must be stairs which they'd missed seeing. Josh and Angel stared at each other.

Chapter Thirty

'Quick!'

Josh grabbed Angel by the hand and rushed her across the floor to one of the vans. Not the nearest one. He tried the sliding door, found it unlocked, and bundled Angel inside, jumping in after her himself. He closed the door as quietly as possible, being careful not to let it bang.

They could still hear the footsteps, but they were no longer overhead. Instead, they were clattering down a flight of stairs positioned in the darkest corner. When the footsteps reached ground level, Angel could hear voices as well, for the first time.

Since, naturally enough, the voices were speaking in Polish, Angel felt that she might as well be deaf. However, she hoped that Josh was making some sense of them.

It was even darker inside the van, with no light coming in from the snow. But it was surprisingly comfortable, as Angel found when she first jumped in, and tripped over something sticking out in her way, onto a bed of some sort, pushed against one of the van walls. She collapsed on top of it, and found that it was covered in soft pillows and a duvet. The thing she had tripped over was a bedside cabinet.

Josh, moving carefully about, found another bed on the other side of the van, and sat down on it in his turn. Standing up to explore further, he found that there were six beds in total. There was something which might have been a lamp on one of the cabinets, but Josh refrained from switching it on, in case it could be seen outside the van by the two men.

Meanwhile, he was listening to their conversation. They were talking about the journey they were about to undertake, and complaining bitterly about the snow, which would make it more difficult.

One of them claimed that there was no need to go that night, that it would be just as well left until the morning. The other, apparently the boss, insisted that it was important to get away now. They had to pickup the girls and bring them back here before morning, before someone important – who it was Josh couldn't gather – arrived to see them.

Still grumbling, one of the men got into the driving seat of one of the vans – the one parked nearest the front – and the large doors, while the other, Josh thought, went to open the doors wide. He got into the passenger side at the front of the van, and Josh and Angel could both hear the sound of the engine starting up, and the van moving off through the doors. Then they heard the man who seemed to be the boss jump down again, pull the doors shut, and, they guessed, get back into his seat beside the driver. With the heavy doors shut, no more could be heard.

'What was all that about, Josh?' Angel asked when silence had come again. Josh told her.

'So, they've gone to pick up some more girls,' Angel said slowly. 'We're in the right place after all. We'd better have a look upstairs.'

'I guess we had. Just remember, though, there may be other people up there, Hawthorne for one, and maybe more. We need to go on keeping quiet and doing without the torch.'

'Right.'

They left the van, which was obviously equipped, they realised, for more victims of the people traffickers, and moved silently over to the dark corner and the stairway.

The stairs were made of concrete – a good thing, since it meant that there would be no creaks, as there might have been with wooden treads. Creeping silently upwards, they reached the first landing and saw light ahead of them, filtering down the stairs from a room with a partly open door. The question now was, should they go on up?

There would be no point in turning back now, Angel decided. It seemed that Josh thought the same thing, for he put one hand on Angel's right arm, and pointed upwards, beckoning her with his other hand. Angel nodded.

They crept on up the next flight until their heads were far enough above the top step to see what there was to be seen. There they both stopped instinctively.

There were voices coming from the room with the open door – voices speaking in English, to Angel's relief. She felt that she had missed quite a lot of the conversation in Polish between the men who had driven off in the other van, even though Josh had given her the gist of it.

It was difficult to make out what they were saying. There was a male voice and a female voice, but the words weren't clear.

'We need to move nearer,' Josh murmured in her ear, so quietly that she could just about hear him. In response she nodded silently.

Moving slowly and very quietly, they continued on up the stairs. Angel noticed that Josh had drawn his gun.

Reaching the top of the stairs, they paused to think and look around. There was another partly open door nearby, which they could reach without passing the room where the speakers could now be heard more clearly. Josh pointed to it, and Angel nodded again.

As silently as ever, they made for the doorway and slipped inside. They could hear the voices, but still not loudly enough for comfort. The man's voice came through more clearly, but the woman's was an indistinct murmur.

He was saying '... I don't know what's been happening here, and I intend to find out ...'

Murmur murmur from the woman.

'... and I mean to find out who's responsible for this mess up ...'

Murmur murmur.

'... there's no use telling me you know nothing about it. Why are you here, then?'

Murmur murmur.

Angel strained her ears, trying to hear the woman's remarks more clearly. There was a strange feeling at the back of her brain that she should know that voice. But the words were still unclear, however much she strained to hear.

The man's tone sharpened. He spoke more loudly. It was clear to both the eavesdroppers, by now, who the speaker was. It was Liam Hawthorne.

'Come on, tell me the truth. What's been happening?'

Abruptly he broke off. Josh and Angel could hear footsteps approaching, and so, evidently, could Liam Hawthorne.

'Who's there?' he called out sharply. 'What do you want?'

The door was pushed open, sending out enough extra light making it clear to Josh and Angel that that was what had happened.

The footsteps continued into the room.

'What are you doing with that gun?' demanded Hawthorne angrily. 'What –!' His voice was drowned out by a shattering explosion.

Angel recognised it at once as a gunshot.

Angel and Josh wasted a moment staring at each other in horror. That someone should shoot Liam Hawthorne was the last thing they would have expected. Or was it he who had shot someone else?

As they stared at each other, they heard footsteps running towards the stairs. Recovering, they ran out of the room where they had been hiding.

Too late. The footsteps had reached ground level and were crossing the open space. By the time one of them could follow, they would have disappeared through the door into the outside world. Instead, both Josh and Angel headed for the room where Liam Hawthorne had been talking to someone. Josh had his gun in his hand, and went first.

The door lay wide open. They went in. On his back on the floor, eyes wide and staring at the ceiling, Liam Hawthorne lay, very dead. His fair hair flopped over his face, which was no longer red, but turning grey as the blood drained out of it.

Standing opposite him, one hand to her mouth and a gun in the other hand which hung down by her side, was Magda.

Chapter Thirty One

'Magda!' Angel burst out.

Josh, more practical, strode forward and took the gun from Magda's hand. He raised it to his nose and sniffed.

'This has been fired recently,' he said. 'Magda, was that you we heard arriving just now?'

'No, I was here, talking to Hawthorne when someone else came in, wearing a scarf round her face, and shot him without waiting for anything – even to speak. She threw down her gun, and I picked it up. It isn't the one you gave me, Angel, that one's still in my pocket, look.'

She reached in to her pocket and produced another gun which she handed over to Angel.

'Yes,' Angel said, turning to Josh. 'This is the gun Magda had. I don't recognise that other one, the one you're holding.'

'So, who was it who came in and shot Hawthorne? And why?'

'That's the question. Magda, tell us what happened. We could hear you and Hawthorne talking, but although we could make out what he was saying, we couldn't make out you. Start with you following him in the car. Did he come straight here?'

'No, he drove to the city centre, where the clubs are, and stopped in a parking spot. But before he got out of his car, I could hear his mobile ringing, and he answered it. I couldn't hear what was said, of course. He talked for quite a while, then he drove off again and this time he headed here. I parked out of sight, and when I saw him go in, I followed him. He left the small door unlocked, so I had no problem there.

'He came upstairs, and I came after him.' She paused.

'But why did you go into the room and start talking to him, Magda, for goodness sake?'

'I don't know, Angel, but I suppose I was just so angry with him for the racket he was running that I felt I had to tell him what a despicable swine he was. I had my gun, but I didn't take it out right then. To tell you the truth, I was afraid of what I might do if I was facing him with a gun in my hand. I wanted so much to shoot him. But I also wanted to catch him and have him punished legally, and have him made to tell who else was involved, and if he had any other girls imprisoned. I'm not sorry someone shot him,' she added defiantly. 'He deserved to be shot.'

'So you went into the room,' Josh interposed. 'What then?'

'He seemed astounded to see me. I think he was expecting some-one else, because the first thing he said, when he heard me coming and looked round, was, "Oh, there you are!" Then he saw me and his jaw sort of dropped, and he said, "Who are you? What are you doing here?"

'I said, "I'm your Nemensis, Hawthorne." And he said, "What are you talking about?" He staggered over to that chair' – she pointed to the chair beside the desk across the room '– and more or less collapsed into it. He wiped his forehead with his sleeve, and said nothing for a minute or two. Then he stood up again, and came over to me, and started saying things like, "I don't know what's been happening here, but I intend to find out."

'I said, "I don't know what you mean. You know all about it, don't you?"'

'I think that must be where you and I came in, Angel,' Josh said.

Angel agreed. 'Yes, that was the first thing we heard, although we didn't hear your answer, Magda. But I had an idea that your voice was familiar, that I'd recognise it if I could make out the words.'

'There wasn't much more. He went on, blaming me for making a mess of things, and stuff like that, and I told him it was his own mess. Then the other woman burst in, like I said, and fired at him before either Hawthorne or I knew what she was doing.'

She was looking pale and frightened. 'I need to sit down, Angel. It's been what they call traumatic, okay?'

She sat down in the chair she had pointed out where Liam Hawthorne had sat a short time before.

Angel gave her a sympathetic look. Then she turned back to Josh.

'It sounds to me as if Liam Hawthorne got a call from someone, and they arranged to meet at the HQ building. Magda thought he was expecting someone and was taken aback to see her.'

'Yes. And it's likely, I guess, that the person who rang him was the one who shot him. A woman, in that case. She knew he was there. She lured him down there with some story, maybe that the police were on their tracks, then she shot him. I don't think it's clear why.'

Now, if Magda had shot him, the motive would have been obvious. No, it's okay, Magda' – as Magda uttered an upset sound – 'I know you didn't. Your gun wasn't used, and I don't think you had a second gun, so calm down. If we knew the motive we'd probably know who it was.'

'This Aleksandra that Lucinda mentioned, do you think?'

'Quite possibly. Thieves falling out, maybe.'

He took out his phone. 'High time I reported this death by shooting to the proper authorities, so they can come round and remove the body and examine the crime scene, guys.' He rang, and they listened while he reported briefly.

'We should have followed the woman who shot Hawthorne straightaway,' Angel said. 'We were too horror stricken by the sound of the shot – as least, I was.'

'Me, too,' admitted Josh.

'But I have an idea,' Angel went on. 'We might be able to follow her footprints in the snow if it's thick enough, and if we act quickly now before they get covered over.'

'Brilliant, honey! Let's go, then.'

They all three – even Magda who seemed to have recovered from her shock and be filled again with enthusiasm – made for the stairs and hurried down and across to the doorway. Once there, Josh stopped them.

'Let's be careful, guys,' he said. 'We don't want to trample over any marks that are left. Let me go first, okay? Then you two can follow on, keeping well over to the side of the tracks. I'll be doing that, too.'

They carried out Josh's plan, moving carefully out through the small door and keeping well to one side.

As it turned out, they could see footmarks still clear on the newly fallen snow. They were small enough to seem like a woman's, but otherwise not distinctive. To Angel's eyes they suggested trainers such as so many people wore now.

'Good, so far,' Josh said. 'Come on, guys, let's see where they lead us.'

They followed the footprints through the streets behind St. Michael's Church, not sure what they would find, but determined to try their best. Who knew where they might lead?

Presently the footsteps went round a corner to an area where a number of cars were parked, covered with a layer of snow that looked like the icing on a Christmas cake.

The footprints led them into the centre of the parking place, and then stopped, at an empty space.

'I think she's beaten us,' Josh said. 'This looks like the place where she got into her car and drove away.'

'Sure, that must be it, Josh.'

Magda looked hopeful.

'Can't we take a picture of the tyre prints and see which type of car they belong to?' she asked. 'Isn't that the sort of thing your *Interpol* mates do?'

'I think you've been watching too much television, Magda,' Josh said. 'It's not as easy as all that. And even if we knew what type of car it is, there might be hundreds of them in Krakow alone. Still it's certainly worth a go.'

He took out his phone and carefully snapped a dozen or so shots of the tyre marks driving away from the empty space where the car had been. Where the footprints they had been following had stopped.

'Okay, that's as much as we can do for now, guys. I'd better get back to the scene of the crime. The cops will be there by now. I shouldn't really have left, but the footprints were important. They'll want a more detailed report than I gave them on the phone. I'll see if they can do anything with these pics, okay?

'Magda, where did you park Angel's car? I'll walk you and Angel round there, and then head back.'

Chapter Thirty Two

They watched Josh disappear in the direction of the HQ building. Then Magda tugged at Angel's sleeve as she was starting to get into the car.

'Wait a minute, Angel! I didn't suggest it to Josh because he needed to get back to the crime scene. But why shouldn't you and I try to follow the tyre marks as far as we can?'

'I'm afraid they'll be jumbled up with lots of other cars before long, Magda.'

'Well, you never know. It's worth a try, isn't it?'

Angel laughed. 'Yes, why not? Like you say, it's worth a try!'

They jumped into the car and Angel took it back the short distance to the parking place where they had snapped the tyre marks.

'Okay, we'll have to go slowly to make sure we follow the right tracks,' she said. 'Can you stick your head out of the window and keep a look out for them, Magda? I'll need to be watching the road.'

Magda pressed the button to open her window right down, and leaned over with her head well out, so that she could see the road ahead.

'Keep going,' she told Angel. 'The tracks lead right ahead.'

Angel drove carefully, on account of the snow. The last thing they needed was a skid and a crash. 'Can you still make out which tracks they are, Magda?' she asked presently.

'No problem. As you can see, there isn't much traffic tonight. People don't want to drive in the snow, maybe be snowed up miles from home if it gets heavier. I can still see the tracks we want quite plainly.'

They drove on. As Magda had pointed out, the road was nearly empty – even here on the main road out of Krakow.

Angel was amazed that the tracks were still so easy to see. She had expected that they would have been covered by fresh snow, or else mixed up with other cars, but they were still there, leading them on.

Suddenly Magda called out, 'Angel! Stop!'

Angel braked. 'What is it?'

'I think that small car ahead is the one we're following.'

'How can you tell?'

'The tracks run into its back. They match up with the ones it's leaving.'

Angel opened her own window, and peered out carefully. She could see what Magda meant. In front of them, a small car was trundling slowly along. As the girls watched, it pulled in to the side of the road. Ahead were crossroads. The car waited. Angel and Magda waited.

'Should we reverse and find somewhere to wait out of sight?'

'Yes,' decided Angel. 'I think we should do that.'

She reversed her own hired car carefully, pulling into a turn off, a few yards back. 'This should do. We don't want to lose sight of her.'

They sat, growing colder and colder, and waited.

It seemed a long time before they heard the sound of a heavy vehicle of some sort approaching from the left crossroad. They watched as it drew up in front of the other car. It was a large van, similar to the one Angel and Josh had heard driving away from the headquarters. Angel couldn't be sure it was the same one, but it seemed probable.

A big man, wrapped in warm clothes which included a heavy jacket and a woolly hat, jumped down from the van and approached the car. In the clear air, they could hear him speaking in Polish.

'Can you make him out, Magda?' Angel murmured as quietly as she could.

'Yes. He's asking why she rang, why they had to come here instead of back to HQ, what the problem is?'

The woman was answering now.

'She's telling him someone got shot at the building. The police will be all over it by now. They have to take the cargo somewhere else.'

Magda was spitting with anger. 'The cargo! She means the girls they've taken!'

'Hush!'

They listened, but there was little else to hear. The woman directed the van driver to follow her, Magda reported.

The big man got back into the driver's seat of the van, and swung it round behind the small car. The car drove off, the van following. Leaving sufficient distance to keep from being spotted, Angel followed in turn.

A fresh, much heavier fall of snow helped them to keep well out of sight. It was as much as Angel could do to see the van ahead. She peered through the windscreen, the wipers going furiously, and kept it just in view.

They had been driving for some time before she realised that they were taking a road which had become very familiar to her in the past couple of days. On each side, the snow hung from the branches of the trees, turning the landscape into a fairytale picture. They were turning off into a side road before Angel became fully convinced that they were heading towards the Hawthornes' country house.

'Magda,' she said, 'do you see where we're going?'

'Where?'

Magda hadn't driven the road quite as often as Angel, so it had taken her a little longer to take it in. However, Angel's hint woke her up to see where she was going.

'We're heading for the Hawthornes'!'

'That's what I thought. But why?'

'I suppose the gang members, like this woman, all know it. They may be hoping to use it as a temporary HQ. They probably don't know that Lucinda is there.'

'And the staff,' Angel reminded her. 'What about them?'

'I don't know. But I would guess that they are part of the gang.'

'Yes, why not? It would have made things safer for Liam Hawthorne if they were,' Angel agreed.

'So what should we do when we get there?'

'Scout around. Watch to see what they do with the girls in the van. Ring Josh and tell him to send the cops out here to arrest the woman and the guys in the van, and maybe the staff as well if they seem to be in it.'

'Okay.'

They drove on, amid the thickening snow. It was as much as Angel could do to keep the van in sight, but from time to time she recognised familiar landmarks. There was the bunch of trees where she and Josh had waited to track Liam Hawthorne as he went to pick up Lucinda at the airport – and where later she, Josh and Magda had waited to see the Hawthornes return from their meal out.

A few minutes later there was the place where she and Josh had talked with Lucinda. They must be nearly at the gates, then.

Sure enough, almost at once she saw the van swing in though the gates, which had been left open. The driver of the small car must have been far enough ahead to get out, open the gates – leaving them open for the van – and then return to the car and drive up to the house.

Angel braked carefully, trying not to skid.

'I think we should stay outside for now, Magda,' she said. 'I want to ring Josh. Or maybe just text him, in fact.'

She took out her phone and spent a few minutes texting busily.

'Okay. I think we should get out of the car, and make our way up to the house on foot. Don't want them to hear a car engine coming!'

'Fair enough,' Magda agreed. 'We can see where they've parked the van, and either check inside it if none of the gang are around, or see if they've taken the girls into the house.'

They got out of the car, wrapping their jackets round them. They had both brought gloves, for which they were very grateful, but Angel envied the woolly hat the van driver had been wearing.

'Now for it,' Angel said. 'Let's get going.'

Chapter Thirty Three

They moved quietly through the gates. The van driver and his mate hadn't wanted to get out of the van into the snow to close them, understandably.

'We'll have to keep to the drive, walk in the wheel tracks,' Angel said softly. 'If we try to walk on the grass, the snow will be so deep we'll trip for sure. But I don't think anyone is likely to see us on the drive.'

Magda, trying not to shiver, agreed. They ploughed off up the drive, deep in snow, but with the wheel tracks of both the car and the van cutting deep furrows which made for easier walking. After some minutes of effort and hard going, they saw something looming ahead of them, and saw that it was the van. It was parked in front of the house, slewed across the doorway.

'Looks like they've skidded,' Angel said.

'Yeah. But not too badly.'

'Shall we have a closer look?'

'I think we should.'

'Let's hope the driver and his mate have gone inside into the warm.'

'It can't be too warm inside the van, for the passengers, if they've left them there.' Magda's indignation sounded in her voice, quiet though she tried to keep it.

'Actually, when Josh and I were hiding in the other van at the HQ building, we noticed the heating system in the van. It wasn't the sort that switches off when the engine stops. It had its own generator. So the girls are likely to be warm enough, at least.'

'In that case, let's get in and join them!' Magda giggled. 'I'm turning into an icicle out here.'

'We'll need to go carefully.'

They approached the van, looking carefully to see if there was anyone in the front cabin where the driver and his mate sat. When they were sure it was empty, Angel moved along the side of the van to where the sliding doors were, similar to the ones which Josh had opened to let Angel and himself climb in to hide in the other van. When open they would give access to the rear compartment.

Angel put her hand gently against the door and pushed sideways. Nothing happened.

'I'm afraid it's locked,' she said. 'That makes it seem as if the girls are still inside, and haven't been taken into the house. I'll have to see what I can do with the lock.'

Angel knew she hadn't Josh's experience and skill in cracking locks, but she was still confident that she could manage well enough. She needed her hands bare to feel what she was doing properly. Taking off her gloves, she gave them to Magda to hold. 'I don't want to risk having them fall out of my pocket and get lost,' she explained. Then, taking out the tools she had brought with her when they left the hotel, crouching over, she set to work.

The lock was a very different one from most of those she had previously tackled. It was more than ten minutes before she was able to stand up again and announce to Magda, 'There. That should do it.'

Retrieving her gloves and putting her tools away, she put both hands against the door and pushed again.

This time, to her relief, she felt the door sliding open beneath her hands.

Inside the van, it was dark. Angel was surprised. She remembered that there had been at least one light in the other van, although she and Josh had been too wary of light leaking out to risk turning it on. But surely, if the girls were here, they would want some light. Lying in the dark was never a pleasant thing, especially for prisoners.

They climbed in, sliding the door shut behind them, and stood for a few minutes listening.

As their ears grew acclimatised, they could hear heavy breathing. It didn't sound like normal breathing, even the breathing of sleepers.

'Drugged,' whispered Angel. 'You can hear it in their breathing.'

Magda nodded, then, realising that Angel couldn't see her, said, 'Yes. That's what it sounds like. How many of them are there, do you think?'

'The other van had beds for six. We should check. You stay here at the doorway and I'll find the light and turn it on.'

She moved forward, feeling her way slowly, until she came to a bedside cabinet with what felt like a lamp on it, and turned it on. The compartment sprang into light.

It showed them six girls, their eyes closed and their faces heavy with drugs, lying on six beds lined up against the opposite walls of the van. They were all young and pretty. Angel's heart was moved with pity to see them lying there so helpless.

'What can we do, Magda?' she whispered. 'I'd thought we could have got them out safely while the gang are all inside the house, but we can't carry six of them, all drugged, back to our car.'

'No.'

Magda looked at her, as helpless as the girls.

'And I don't think we should try to bring them round, even if we could. It might be very bad for them.'

Angel stood looking at the drugged girls, thinking desperately.

An idea sprang into her head.

'Listen. Suppose we drive off the van with them all still in it? We could probably meet up with Josh and his mate Joe, the Inspector, somewhere along the road. They ought to be well on their way by now, with other reinforcements. What do you think?'

'Brilliant, Angel!' said Magda enthusiastically. "Do you think you could manage to drive the van?"

'Why not?' asked Angel lightly. 'I don't have a license for Heavy Goods Vehicles, but I don't suppose the cops'll worry too much about that. I don't see why it should be especially difficult.'

'Okay, then. Let's do it!'

'You had better stay with the girls, in case they start waking up. You'll be able to reassure them that they're being rescued, not taken to the Middle East. You speak the language, too.'

Hugging Magda briefly, she slipped out of the van door and headed round to the driver's compartment.

She was glad to see that the door wasn't locked. But would the keys be in the ignition?

Angel knew how to start up a normal car without keys, but she wasn't sure if her skills would work on a heavy van. Possibly. Or possibly not.

To her relief she saw as she swung herself into the driver's seat that the keys were in place. The man must have thought that his van was safe enough in the grounds of a private house, especially in a snow storm.

She settled herself into the seat, then hesitated. It might be a good thing to check where exactly Josh was, and to arrange a meeting point. She opened her phone and rang his number.

'Josh?'

'Hi, Angel honey.'

'I'm taking the van with the six girls in it. We're starting from Hawthorne's house. I'd like to meet you along the road. Where would be a good place? Or are you nearly here by now?'

'Just leaving Krakow. How about the turnoff from the main road?'

Angel breathed a sigh of relief. Josh, being his usual self, hadn't wasted words. She followed his example.

'Great. I'm leaving now.' She clicked off the phone and turned the key in the ignition. The van gave a jerk. Angel released the clutch, accelerated, and felt the heavy vehicle move forward.

Snow had piled up round it, in front of the wheels. But so far it hadn't hardened into any serious blockage. Angel upped the speed, and the van continued to move. She turned it in a semicircle until it faced out along the drive again.

In a short time it was travelling as fast as Angel thought safe, covering the distance to the open gate without much trouble.

Above the noise of the engine she began to imagine that she could hear shouts behind her. Had the van driver come out and found his vehicle missing, in fact disappearing down the drive?

Angel just hoped she was imagining it. She drove on, increasing the speed as much as seemed wise.

But she was well away now, and no one following her on foot could overtake the van, she was confident. It might not be moving at top speed, but it was a lot faster than any man – or woman either – on foot.

It was as she pulled through the gate, congratulating herself that things were going well, that she heard, back at the house, the sound of another engine starting up.

Chapter Thirty Four

Angel mentally kicked herself. It would have been so simple to find the woman's car where she had parked it and disable it. She knew half a dozen ways of putting a car out of action. Instead, she had driven off, making enough noise to alert the gang, and they had had the sense to pile into the car and follow her.

It seemed that speed was her best chance now. If she could reach Josh before the car overtook her, everything would be okay.

She wondered briefly if she should stop long enough to disable her own car before her pursuers found it and made use of it. Two cars following might be more tricky than just one. But she decided against it almost at once. The car was too close behind her for her to risk losing any time. The drive was a long twisty one, which meant that she had a decent start, but not enough of a start to waste the few minutes it would take.

Angel drove on.

Behind her in the van there was silence. None of the girls had woken up yet, she was fairly sure. The wall between the driver's compartment and the rear area wasn't sound proofed. She would be able to hear if Magda and the girls were talking. There was nothing, which was probably just as well. It would panic the girls, and possibly Magda, too, to hear the car pursuing them. They would all be in a groggy state, recovering from the knock out drugs they had been fed, and much less resilient than they might normally be. Probably Magda would be less upset, though. So far, she'd been through some of the stuff of nightmares, and had bounced back every time.

Was the car coming closer? Angel strained her ears to listen above the noise of the van's engine. No, it seemed still quite far away. She put down her foot and drove faster. She had passed the trees where she and Josh had waited for Liam Hawthorne, by now. Still a bit to go before she would reach the main road. She looked forward eagerly to meeting up with Josh. Perhaps he would reach the turn off before her. In that case, he would surely keep going, along the dirt road, until he saw her. She might see him any minute. Angel's heart lifted at the thought.

The snow was thicker than ever. It was getting hard to see out of the windscreen, even with the wipers going full blast. But it would be a mistake to slow down. She could hear the engine of the following car and it seemed closer behind her than before. There must be something she could do. Could she take advantage in some way of the snow?

Picking what she thought was the best idea out of the number crowding in her brain, she deliberately slowed down. She hoped she wasn't doing something stupid.

As she heard the car approaching nearer, she slowed further. Then, acting quickly, she put the van into reverse, pressed hard on the accelerator to put on speed, and backed hard into the following car, going as quickly as she could go.

There was a splintering crash, followed by shrieks and shouts. Then silence.

Angel had done what she'd hoped to do. She had used the van as a weapon to destroy her pursuers.

Changing back into first gear, she moved the van away from the car, disentangling the two vehicles insofar as she could. Then she braked, took out her gun, and sprang lightly out of the driver's compartment.

Behind the van, several yards back now that Angel had pulled away from it, the small car had turned on its side and was obviously badly wrecked. The driver, the big man who had driven the van, was unconscious. How badly he was injured, Angel didn't know.

The second man, who had been beside him in the passenger seat, had a broken arm. The bone protruded clearly, white and unpleasant to see. His legs were trapped under the dashboard. It wasn't possible to tell how badly he had been hurt, apart from the arm.

As Angel paused to look at the crash, someone scrambled out of the back of the car and ran cross the snow. It was the woman who had shot Liam Hawthorne. Her face was still wrapped in the scarf which had covered it earlier and kept Magda from seeing her well enough to recognise.

Angel started to give chase, then thought of Magda and the girls.

Turning back to the van, she could see that it had suffered very little damage from the collision with the smaller vehicle. She went to the door and pushed it along to open it. Stepping inside, she pulled the door shut behind her to keep the heat in.

Magda's sleepy face looked up at her. She was lying back on the easy chair, the only one, which was next to one of the beds, with a cushion pushed behind her head. The drugged girls slept on.

'Angel,' Magda said by way of greeting, 'have we arrived? Have we met up with Josh and his cop friends yet?'

'No,' Angel was beginning, when she heard a voice outside calling her name.

'Angel! Are you there?'

It was Josh's voice. Angel pulled open the van door again, and jumped thankfully down to where Josh's arms were waiting to embrace her.

'Josh! I'm so glad to see you!'

'Honey, what's been happening?'

Angel explained as quickly as she could.

'These girls need to be taken to hospital, so a doctor can check them over. And the two men in the car need a doctor, too, although they certainly don't deserve it.'

'One of them – the driver – is past medical help,' Josh said drily. 'And the other one will have to be cut out of the car. His legs are trapped under the dashboard. Joe is sending for technical help for that.'

'The woman got away across the fields,' Angel said. 'If the cops are quick enough they might catch her, though I doubt it.'

'I think you and Magda both need a bit of comfort,' Josh said. 'Let's go back to the house and see if we can find you some food and some hot coffee, babe.'

'That would be perfect, darlin'. And can we leave the girls to Inspector Joe to look after?'

'Sure we can. Joe brought a whole team with him, paramedics among them.'

'I've just remembered. There may be some staff inside the house who are working with the gang. Magda and I thought it was very likely that Liam Hawthorne wouldn't employ honest men and women who would see what he was up to and give him away.'

'You've got a point there, honey. But we can safely leave them to Joe as well.'

'Oh, and Josh, I nearly forgot about Lucinda! She must be in there somewhere! Dear knows what's been happening to her.'

'Okay, we'll go and check it out. I think she's probably okay, but we'll find out.'

There was a clatter of footsteps and implements arriving at the van, and one of the paramedics put his head round the door.

'Some patients for us here?' he asked cheerfully. He spoke with a broad American accent, as many Europeans do, who have learnt their English as much from the movies as from school. He must have known he was going to be speaking to the American, Josh.

'Six girls who've been drugged,' Josh said. 'Your job is to get them to hospital where a doctor can have a look at them, guys.'

'Will do,' said the cheerful one, and he came on inside the van with several colleagues.

'Come on, Magda,' Angel said. 'Time you and I left.'

They jumped down from the van, and Josh drove them back to the house through the still falling snow.

Angel hadn't been there since Liam Hawthorne's party, when she had gone back to see if Magda was still there. It was still the magnificent home it had been then, but the coloured lights and bunting had been taken down. It looked more sober, but still magnificent.

'I think the first thing we should do is to look for Lucinda,' Angel said.

'No,' Josh said firmly. 'The first thing you two should do is sit down comfortably while I make you some coffee. I wouldn't mind some myself, come to think of it. Joe and his men are rounding up any staff there are, and they'll find Lucinda while they're doing that.'

Angel – whose experience driving the van, and then crashing it into the car, had indeed left her feeling rather shaken – knew that she could do with a cup of coffee too. The information that the driver of the car had been killed in the crash – which she had deliberately brought about – had added to her trauma. She noticed that her legs felt shaky.

Along with Magda, she followed Josh to the warm welcoming kitchen with its wood burning stove sending out splendid heat, and collapsed into a soft chair.

Angel on Guard – *Gerry McCullough*

Chapter Thirty Five

Angel sipped happily at the hot coffee when Josh handed it to her, but after a few moments her thoughts returned to Lucinda.

'Josh, it's all very well to say that we can leave Lucinda to Joe and the other cops. But I feel responsible. Okay, I'll finish this coffee – which is very welcome, and thank you for it, darlin' – but then I'm going to look round for her myself, starting with her bedroom. If Joe is focussing on the staff – if any – he might not get around to looking in Lucinda's room for a while. I just have a bad feeling about her. Supposing she's there, tied up or drugged or something?'

'Okay, honey, I won't try to stop you.'

'I'm going, too,' Magda said firmly.

'Do you want me to come?'

'No, Josh, darlin', there's no need for an army.'

'Then I'll go and find Joe and see what he's up to, and if he needs any help.'

He collected up the three coffee mugs and put them in the dishwasher, then they left the kitchen. Josh headed for the big living room downstairs, and Angel, followed by Magda, made for the staircase.

Neither girl had much idea where Lucinda's room might be, but at least they had seen some of the upstairs rooms before, and could rule out those which weren't bedrooms.

They moved up to the next floor, and tried several doors, all of which opened at a turn of the handle. No sign of Lucinda in any of them.

Presently they came to what was obviously Liam Hawthorne's bedroom, and felt they must be getting warmer.

'I should guess husband and wife have rooms near each other, since we can tell from Liam's room that they didn't actually share,' Angel said.

'What's the point of being married and not sharing a room?' Magda wondered aloud.

'Your guess is as good as mine. But you remember that in the house near Holywood, Lucinda obviously had a room of her own. They must like the opportunity to have some privacy, I suppose.'

Near the room which had been Liam's they came to a door which didn't open when they tried it.

'Locked,' Angel said. 'This could be it.'

She took out her picklocks and began to work on the door.

'Should we knock?' Magda suggested.

'Let's just see if we can get the door open, first.'

Angel continued to work away, in silence. Suddenly there was a sharp click.

'Done it.'

'Great.'

Angel turned the handle and gave the door a considerable push. It opened easily, and they went in.

They were in a spacious, handsomely furnished room, with twin beds, a couch and two easy chairs over to one side, a door which clearly led to a bathroom, and a built in wardrobe with a matching chest of drawers in an antique style.

Lying on one of the beds was Lucinda Hawthorne. She was tied hand and foot, but not gagged, and her eyes opened wide as she saw them.

'Angel!' she exclaimed in a faint, croaky voice. 'I'm so glad to see you! What's going on? Who were those people who burst in and tied me up and locked my door?'

'First, let's get you untied, Lucinda.' Angel went over and began to work on Lucinda's bonds.

'I've been struggling to loosen the ones on my wrists,' Lucinda said. 'I think I'm nearly there. Then I could have unfastened my legs, I think.'

'The ropes on your wrists are certainly quite loose. Good for you, Lucinda.' Angel deftly completed the untying of the ropes, and Lucinda sat up, rubbing her wrists and ankles.

'Now,' said Angel finding a chair to sit on and pulling it over nearer to Lucinda, while Magda plumped down on the bed, 'tell us about it. What happened? And did you recognise any of those people?'

'There were three of them,' began Lucinda. 'Two men and a woman. They were all Polish. They spoke Polish to each other, and besides, they looked Polish. No, I didn't recognise any of them. I was lying down on the bed, thinking about getting ready to go to sleep, and wondering how soon Liam would come home, when I heard footsteps pounding up the stairs, and they burst in through the door. They said something in Polish, but of course I couldn't understand a word. I asked them who they were, and what they wanted, but they didn't answer.

They had some rope with them – I think they must have found it in the conservatory, Liam keeps some there for tying up the flowers – and, anyway, they started tying me up. The men did, the woman gave orders. Then they went, locking the door behind them.'

'Can you describe them? Especially the woman. The men are out of the picture now.'

'She was wrapped up so I couldn't see her face. She was taller than me, about your height, Angel. Oh, and one of the men, the bigger, burly one, called her Alex. It made me wonder if she was the one Liam's email was addressed to. Liam might be able to tell you more about her, if he was willing to.'

It dawned on Angel that Lucinda didn't know her husband had been shot – shot dead. With so much else happening, she had almost forgotten that. She would have to tell Lucinda. Or someone would.

No, it would be better coming from her than from a policeman. Certainly, she would have to talk to policemen about it afterwards, but first it should be broken to her gently, by someone who was a sort of friend.

'Lucinda,' she began gently, 'I'm afraid I have some very bad news for you. Magda, maybe you could move over a bit? Thanks.'

She went over to the bed where Lucinda was sitting, found room to sit beside her, and took Lucinda's hand. Then she put the other arm round her.

'Tonight your husband Liam was in the room in an old building in the city. Magda was there, talking to him. I had just arrived, with my friend Josh, and we heard them talking as we came nearer. Then a woman, wrapped up as you described, came in, shot your husband and then ran out again. I'm afraid he's dead, Lucinda.'

Lucinda wailed out one word, 'No!' Then she threw herself down on the bed, buried her face in her hands, and began to cry in huge heaving bursts.

'I think it must have been the same woman who came here with the two men and tied you up.'

Magda can tell you more about what happened than I can, if you want to ask her.'

Lucinda stopped heaving with an effort, and looked up at Magda.

'You were in the room when he was shot?'

'Yes, we were talking. He asked me what I was doing there. I think he was expecting to meet someone, and it wasn't me – I was a surprise to him.'

'Did you recognise her? Could you describe her any better than I was able to?'

'No, your description fitted what I saw. I couldn't do any better.'

'You should lie down now, Lucinda. Do you have anything to take, paracetamol or anything like that? You need to sleep and calm down. Magda and I will go and tell the inspector what happened to you, but we'll ask him to leave questioning you until the morning.'

'There's some stuff in the bathroom cabinet I take to help me sleep,' Lucinda said. 'I put it away there earlier when I unpacked.' She looked wretched. Angel felt immensely sorry for her. She brought back a couple of tablets and a glass of water, and gave them to Lucinda.

'When you've swallowed those, you should get yourself into bed. I'll fetch you a nightie. Is there one in this drawer?' She moved over to the decorative chest of drawers positioned against the wall nearest to Lucinda's bed.

'Yes. Second drawer.'

Angel produced a flimsy nightdress in shades of blue and lilac, and handed it to her.

'Can you manage? Or do you want me to help you?'

'I'm okay. I'll go into the bathroom and get ready. But you won't go, will you, Angel? You'll stay with me?'

'I'll wait until you're tucked up in bed, Lucinda,' Angel promised. 'But then I'll have to go and talk to the inspector.'

'No! No! You mustn't leave me, Angel!'

'Go on into the bathroom, Lucinda,' was all Angel said, and Lucinda went in obediently. But when she came out again shortly afterwards – washed and changed into the nightdress – she began to plead with Angel again to stay with her.

'Magda,' Angel said at last in desperation, 'why don't you go and find Inspector Joe, and Josh, and explain the situation to them?'

'Magda, I need you to stay, too,' Lucinda wailed. 'I'm terrified to be left here by myself – I need both of you in case those people come back.'

'I'll come back here when I've spoken to the police, Lucinda,' Magda promised. She and Angel exchanged glances. They seemed to be stuck with an hysterical woman who clung to them both.

'Okay, Magda, you go on. I'll stay here till you get back,' Angel said.

Magda slipped quietly out of the room.

Angel sat down on the chair where she had been sitting previously, while Lucinda climbed into bed.

'Try to sleep, Lucinda,' Angel advised her gently, and Lucinda lay back and closed her eyes. But a moment later she opened them again.

'What was Liam doing in an old building?' she asked, a puzzled frown on her face. 'He said he was going to a night club.'

'We think he got a text message from someone, asking him to meet them there. He went there because of the message. The police should be able to find the message on your husband's phone.'

'And what was this old building? Why should anyone want him to meet them there?'

'It was the headquarters of the people trafficking gang – or so we think,' Angel told her. Then she wished she hadn't, for Lucinda burst into another bout of tears, covering her face with her hands again.

It was a relief to Angel when at last she heard footsteps on the stairs. Magda coming back to share the load.

Chapter Thirty Six

It was not only Magda. It was Josh as well. Angel was inexpressibly relieved to see him.

'Oh, Josh!' she said, springing up from the chair and putting her arms round him.

'Hey, hey, honey,' Josh said, hugging her back for a moment. 'What's the trouble?'

'Lucinda's so upset about her husband.'

'Of course she is.' Josh put Angel gently back in her chair. 'Mrs Hawthorne, you have my warmest sympathy. I can only say, we'll do everything we can to catch the woman who shot him, and who tied you up, if that was the same one.'

'It sounds like it,' Magda said. 'Lucinda's description of her matches what I saw.'

'I'll see that the description goes out to all stations tonight,' Josh said.

Lucinda stared at him. 'How can you do that?' she asked. 'It would take a policeman to authorise that, surely?'

'Ah.' Angel tried to hide her embarrassment. 'Sorry, Lucinda. I didn't tell you. Josh works at *Interpol*. He's here to track down the guys running the people trafficking gang. He's helping the local cops. I should have said, but he doesn't want it spread around.'

'Oh,' Lucinda said. She seemed to have nothing else to say.

'I haven't come here to distress you more tonight, Mrs Hawthorne, just to express my sympathy and my assurance that we're doing everything we can to catch these guys. Come on, girls, we'll leave Mrs Hawthorne to get some sleep.'

He took Angel's arm and started for the door, but was halted in his tracks by a loud wail from Lucinda.

'No, no, Angel, Magda, you promised you'd stay! Don't leave me here alone!'

Angel looked despairingly at Josh.

'Josh, I can't leave her.'

'And neither can I,' put in Magda.

'It's okay, Lucinda, we'll stay with you.'

'It's your choice, honey. But I need to go. I want to get Joe started with the description both Magda and Mrs Hawthorne have given, and see what they can find. I'll see you in the morning, babe.'

He went out, and Angel leant back in her chair and wondered if she would get any rest that night.

But Lucinda, happy that she was not to be left alone, had closed her eyes and looked as if she was falling asleep already.

'This is all very well,' hissed Magda, 'But where are you and I going to sleep, Angel?'

'Pillows and duvets in the cupboard on the landing,' muttered Lucinda sleepily. 'One of you can take the other bed, and one of you the couch.'

She turned over and went to sleep.

'You can have the bed,' Angel said. 'I'll nip out and get a duvet and pillows for the couch.'

'We'll toss for it,' Magda said, producing a coin from the purse in the pocket of her jeans. 'Winner gets the bed.'

The coin spun. Angel said, 'Heads.'

Magda showed the results to her with satisfaction. 'Tails it is, Angel. I get the bed. But just to show how generous I am, I'll get you the pillows and duvet.' And she went onto the landing to fetch them.

Ten minutes later, the only sound in the room was the gentle breathing of the sleepers.

Chapter 36

Angel woke up with a start several hours later. Something metallic and cold was pressing against her cheek.

'What –' she said, still half asleep.

'Keep quiet.'

The voice, guttural and harsh, sounded familiar, yet different.

'Stand up and put your hands behind your back.'

Angel, aware now that the cold object against her cheek was a gun, obeyed. The room was in darkness.

'Magda?' she said. 'Are you okay?'

'Not exactly,' came Magda's voice with a rueful note in it. 'My hands are tied, and I've been threatened with a gun. It's getting to be a regular thing.'

Angel laughed, mostly from relief. For a few minutes she had been afraid Magda had been shot. The person with the gun seemed happy to shoot without hesitation as it occurred to her.

'Be quiet!' the voice said.

Angel was quiet.

She wondered at the woman's nerve, coming back when she must know the police were searching for her everywhere. Angel considered the possibility that Josh might have arranged for someone to stand guard on the house, someone who would hear the noises and come to investigate. But, no. It wouldn't occur to Josh, any more than it had to herself, that the woman would come back. The only one who had feared it was Lucinda. That was why she had begged Angel to stay. The only one on guard was Angel herself. And Magda, of course. Why should she come back? Was she intending to kill Lucinda?

Angel risked a look round at the other bed where Lucinda should be sleeping, but it was too dark to see much. All the same, it seemed to Angel that there was no shape of a sleeper in the bed. Where was Lucinda, then?

'Put your shoes and jacket on,' the woman said. 'Magda put hers on as I instructed her before I tied her hands. If you cause me any problems I'll shoot Magda first, then you. So hurry up.'

Angel knew that the best time to resist an attacker was right at the beginning. If she allowed herself to be tied up, it would be much harder. But the gun was now pointing at Magda, and Angel couldn't risk it. If the woman had kept it pointed at her, she would have tried something. It wouldn't have been the first time she had disarmed someone holding a gun on her. But Magda being threatened made it different.

She bent down to get her shoes, and sat on the bed to put them on. 'What about my jeans?' she asked coolly. 'If we're going somewhere where I need shoes and a jacket, I could do with jeans as well.'

'Okay. Just be quick.'

'Where's Lucinda Hawthorne?' Angel asked.

'Drugged and lying in the bathroom,' the woman said. The more she talked, the more familiar her voice sounded. It was a harsh, cold voice – frightening if you were the sort of person to be easily frightened, which, Angel told herself firmly, she wasn't. She rather thought it was a voice which was successfully disguised.

But if it was vaguely familiar, it must be someone who Angel had met since this business started. She remembered how Magda's voice had sounded familiar to her. She had a good ear for voices. Who could it be this time? Someone who had been working with Liam Hawthorne, and who had then turned on him and shot him?

It must be someone with connections to Poland, she thought. In her mind she ran over the names of the women she had met, or had heard speaking, since the start – Elena, Magda, Lucinda – all very unlikely. Then there was Sandy, the lead singer with *Rock On*, who seemed to know Liam Hawthorne well. Was Sandy short for Aleksandra? Or the woman Liam had called Stella, at his party. They had seemed very close. Could she use Aleksandra as a code name? Or there were other women at the party – women Angel hadn't been introduced to, but whose voices she had heard. No one seemed definite.

No other possibilities came to mind.

'Okay,' she said finally. 'Ready.'

If she could get the woman to keep talking, she might eventually recognise whose voice it was. 'Do you want me to turn around so you can tie me up?' she asked.

'Yes.' The woman must have recognised the danger of speaking too much, for she said nothing more. Instead she seized both Angel's wrists in one hand, clamped them against her own chest, and wound rope round them, keeping hold of her gun. Angel was surprised at the skill she demonstrated and the speed. In no time her wrists were tightly bound.

'Move,' the woman said. Pushing Angel with her free hand and holding Magda by her arm, she hurried them out through the door, which Angel now saw had been left open deliberately.

Keeping behind them, she herded them down the stairs and towards the kitchen. The door there had not been left open, but without much effort she used a spare hand to turn the handle and push them through. It was clear that she intended to take them outside. That would be harder, because the back door, leading out from the kitchen, had been bolted by the police before they left the house. However, the woman, displaying once more her considerable dexterity, pulled open the bolt and took them out into the night.

The air was crisp and cold. Above them, the stars were shining in beauty on the fairytale world – trees and bushes outlined in snow and large smooth spaces which were the Hawthornes' front gardens. The stars were throwing down enough light for them to see where they were going. The snow had stopped falling, and the sky was clear.

The woman still kept behind them, but Angel caught occasional glimpses of her as when they came to a twist in the path they were following. It was only enough to tell her that, as in her previous appearances, the woman was thoroughly wrapped up, and that a scarf hid her face from view.

'What are you going to do with Lucinda?' Angel ventured to ask presently.

'Lucinda?' The woman laughed. 'Don't worry about Lucinda. She's okay.'

'Are you going to shoot her?'

'No, why should I hurt Lucinda? Now shut up.'

It was bitterly cold. Angel found herself shivering in spite of her warm jacket. The stars were throwing enough light for her to see that they had come round the house from the back door and were now going down the winding drive. In another short while they had reached the gate. It was open, left that way by the departing police.

The woman bustled them out through it. Suddenly Angel realised where they were heading. Her own hired car, left here what seemed like a long time ago, was still where she had parked it, its roof covered in snow inches thick, like – as she had thought before about other cars – the icing on a Christmas cake. Its engine might be too cold to start, but clearly the woman didn't think it would be.

'Keys,' she snapped at Angel.

'Right pocket,' Angel said briefly.

The woman realised that Angel with her hands tied was unable to get the keys herself. Still aiming her gun at Magda, she reached into Angel's right hand pocket to retrieve the keys. While her hand was still in Angel's pocket, Angel seized her opportunity. Quick as a flash she bore down on the woman's arm, trapped inside the pocket, swung round and knocked against the gun in her other hand. The gun exploded as the woman pulled the trigger, but it was no longer pointing at either Angel or Magda. The bullet soared harmlessly into the sky as the gun fell to the ground. Angel kicked out at the woman, catching her on the jaw and sending her flying.

'Quick, Magda!'

Magda jumped forward, tied though she was, and put her foot on the gun.

'Got it!'

'Good girl!'

Chapter Thirty Seven

The situation had changed for the better, but both girls were still bound at the wrists.

'Get up!' Angel ordered the woman. 'Now, you're going to untie us or else I'm going to go on hitting you until you do.'

Her words had an immediate effect. The woman scrambled to her feet, looked round desperately for her gun and saw that Magda had it under her foot, impossible to grab.

Reluctantly she began to untie Angel's ropes.

'Good,' Angel said briefly. 'Now Magda's.'

'Why don't you untie Magda yourself?'

'Because I've more sense than to give you a chance to get that gun back while we're both occupied. Go on, do it.'

A few minutes later, Magda's hands were also free. Stooping down quickly, she took hold of the gun and levelled it at the woman.

'Shall I shoot her, Angel?' she asked.

Not quite sure if she was serious or not, Angel said, 'That's something we'll have to think about, Magda. On the whole, I think we'd better let the police have her.'

'Oh.' Magda sounded disappointed. 'So, do we take her back to the house, or call the cops from here? It's sort of cold to wait around for them to come.'

'We'll go back to the kitchen and throw some logs on the stove,' Angel decided. 'And we'll check on Lucinda, untie her and make sure she's okay. But I'll text Josh first.' She took her mobile from the pocket of her jacket and began texting. 'Don't take your eyes off her, Magda, while I do this.'

'No way.'

The text sent, Angel pushed the woman back towards the house, while Magda and the gun followed.

'When we get into the heat of the kitchen, we'll unwrap this lady and see who or what we've got under the coats and the scarf,' Angel added cheerfully.

They had almost reached the kitchen door when a man's voice spoke out of the darkness.

When Josh got Angel's text message he was at the hospital where Szczepan Kowalski had been taken with his broken leg.

Joe had told him that it looked as if Szczepan was about to open up. He was hopeful that he and Josh could get more info from him. Of the three they had arrested, Szczepan was the one who knew most. Shorty might know something, too. Shuggie, Joe thought, was only a gofer, with little or no inside information. Shorty was a Belfast hard man, unlikely to break, but Szczepan was another matter.

Josh sat with the Inspector at Szczepan's hospital bed, and questioned him.

'So, Szczepan, how did you get involved with this people trafficking gang? Who introduced you to the boss?'

'You'd like to know, wouldn't you?' Szczepan's voice jeered.

'It might help you,' Inspector Buczek said. 'You're in for a long sentence. Help us and we'll put in a word for you, maybe get it reduced for cooperation.'

Josh could see the struggle going on in Szczepan's eyes.

'After all,' Josh said reasonably, 'the boss man is dead, now, isn't he? Liam Hawthorne. Dead and done for.'

'He can't get at you now, Szczepan,' Joe put in.

'Dead? That's all you know!' Szczepan burst out. 'Liam Hawthorne was just a fall guy – he was set up to come to that place that used to be the headquarters. Then the boss shot him – haven't you realised that yet?'

Josh and the inspector exchanged glances. Was Szczepan telling the truth? Or was this a trick?

'So you don't know what you're talking about when you say the boss can't get at me now! If I tell you any more, I'll be shot, too!'

If Szczepan was telling the truth, Josh realised, Angel was in serious danger. The woman who had shot Liam Hawthorne was loose somewhere around the Hawthorne house.

His phone told him he had a text. Looking down at it, he saw that it was Angel. He read it and breathed a sigh of relief. She had come up against this woman, but had turned the tables on her. Typical of Angel, Josh thought with a grin. He would get along there as soon as he could.

Meanwhile, he turned back to questioning Szczepan.

'I've just got a text,' he told the man. 'The woman who shot Hawthorne is a prisoner. She'll soon be joining you in jail. So the more you tell us now, the shorter you jail time is likelier to be. And the harder it will be for her to get at you.'

Szczepan's face changed. 'Maybe I could tell you a little more,' he said.

Chapter Thirty Eight

Outside the Hawthornes' house, Angel and Magda heard a voice they both knew.

'Stand still. I have you covered. Turn around slowly and hand over the gun.'

Angel froze. She recognised the voice at once. It was Pete Gillespie. The cop who Magda had distrusted, but whom both she and Josh had thought was honest. How wrong they had been.

Magda let out a startled cry, as the woman turned back to her and seized the gun from her unresisting hand.

'I owe you an apology, Magda,' Angel said. 'I didn't believe you when you said this man was a crook.'

Pete glared at her. 'More fool you,' he said.

Angel remembered something which she wished she'd thought of before. Elena had mentioned a man called Pete taking them to the airport and putting them on the plane to London. As Pete said, more fool her to have forgotten that.

Pete turned to the woman.

'Good work, boss,' he said.

He seemed disposed to talk. 'I know you didn't expect anyone else to turn up, Angel. But, you see, I've been waiting for your little party to arrive at the car. We're scheduled to drive to a private air-field nearby – the Eastern Airfield – to meet a client from Saudi Arabia, who's expecting a cargo of girls tonight. He has his plane waiting to take off with them, and he's ready to pay a very pleasant amount for them, which is what matters. So I can't let you capture my partner, can I, and spoil the whole business arrangement?

'You've killed most of the rest of our associates – or put them in prison. And now you've taken away our cargo. But although there are only two of you, you're top quality – both blonde which is what they like in that part of the world – so I hope the client will be happy enough with you to pay up without complaints.

I don't mind telling you all this because you'll be leaving us in a very short time, on your way to shine in the Gorgeous East. Come on, turn around, back down the drive again.'

So the woman had come to take them as replacements for the girls rescued from the van. Angel was horrified that Magda should be threatened with a repeat of the things she had already gone though. As for herself, she couldn't help being quietly amused at the fact that the plan she had suggested to Josh, that she should get herself captured as one of the girls, was actually happening without any planning on her part.

Of course, it was a pity that it was happening without any arrangements being made for her to wear a wire and record what was said as future evidence.

Meanwhile, their captors were hurrying them down towards the gate. It occurred to Angel that she should have got her car keys back from the woman, but it was a bit late to worry about that now. She assumed that the plan was still to leave in Angel's car. But it turned out that that was not the case.

Parked not far from the place where her car was, a large shiny black Mercedes – also iced with a white decoration of thick snow – looked ready for action, weather or not.

'I got her keys,' the woman told her partner. 'I intended to get into her car and disable it, in case anyone tried to use it to follow us.'

'Good. But I imagine anyone who turns up will have their own car,' the man said.

'Also, there was no sign of you when I got here, Pete. You were late. What happened to you? I like to be able to rely on people to

214

do what they're supposed to do. I decided to take her car and head to the airfield by myself, if you didn't turn up soon.'

'Ah, but I did – and in the nick of time, don't you agree? You do realize that the roads are clogged with snow. It makes for slow going, even though there's no traffic – partly because it's the middle of the night, but mostly because of the snow. But I got here in time, in spite of that. How would you manage without me? '

'Don't fool yourself, Pete – I could manage.'

Pete said nothing. The harsh, cold voice in which the woman had spoken had taken the wind out of his sails.

'Okay, girls,' he said at last. 'The doors are unlocked. Get in the back. And remember that there's a gun on you. Don't take any silly risks.'

The party halted. The woman opened the back doors of the car and ushered both girls inside, slamming the door on them and getting into the passenger side at the front. The man kept his own gun steady on the girls until his partner was comfortably settled, twisting round in the front seat with her gun aimed at her prisoners. Then he himself got into the driver's seat, and lowered his gun.

The car started.

So far there had been no opportunity to escape. Angel was determined that at whatever risk she wouldn't allow herself to be meekly shepherded into the plane. There was bound to be something she could do.

There was also the fact that she had texted Josh, and that he would be on his way as quickly as he could come. And, knowing Josh, she expected that in spite of the snow on the roads, that would be pretty quick.

Nevertheless, as she sat beside Magda, her mind was turning over various plans. It mainly depended on what opportunities came up.

Should she try to wreck the car? No, she and Magda might get hurt as well as the crooks.

Should she go for the woman, wrest the gun from her? Easier said than done. In the confined space of the car, if the gun went off someone would be hurt. Probably herself or Magda, since the gun was aimed in their direction.

She continued to think.

If she waited until they reached the airfield, and got out of the car, the chances were that Pete would have his gun on them as well as the woman. In fact it was quite likely that others would be there, bodyguards of the client, also heavily armed. Not a good situation for an effort at escape.

Waiting for Josh to arrive was not an option. Pete had remarked that the bad roads, thick with snow, had held him up. They would hold Josh up, too, excellent driver though he was. By the time he got there, he might be able to do nothing but wave the plane good-bye – if even that.

Angel made up her mind. There was only one thing for it, and the sooner the better.

Chapter Thirty Nine

'This is a bad road, even without the snow,' she remarked casually, addressing herself to the woman. 'You may not be familiar with it. I am. I've driven up and down it I don't know how many times in the last few days.

Not the last time, but the one before that, there were the remains of a wrecked car scattered all over the road, and we ruined a tyre on part of it, and had to stop to change it. It was a miracle we weren't completely wrecked ourselves. I hope Pete's looking out for stuff like that.'

It hadn't actually been on this road, she reflected, but on the side turning Josh had taken as a short cut – but there was no need to tell them that.

It was hard to tell from the woman's face, completely covered, except for the eyes, by her scarf, but she moved slightly, and Angel was convinced that she was worried. Pete showed no signs of concern, but he was not Angel's target.

'Of course, it hadn't been snowing then, so it wasn't so hard to see obstacles in the way. Now that the snow has covered everything up, I should think it would be nearly impossible – look out!' she shouted – almost screamed – and half rose from her seat.

The woman started back, turning her eyes towards the driver and the view out of the windscreen. For a few seconds her gaze was no longer fixed on Angel. It was enough.

Completing her movement upwards, Angel leaned forward and seized the gun by the barrel, holding it tightly so that the woman couldn't press the trigger. With her other hand she chopped the woman's

The woman's grip on the gun slackened, and Angel it of her hand. A second later she was holding it against , below his right ear.

'Sit down and don't move unless you want me to blow his head off,' Angel said. 'You, Pete, pull in at the side as soon as possible.'

Her orders were obeyed. Pete, feeling the cold metal of the gun against his neck, knew he was helpless for the time being. Like Angel earlier, he knew that any attempt to grab the gun would be disastrous for himself.

Angel knew she had him. Her only concern was the woman. Did she care if Pete was killed? Did she think she could handle matters by herself, without him? Would she try to get the gun off Angel, regardless of what happened to Pete?

Angel could only hope not.

The car was pulled in at the side of the road.

'Now get out,' Angel said, speaking to the woman. 'You first.'

The woman did as she was told. As soon as she had closed the door behind her, Angel told Pete, 'Now drive on again.'

She waited until he had driven a few miles, then said, 'Pull in again.'

'Magda, I want you to get out first and I'll give you the gun as soon as both Pete and I are outside. I'll need you to hold him up until I get into the driver's seat. Make sure you keep at a good distance from him, we don't want him jumping you to get the gun back, okay?'

'Okay.'

Pete pulled the car in again. 'Josh told me you were some girl, Angel, but he didn't tell me the half of it.'

'Shut up. Stay where you are until I tell you to move.'

Magda slipped out of the car and stood waiting for the gun.

'Now get out,' Angel ordered Pete, still holding the gun on him. Pete did as he was told. 'Take your own gun out of your pocket, and put it on the ground. Then walk away from it.'

Angel got out in turn, on the same side as the other two, and ad the gun delivered to Magda before Pete could look round to see what was happening. Magda, standing at a safe distance, levelled the gun at him, while Angel picked up the gun Pete had put on the ground and stowed it in her pocket.

Magda, still pointing her gun, said, 'Don't move, mister. I'd love to pull this trigger. In fact, I think that would be a good idea. How about it Angel?'

Angel climbed into the driving seat. 'Not in cold blood, Magda. We'll maybe find a better time.'

She turned the engine on and started the car up. 'Now, Pete, start walking. And don't stop. I'm afraid both you and your partner will be pretty cold, but walking warms the blood.'

She waited until he had gone some distance, then said, 'Into the car, Magda, quick.'

Magda jumped in, the gun in her hand still steady on the retreating back of Pete Gillespie. Angel accelerated away.

'With the roads so empty of traffic, it's not likely either of them will get a lift,' she said. 'I'm going to get up to the main road, and then I'll stop for long enough to text Josh. He probably knows where this airfield is that they mentioned. It would be good if he was able to get there and to identify that plane. He ought to be told about Pete Gillespie, too.'

'Yeah, good idea. Don't you think we should try for the airfield ourselves, Angel? In case Josh is held up by the snow on the roads, and doesn't get there in time?'

'How would we do that, Magda?'

'Pete Gillespie gave away the name, remember? The Eastern Airfield.'

'So he did. As he said himself, he didn't need to hide anything from us, because we'd be flying out of the country and unable to give anything away, in a short time.'

'So we know where to go.'

'Do you know where it is, Magda? This being your native country-side?'

'No, I have a vague idea, but that's all. But we could put it in the SatNav.'

'Great idea!'

'Okay, when you stop, I'll put it into the SatNav while you ring Josh.'

Angel drove on until they reached the main road, and she felt they'd put sufficient distance between themselves and the walkers in the snow. She rang, and listened while the phone rang, but there was no answer. The phone switched to voicemail. 'Okay,' Angel said, mostly to herself. 'Too bad.'

The signal came for her to speak, and she began. 'Josh, your mate Pete Gillespie is a traitor – part of the gang. One of the leaders, in fact. We were about to take the woman into the house when he came up behind us and told us at gunpoint to let her go and drop the gun. Then he took us off in his car, a Mercedes. He explained that they had a client from Saudi Arabia waiting in his private plane for the cargo we'd taken off him, and said he was going to hand over me and Magda instead.

We managed to get the gun back and put him and the woman out in the snow – poor things!– and we drove as far as the main road and stopped to let you know. Now we're going to drive to the air-field – which he told us is called the Eastern Airfield – and see if we can hold up the plane and capture the client. Hope to see you there, darlin'!'

'Okay,' she said to Magda, closing her phone. 'Have you set it up? Which way does the SatNav want us to go?'

'Straight on and turn left in a kilometre.'

'Okay. Will it tell me what to do next?'

'Yes, but in Polish. I'll translate for you.'

They drove on for a kilometre, then the SaNav spoke. In Polish.

'Turn left,' Magda said. 'Drive for three kilometres.'

They followed the SatNav's instruction for another ten minutes.

Since they had left the main road with its lights, all around had been darkness, lit up only by their headlights and the gleam of starlight on snow. Suddenly there were lights off to one side, well ahead.

'Do you think that's it, Angel?'

'I think it is.'

'Turn in at the next turn on the right,' said the SatNav, translated by Magda.

Angel turned in. 'You'd better turn that off, now, Magda. We don't want unnecessary noise. I'll switch the car off before we get too close.'

They were in a wide, snow covered space with three small buildings in the distance. Angel turned off her headlights and drove cautiously nearer. The light was coming from two places, enough light for her to drive without risk.

First, there was light from the buildings, two of them large enough to be hangers holding aircraft, and the other probably a workshop holding equipment and benches with enough space for the mechanics to work. Secondly, a string of lights on what must be the runway.

They could hear the sound of a machine at work, and as they drew nearer they could see that it was a snow plough moving on the long track, presumably clearing away the snow and leaving a path for the takeoff of the client's plane.

There was no plane in sight, and Angel guessed that it was still inside one of the hangers. She pulled up at a distance from the runway and the hangers which would make it hard for the people working there to see her.

'Okay, Magda. Keep your gun ready. Let's go.'

They climbed out of the car, closing its doors as quietly as possible, and set off across the airfield.

Chapter Forty

The first thing would be to dodge successfully round the snow plough on the runway. Angel wanted to get a good look inside the hanger, to see the number on the plane, and if possible to see the pilot and the owner. They moved along, keeping well away from the machine, until they had passed it. Then they approached the runway more closely.

'We'll have to cross it to get to the hangers,' Angel said. 'Not a sound, now.'

Almost holding their breath, they came up to the edge of the runway. The lights were now shining directly on them, revealing their presence to anyone who glanced in their direction.

'Quick!'

They darted across the runway, reached the other side, and kept on moving quickly until they were out of the direct beam of the nearest lights.

Angel drew a deep breath. 'Whew!'

They stood still for a moment, assessing their chances of getting to a position where they could see into the hangers – or at least into the right one, the one holding the client's plane. The hanger on their right was quite close. Its large folding doors had been flung wide open. It was likely to be the one currently in use.

'Come on.'

Together, they moved carefully up to the edge of the building.

'I'll look first,' Angel said. 'If we both look, they're more likely to see us, right?'

Magda nodded.

Angel advanced her head just enough to be able to see around the edge of the door with one eye. Yes, there was a plane there, obviously set up ready for action. There were two mechanics moving round it, checking various things, getting ready for takeoff. A plump, brown skinned man wearing an expensive dark blue suit was lounging against the wall beside the plane, watching them with interest. The client?

Angel took a good look at him. The overall first impression was of someone small and fat. In spite of his well cut suit, he was carrying far too much extra weight. Too much champagne, too many elaborate and expensive meals, she decided. There was something unpleasant about his face – the self satisfied, complacent expression of someone who cared about no one but himself. She drew back and motioned to Magda to have a look.

Magda's face, when she in turn finished looking and drew back, said it all. Disgust and anger fought for victory in her expression.

Angel moved away, and Magda followed.

When they were far enough away not to be heard over the noise of the airplane's engine tuning up and the farther away snow plough, Angel spoke.

'Did you recognise any of them, Magda?'

'The fat guy looked a bit familiar, I think. But I can't think who he is.'

'I can,' Angel said grimly. 'I've see him on television, recently, in connection with hostage taking. He's Sheik Abu Hassan. A multi millionaire, with a reputation for involvement in drugs and guns. He was online claiming that he had had nothing to do with the hostages, that they'd been taken by some terrorist group that he was trying to put down. I don't think the interviewer believed him.

'And the hostages, now that they've been rescued, told a different story. But he couldn't be arrested by our police, he's a citizen of a small state which protects him, as long as he stays there.'

'He's not there now,' Magda pointed out. 'Couldn't we get him arrested here?'

'Possibly. We'd need evidence that he was involved in the people trafficking.'

'Why don't you take a pic of him beside the plane, anyway? It would be a start.'

Angel agreed. Opening her phone she moved back to her previous viewpoint and snapped several shots.

She was aware that it was only too possible that the Sheik would notice her, but as it turned out, just as she took the shots his attention was distracted by his own phone. He opened it and said, Hello?' in a soft, smarmy voice.

He stood listening for several minutes, then said, 'So where are you? I'll send Antoni.'

Snapping the phone shut, he said to one of the mechanics, 'Fetch Antoni for me. You know where he's parked, behind the hanger.'

The mechanic came towards the doorway, and Angel and Magda swiftly retreated a considerable distance into the darkness. The mechanic came out, hurried round the corner of the hanger, and in a few minutes came back with another man – clearly Polish – tall and good looking with dark hair and brown eyes.

'Antoni, I want you to take the car and collect my business partners. They're stranded in the snow some kilometres down the side road that turns off not more than another kilometre along the main road. Bring them back here. If you have any problem finding them, ring their number and get more instructions. Here – I'll text it to you. Okay? Get moving.' The Sheik, speaking to an employee, now used a loud harsh voice which Angel and Magda had no difficulty in hearing.

Antoni saluted smartly and made his way back to the car behind the hanger, and Angel said quietly to Magda, 'Good thing they seem to communicate in English. I suppose the Sheik doesn't know enough Polish.'

'Yeah.' Magda looked at her. 'Here's a problem for us. Pete, or the woman, must have rung him.'

'I should have taken their mobiles,' Angel said ruefully. 'I was too concentrated on the guns to think of anything else right then. A mistake.'

'Oh, I don't know about that. If they get together, there's more chance of getting some evidence, right?'

'I suppose so. We could do with Josh getting here.'

'So, meanwhile, what's the plan?'

'We'll move back and try to overhear some more. I mean to turn my phone on to video them, with sound. That way, we'll have all the evidence we need, I hope. Depending on what they all say. We really need to find a place where we won't be seen when Antoni arrives back. Or before that, of course. Let's go around the back of the hanger and see if there's somewhere we can get inside.'

They started off around the corner – looking out for other cars and drivers parked at the rear – and were relieved to see none.

'Antoni will probably be about half an hour, or anyway twenty minutes, I suppose,' Angel said thoughtfully. 'All the same, we want to find that hiding place as soon as possible.'

The hanger was a ramshackle building which had been there for many years, to their relief. This made it more likely that there would be gaps in the woodwork where time and weather had warped it, where they could manage to get through. It took them five minutes or so to identify a gap, between two worn and damaged planks of wood, which might allow them through.

'We'll look first,' Angel said. 'No use struggling through right into the Sheik's line of sight, or the mechanics' either.'

'True.'

Angel unfastened her jacket, putting the gun into the pocket of her jeans, but kept on her gloves. The likelihood of getting her bare hands scratched on the damaged wood, from splinters, was too high to take the risk. She carefully eased the planks of wood further apart, and put her eye to the improved gap. She was looking out at piles of spare parts, heaped on tables, at discarded coats and other clothes, at what looked like rubbish.

'This looks safe,' she reported. 'Take a look and see what you think.'

Magda in turn peered through the gap.

'Yes, I think we'd be well concealed if we get through here,' she agreed. 'But what about our coats, Angel? I quite see that we want to make ourselves as unbulky as we can, but we'll need them once we're through if we aren't going to freeze to death.'

'We'll push them through first,' Angel decided. 'Then we go after, and put them on again.'

'Right.'

Angel gathered up the two jackets and pushed first one then the other through the gap.

'Okay,' she said. 'Here goes.'

Chapter Forty One

It wasn't too easy, but Angel finally managed to get herself through. Standing out of the way, she waited while Magda, in turn, wriggled through. This took a little longer, for Magda – although certainly not fat – was big boned, built on a more substantial, sturdy frame than Angel's slim, graceful, light-boned figure. Eventually they were both through, and putting their jackets back on. They stood for a minute or two, looking about for the best place to conceal themselves.

'We want to get as close to them as we can,' Angel whispered. 'No point in being here if we can't make out what they're saying. No use recording a blur and a mumble of sound.'

They moved forward among the piles of rubbish until they could see the Sheik and the plane. The mechanics were inside the plane for a lot of the time, but were also to be seen moving around the outside, checking this and that. Angel, who knew a little about planes, thought they seemed to be doing a good job.

Presently Sheik Abu said in his loud harsh voice, 'Aren't you nearly finished, yet?'

One of the mechanics, not the one who had acted as errand boy to fetch Antoni, but the other one who seemed to be in charge, climbed down from the wing where he had been adjusting the fuselage, and said, in a not particularly subservient voice, 'We want to make sure there are no faults. I don't suppose you want to crash? We've added a few things to allow for the snow, particularly on takeoff along the runway. Most planes in the main airports are grounded at the moment, but you've insisted on being ready to leave tonight. It takes extra work.'

The Sheik shrugged and said nothing, showing no sign of gratitude, and the man climbed back up.

It was the first time Angel and Magda had got a close look at him, and Angel saw Magda's face change. She pulled at Angel's sleeve.

'That man! The mechanic in charge! I know him!'

'You do?'

'Yes, his name is Jan Nowak. He was in my class at school. I always thought he was a good guy. What's he doing here, working for these villains?'

'Maybe he doesn't know anything about them? Maybe he's only carrying out his usual job, looking after the aeroplanes that use this airfield?'

'Wouldn't that be great? It would mean that he would help us if we told him what these people are involved in.'

'But could we risk it? Supposing he's gone to the bad since your school days, Magda? If we let him know we were here, would he give us away to the Sheik?'

'Who knows?' Magda agreed regretfully. 'We'd better say nothing. But we could keep it in mind if we got caught, that there's at least a chance he would help.'

'Hush.'

They listened as the sound of a car engine came nearer and stopped. Then there were voices and the sound of footsteps approaching. Angel turned her phone on to record.

'Ah, my dear Pete.' The Sheik's voice had changed from the harshness of his address to his staff into a more pleasant, almost respectful tone. 'I'm glad to see you've got here. And this is your partner?'

'His boss,' the woman said. The harshness of her voice was, if anything, more pronounced. Pete laughed.

'Certainly, my boss. You two haven't met before.'

'And am I to know your name, madam?'

'No one hears my name,' the woman said. 'I'm known as *Top Cat*. I don't intend to give anyone the opportunity to give me away.'

The Sheik coughed and changed the subject. 'And when am I to see your cargo? It was coming separately, in a large van, I understand?'

Pete sounded uneasy. 'It's not just as simple as that, Sheik. There've been a few hitches.'

'Hitches?'

'The cargo was hi-jacked. The van was stolen with the girls still in it, and handed over to the police.'

'So, what was the point of coming here with nothing for me? You promised me six attractive girls, now you say you have nothing.'

'Wait a minute, wait a minute, Sheik. The boss grabbed a couple of other girls, not six, okay, but really top notch. Blonde and beautiful.'

'Ah. That sounds better.'

'But while we were driving here one of the girls pulled a gun on us and put us out of the car and drove off with it. That's why we were stranded.'

The sheik's face grew red with anger. He exploded into rage. 'You incompetent fools! What use is that to me? Why did you come here to tell me this rubbish, this failure to supply the girls I need? If you think I'm going to pay you anything for not bringing me girls, you're both fools!'

Again Pete tried to interrupt, but it was the woman's voice which cut through the Sheik's outburst.

'Stop talking nonsense. We came here to show you how you can get these two girls back. I always carry a tracker in my pocket in case I need to use it. When the girl told us she was going to put us out of the car, I got it out and attached it to the car door before I got out, and I switched it on. I can tell you exactly where the car went. Do you want to stick by our deal and pay us for this information or not?'

'But – but – what use is the information if the girls are on the other side of Krakow by now?'

The scarf hid the woman's expression, but Angel was sure she was smiling nastily. 'None. But they aren't on the other side of Krakow.'

'So – where are they?'

'Do we get paid?'

'Yes, yes, if the info is of any use. If they are nearby and can be taken again.'

'They are very nearby. Or their car is. As for taking them again, there are three of us, plus your driver – if he can be trusted to help – or the mechanics. That should be enough.'

'Not the mechanics. They're not mine – they work for the airfield. But Antoni, yes. Stop holding back, woman. Tell me where they are?'

'Produce the money first.'

'I'll produce it. But you needn't think you'll leave with it until I have the girls.'

'Fair enough. So, where is it?'

'Here, in the plane.' The Sheik sounded sulky. He'd been bullied into an agreement he was less than satisfied with. All three of them climbed into the plane and Angel could just see the Sheik lifting a heavy looking bag from one of the overhead lockers. He came back out of the plane, followed by Pete and the woman, set the bag on a nearby bench, and opened it just wide enough for them to see the piles of banknotes inside.

Angel couldn't tell how much at the quick glance which was all she could manage to get before the Sheik snapped it shut again, but she was surprised at the amount it seemed to be. She hadn't realised she and Magda were worth so much.

'Okay, that'll do.' The woman paused tantalisingly.

'So, where is this car?'

The woman laughed. Then she said, 'The car is parked a few hundred yards from where we're standing. They must have driven straight to this airfield.'

Angel's mouth fell open. What should she do now?

Chapter Forty Two

'If I might advise, I would suggest you get your driver in here now,' Pete said smoothly, 'and you and he have a look at the car. We should stay here. They probably aren't still in the car. They could have come over to this hanger to check out the plane. It would be typical of Angel Murphy to do that.'

The Sheik gave him a hard look. His face was creased with angry frowns. 'I don't entirely trust you, Pete, or your woman friend. I should warn you that even though these mechanics don't work for me, I have warned them to be on the look out for anyone trying to steal my valuables – particularly my briefcase – and they will not allow you to enter the plane or to steal it. They are honest men. Are you armed?'

'Our guns were stolen from us when we were evicted from the car,' the woman said. Not happily.

'In that case, it will be safe to leave you here. Michal! Fetch Antoni, at once.'

The other mechanic – not Magda's classmate Jan – climbed down from the plane and trotted off obediently, and a few minutes afterwards reappeared with Antoni striding behind him.

'Antoni, I want you to come with me,' the Sheik said. 'Michal, you get back to your work.'

With a final glance of warning at his business colleagues, he took Antoni and went out by the door of the hanger to find the car. What he intended to do if he found the two girls there armed with the guns they had taken from Pete and the woman Angel wasn't sure. Clearly he hadn't thought out his plans sufficiently.

When Josh got Angel's second message, he was already in his car, heading for the Hawthornes' house.

It came as no shock to him to hear that Pete Gillespie was part of the people trafficking gang, and, moreover, very high up in it. Szczepan Kowalski had given them that information as they continued to question him.

He was interested to hear that the meeting with the Middle Eastern client was to take place at Eastern Airfield. He knew the airfield in question, and realised that he had passed the turn off to it in his headlong rush to reach Angel at the Hawthornes' house, which was where he thought she was. Until the second message came.

The best thing would be to head straight for the airfield and meet Angel and Magda there. Meanwhile, however, he pulled in and took the necessary time to ring Inspector Buczek.

'Joe? Another message from Angel. You'll need to get a strong team together and go straight to Eastern Airfield. If you get there in time you should be able to arrest the client from the Middle East. I'm on my way there now. Hope to see you there quickly.'

Joe's response was satisfactory. Josh rang off with every expectation that Inspector Buczek with a sufficiently strong team would reach the airfield not to long behind him.

When the Sheik and Antoni had gone out to find the two girls, or at least their car, the woman turned towards Pete.

'Okay,' she said in her harsh guttural voice. 'We may not have guns, but I have a knife in my ankle sheath. Let's move fast. I'll deal with the mechanics, you grab the loot, and we'll get out fast to the Sheik's car. We can't risk him not finding the girls and refusing to pay. Or trying to cut down the amount because it's two instead of six. Get moving.'

'Not just now,' Angel said. She and Magda, guns in their hands, emerged swiftly from their cover behind the piles of equipment and rubbish. She came over – not too close – to the man and woman, and showed them the gun, aiming it at the woman's central mass, while Magda willingly pointed her own gun at Pete's stomach.

The woman said nothing. Pete let out a groan, and said, 'I might have known.'

'Throw down that knife,' Angel said. 'Quick, if you want to survive this.'

The knife clattered across the floor of the hanger.

'Now,' Angel said, 'Sit down over there.' She pointed across to the back of the hanger, not too near the piles of stuff, for she didn't want to run the risk of them finding something to rub the rope against and free themselves. And not too far into the darkness. She wanted to be able to see what they were doing. But well out of the line of sight of anyone coming in through the hanger door.

'Magda is going to tie you up, while I point both these sweet little guns at you. I'm a good shot, so don't take any risks. Magda, I'm sure you'll find lots of rope around in these piles of equipment.'

'Yeah, I can see a coil of it from here. The knife will come in handy for cutting it to the right lengths.' Magda handed over her gun to Angel. Angel stood pointing one gun at each of the crooks, and Magda went to work tying them up, careful not to get between Angel and her gun and the two crooks.

'Take the woman first.' Angel continued to point the guns. 'You needn't shout for help,' she advised their prisoners. 'These mechanics are honest men, as your friend the Sheik pointed out, and all we'd have to do to get them on our side would be to tell them just what you and your gang have been up to. One of them is a friend of Magda's, what's more, so he'd certainly believe us.'

'Do you think we should gag them?' Magda suggested. She had finished with the woman and moved on to Pete Gillespie. 'I think this is tight enough.'

'No, no gags yet. I want to hear what this woman has got to say. We've heard enough from her already, but there's much more to come.'

'We don't want them shouting to warn the Sheik when he comes back,' Magda objected.

'True. Well, we'll try to get the gags tied before he comes. You can gag Pete now. I've heard all I want to from him.'

'I should think so, the slimy, deceitful pig.' Magda shoved a handful of cotton pieces into Pete's mouth, and tied it in place. Then she walked over to Angel and retrieved her gun.

'What I think you should do now, Magda,' Angel said, 'is to climb up into the plane and explain the situation to your old friend Jan, and to the other man, Michal, wasn't it? I think we should be sure our flanks are covered, as the generals say.'

'Good idea.'

Magda climbed into the plane, and Angel could hear the shouts of surprise. They sounded pleased. Then Magda's voice, speaking at some length. She heard what seemed to be exclamations of outrage, and someone cursing in Polish – or so Angel assumed from the tone of voice. Then Magda laughing.

A few moments later, Magda climbed back down.

'No problem,' she told Angel, smiling in amusement. 'I don't think I'll tell you what Jan said he would like to do to these two people, or you will think my countrymen are barbarians! But it's clear that we can rely on them completely.'

The horrified expressions on the faces of both Pete and his companion made Angel, in her turn, burst out laughing. 'I think we won't let them loose on these guys just yet, but you might keep it in mind, both of you, that we can if we choose to. So if you're thinking of any clever tricks, think again, right?'

'Jan suggested that we should let him and Michal haul them up into the plane where they can look after them. I think he was really looking forward to the opportunity. But I said you wanted to question them first.'

'Good. Yes, so I do.'

Angel went over towards the prisoners, and leaned against the nearest bench in a relaxed, casual manner.

'Well, let's get on with it,' she said. 'You've done a good job of keeping your identity a secret, *Top Cat*,' she said. 'But there have been a few little slips and indications. Especially your voice.

Oh, you did a fine job of disguising it, but every now and then you reverted to normal, or nearly so. I knew you were someone whose voice I should recognise, but it wasn't until I heard you talking to the Sheik – not knowing I was listening, and not needing to keep your voice so hoarse and guttural – that I really knew.'

She leaned over and twitched the scarf from the woman's face. 'I think it's about time we had this scarf off and the hat as well, Lucinda,' she said, pulling off the woolly hat.

Chapter Forty Three

Magda stared in amazement as the lovely face and curly red hair of Lucinda Hawthorne emerged from the effective, disfiguring disguise she had worn. She looked as beautiful as ever. Only the expression on her face, the mouth twisted and the eyes gleaming fiercely with hatred, showed that this was the same person Magda had seen shoot her own husband and kidnap two people at gunpoint.

'A bit of explaining is due, Lucinda,' said Angel. 'Why did you shoot your husband?'

'Haven't you worked that out yet?' Lucinda asked contemptuously. 'I'd set him up as the fall guy. Told you a string of lies about him, even told you that the computer I let you look at was his, not mine. But I thought you were getting too close to the truth. It seems I was wrong there – you hadn't a clue it was me who was running the trafficking. I thought it was time to get rid of him before he started talking to you, telling you things that would contradict the lies I told you.

'For instance he might have told you I'd been over to Poland regularly and kept a car here. My mistake. And I put in a red herring, an imaginary woman called Aleksandra. There's no such person, actually.'

Angel stared at her. She found it hard to believe that any woman could have treated her husband like that, as a useful tool to be discarded when his usefulness ceased.

'And I suppose it was you who shot those people in Belfast? Your own men? Why did you do that?'

'No. I didn't shoot Jackson. I shot Jason and Bobby because I thought they had killed him. He was my lover, in case you want to know. It was him I was crying for when you broke into my house and found me there in tears. A weak way to behave, but I really loved him.' She bit her lip, and for a moment the fierceness left her face, to be replaced by a look of tremulous grief.

Magda coughed. 'Angel.'

'Yeah?'

'I tried to tell you this before, but I couldn't bring myself to. It's time I came clean. It was me who shot Jackson Morrison.'

'What!'

'Yes.' Magda forced herself to go on. 'He was about to rape me. I'd pinched Slimey's gun, and for the first time I was able to protect myself – and the other girls. So when he started to take hold of me I shot him, and ran.'

'I can't blame you for that, Magda,' Angel said.

'I told the other girls to come away while we could. I threatened Brutus – the other guard – and he could see that I meant it. When the girls and I ran, he bolted too, in the other direction.'

'You –! You –!' Lucinda spluttered unable to produce the right words at first. 'You killed Jackson! If I'd known that when I had my hands on you! I'd have – I'd have –!' She broke into a stream of curses.

'Stop that!' Angel ordered. 'Do you want me to shoot you right now?'

Apparently Lucinda didn't. She was silent.

'What I don't understand,' said Angel presently, 'is why you sent me and Magda out here. Even paying for our expenses, fares and hotel and stuff. Weren't you worried we might find out too much?'

'I was a fool. I thought you were not very bright young girls who wouldn't have a clue what was going on, but I also thought you'd be better over here out of my way than in Belfast, where you'd managed to ruin the local end of the business. More by luck than by judgment, I thought. I also thought Szczepan could take care of you easily. But just in case, I sent Shorty and Shuggie out after you to give Szczepan a hand if he needed it.'

'The three bears,' Angel put in. 'But Goldilocks ate all their porridge.'

Lucinda glared at her, but shrugged it off and went on talking. 'And the next thing I knew, you'd wrecked half my business and had most of my team arrested, and were starting to suspect Pete Gillespie! How on earth did you get onto Pete?'

'That was Magda,' Angel said. 'She'd seen him with Szczepan when she was being persuaded to come over to Belfast. But you're wrong if you think we suspected him. We'd decided he had nothing to do with it until he jumped out with a gun when we reached your house.'

'Another mistake,' Lucinda said. 'On the other hand, he needed to get me free. He should have hidden his face like I did.'

Angel was starting to wonder why Lucinda was talking so freely. Was she trying to gain time until the Sheik came back? Probably.

'All right,' she said briskly. 'Time you guys were safely stowed away in the plane. Magda, give Jan and Michal a shout.'

But before Magda could obey, they heard footsteps at the door.

'Quick. Stand on the left side of the doorway, out of sight. I'll be on the right. Lucinda, if you warn the Sheik, I'll shoot you. As I told you before, I'm a good shot.'

She darted to the right side of the doorway and stood there, gun aimed at Lucinda. Magda, moving equally quickly, took up her position on the left side.

The footsteps drew nearer. The door was pushed further open, and the Sheik came in, complaining loudly.

'No sign of them near the car. I left –' He stopped speaking as he caught sight of the two prisoners at the back of the hanger. 'What –? '

Almost before he had ceased speaking, Angel stepped forward and put the gun to his neck under his left ear. The Sheik jumped convulsively, then froze.

'Walk forward,' Angel commanded him. 'Keep your hands where I can see them, above your head. I want you all together, easy to cover, you understand?'

She pushed the gun against his neck and he began to move forward towards the prisoners on the floor. Angel followed. 'Magda, aim at Lucinda, since I'm busy with the Sheik.'

Magda moved forward after her.

'Wait, Magda!' said Angel sharply. 'Stay in your position. Don't forget Antoni is still out there. He may come after his boss any minute.'

As Magda began to retreat towards her post at the door, they heard a slight sound and saw a movement.

It was Antoni. Tired of looking for the girls with no clue as to where they might be, he had decided to follow the Sheik.

'Magda! Look out!' Angel shouted.

Too late.

Antoni slipped through the doorway and seized Magda from the rear. One hand knocked her gun to the ground. The other arm was twisted round her neck, making her helpless.

'Do you want me to break her neck?' Antoni asked in a soft, reasonable sounding voice. 'If you don't, drop that gun.'

Chapter Forty Four

Josh, driving furiously in spite of the snow, reached the airfield while Angel was still recording the Sheik's conversation with Lucinda and Pete.

Instead of driving into the airfield as Angel had done, he parked outside and well away from the lights, off the road behind some bushes. Getting out of the car, he made his way cautiously across the wide space on the near side of the runway, gun in hand.

He could see the two hangers, and the lights shining from one of them. Circling silently round the buildings, his footsteps muffled by the snow, he spotted the Mercedes parked where Angel had put it at the back, out of sight, and remembered that she had hijacked the car from Pete and his boss lady and was no longer driving the small hired vehicle.

He also found, not far away, the car which had brought the Sheik and later the two crooks, and identified it as the type of flashy car a wealthy Middle Eastern client might well use.

It was time to find a way into the building without being seen. He began to scout cautiously for such a way.

Inside the hanger, Angel's response to Antoni's threat to break Magda's neck was not what he had wanted.

Instead of dropping the gun, Angel lowered it. It was now pointing at the floor.

'Drop it, I said!' Antoni barked, his voice suddenly sharp and frightening.

Angel took only a second to consider. Surely Josh would be here soon. And there were the two guys in the plane, Magda's friends.

She dropped the gun, and saw Antoni's arm relax unintentionally. Very slightly. Enough to allow Magda to speak?

She tested it.

'Magda, are you okay?'

'Yes.'

But as Magda spoke, Angel saw Antoni's arm tighten again. No way Magda could call her friends. But they understood English. They had understood the Sheik earlier when he had spoken to them. It didn't have to be the Polish-speaking Magda who called them.

She opened her mouth, took a deep breath, and was about to let it out in a loud shout when she saw something out of the corner of her eye. She paused. Someone was moving in the piles of rubbish and tools at the back of the hanger, Angel felt sure. It had to be Josh.

'What do you want?' she asked Antoni. 'I've dropped the gun. What now?'

'Kick it over to my boss.'

That would not be a good move. She knew why Antoni had ordered it. He wanted the gun moved to a safe distance. If the Sheik came forward to pick it up in its present position, he would be between Angel and Antoni, and Antoni would be unable to see what she did. There would be every chance for her to grab the Sheik and hold him as a rival hostage for Magda's release. The Sheik was fat and flabby. Angel had no doubt of her ability to take hold of him and keep him as much her prisoner as Magda was Antoni's. Then they could trade, perhaps. Antoni also was in no doubt that she could do this. He didn't intend to risk it.

Meanwhile Josh – if it was Josh – could pick his moment for attack, if she had the Sheik.

'Suppose it goes off when I kick it?'

'Why should it go off? Okay, pick it up instead – by the barrel! – and bring it over to him.'

Angel bent down and started to pick up the gun. The Sheik, not understanding the risk as clearly as his driver had done, moved forward eagerly to take it from her.

Judging her moment, Angel waited until he was at the right distance. Antoni came forward.

'No, boss, you stay well back,' he said anxiously. Once again the arm round Magda's neck slackened.

This time Magda didn't waste her opportunity.

'Jan! Michel!' she shouted, loudly enough to be heard clearly inside the plane.

Three things happened at once.

The Sheik turned his head in alarm to see what the shout was for, and Angel's foot shot out and caught him under the chin. He collapsed helplessly on the ground, a bundle of unconscious flab. Antoni, throwing caution to the winds, rushed forward to try for Angel's gun.

Two hefty Polish mechanics came leaping down from the plane and looked round them to see what they should be doing.

And Josh, picking his moment perfectly, hurled himself out from behind the equipment benches and jumped on Antoni's back, wrapping his arms round him ferociously, squeezing the breath out of him.

'Josh!' Angel cried out. 'Oh, thank goodness!'

'Magda, are you okay?' Jan called over to her in Polish.

Magda grinned at her would be rescuers. 'Fine now, guys,' she answered, also in Polish. 'You jumped in just at the right moment.'

'Josh, we have video on my camera of these crooks talking which should be enough to put them away for any number of years,' Angel said, breathlessly. For Josh, handing over Antoni to Jan and Michel, was enveloping her in an equally breathtaking hug.

'Good,' he said. 'You can tell me all about it later. Right now, the plan is to arrest these villains and get them out of here. And we can get back to civilisation.'

He turned towards the door of the hanger. 'Joe!' he called. 'Are you and the boys there? Come and collect these people. They're all yours.'

The Inspector and a dozen or so of his men hustled in from the airfield where they had just arrived, ten minutes later than Josh, who had not been prepared to wait for him or anyone else.

'Great job, Angel. And you, too, Magda,' he greeted them, before beginning to start his men on the process of cuffing the Sheik and Antoni, and pulling Pete and Lucinda to their feet.

Five minutes later, the hanger was empty, except for Magda, Jan and Michel, chattering together in one corner while they asked questions and she answered. In a few moments they climbed up into the plane.

And Angel and Josh – in another corner – were interested in no one but each other.

'Now, honey,' Josh said, as he at last released her from a *Guinness Book of Records*-breaking kiss, 'Now, honey. Now that I've got you to myself at last, I believe you and I have things to discuss.'

'No discussion necessary, Josh,' Angel told him. 'That question you were asking me? Well, the answer is yes. Yes, yes, yes!'

About the author

Gerry McCullough has been writing poems and stories since childhood. Brought up in north Belfast, she graduated in English and Philosophy from Queen's University, Belfast, then went on to gain an MA in English.

She lives in Northern Ireland – in a converted stone-built cottage in the heart of Co. Down – has four grown up children and is married to author, media producer and broadcaster, Raymond McCullough, with whom she co-edited the Irish magazine, *Bread*, from 1990-96. In 1995 they also published a non-fiction book called, *Ireland – now the good news!*

Over the past few years Gerry has had more than one hundred and thirty short stories published in UK, Irish and American magazines, anthologies and annuals – as well as broadcast on *BBC Radio Ulster* – plus poems and articles published in several Northern Ireland and UK magazines. She has also read from her novels, poems and short stories at many Irish literary events.

Gerry won the *Cúirt International Literary Award* for 2005 (Galway); was shortlisted for the 2008 *Brian Moore Award* (Belfast); short-listed for the 2009 *Cúirt Award*; commended in the 2009 *Seán O'Faolain Short Story Competition*, (Cork) and shortlisted in the 2015 *Harmony House Poetry Competition*, Downpatrick. In 2016 she also won the *Bangor Poetry Award* for her poem, *Summer Passing*.

Gerry currently has a total of nineteen books in publication –

Stand alone romantic suspense novels (4):

- *Belfast Girls* (November 2010, re-issued July 2012)
- *Danger Danger* (October 2011)
- *Johnny McClintock's War* (August 2014)

- *Roundabout* (July 2020)

The Angel Murphy thriller series (3):

- *Angel in Flight* (June 2012)
- *Angel in Belfast* (June 2013)
- *Angel in Paradise* (January 2017)
- Angel on Guard (October 2023)

The Hel's Heroes romantic comedy series (2):

- *Hel's Heroes: a romantic comedy* (June 2015)
- *Hel's Heroes 2: Christie and the Pirate* (March 2019)

Short story collections (7):

- *The Seanachie: Tales of Old Seamus* (January 2012)
- *The Seanachie 2: Norah on the Beach & other stories* (September 2014)
- *The Seanachie 3: Seamus and the Shell & other stories* (August 2016)
- *The Seanachie 4: Paddy and the Snake & other stories* (June 2019)
- *The Seanachie 5: Seamus Makes a Mistake & other stories* (November 2021)
- *The Seanachie 6: In the Bluebell Wood & other stories* (September 2023)
- *Dreams, Visions, Nightmares* – a collection of eight literary and award-winning Irish short stories (January 2016)

Fantasy novels (2):

- *Not the End of the World* – a comic, futuristic fantasy novel (February 2016)
- *Lady Molly and the Snapper* – a young adult novel, time travel adventure set in Dublin and the open sea (August 2012)

Belfast Girls

The story of three girls – Sheila, Phil and Mary – growing up into the new emerging post-conflict Belfast of money, drugs, high fashion and crime; and of their lives and loves.

Sheila, a supermodel, is kidnapped.

Phil is sent to prison.

Mary, surviving a drug overdose, has a spiritual awakening.

It is also the story of the men who matter to them:–

John Branagh, former candidate for the priesthood, a modern Darcy, someone to love or hate. Will he and Sheila ever get together?

Davy Hagan, drug dealer, *'mad, bad and dangerous to know'*. Is Phil also mad to have anything to do with him?

Although from different religious backgrounds, starting off as childhood friends, the girls manage to hold on to that friendship in spite of everything.

A book about contemporary Ireland and modern life. A book which both men and women can enjoy – thriller, romance, comedy, drama – and much more ...

"fascinating ... original ... multilayered ... expertly travels from one genre to the next"

Kellie Chambers, Ulster Tatler (*Book of the Month*)

"romance at the core ... enriched with breathtaking action, mystery, suspense and some tear-jerking moments of tragedy.

Sheila M. Belshaw, author

"What starts out as a crime thriller quickly evolves into a literary festival beyond the boundary of genres"

PD Allen, author

"a masterclass, and a vivid dissection of the human condition in all of its inglorious foibles"

WeeScottishLassie

Danger Danger

From the author of **Belfast Girls**

Gerry McCullough

Two lives in parallel – twin sisters separated at birth, but their lives take strangely similar and dangerous roads until the final collision which hurls each of them to the edge of disaster.

Katie and her gambling boyfriend Dec find themselves threatened with peril from the people Dec has cheated.

Jo-Anne (Annie) through her boyfriend Steven finds herself in the hands of much more dangerous crooks.

Can they survive and achieve safety and happiness?

Angel in Flight:

the first Angel Murphy thriller

Is it a bird? Is it a plane? No, it's a low-flying Angel!

You've heard of Lara Croft. You've heard of Modesty Blaise. Well, here comes Angel Murphy!

Angel, a *'feisty wee Belfast girl'* on holiday in Greece, sorts out a villain who wants to make millions for his pharmaceutical company by preventing the use of a newly discovered malaria vaccine.

Angel has a broken marriage behind her and is wary of men, but perhaps her meeting with Josh Smith, who tells her he's with Interpol, may change her mind?

Fun, action, thrills, romance in a beautiful setting – so much to enjoy!

"it's a fast-paced read, ... exciting, and you can not put this book down"
Thomas Baker, Santiago, Chile

"I could not stop reading! ... a gripping thriller from beginning to the end"
SanMarie Lamprecht

"a fast-paced, exciting read. From the moment I read the first line, I was hooked"
Cheryl Bradshaw, author, Wyoming, USA

"a sassy bigger then life heroine in an action packed adventure thriller in Greece"
Book Review Buzz

Johnny McClintock's War:

One man's struggle against the hammer blows of life

The story of one man's struggle to maintain his faith in spite of everything life throws at him.

As the outbreak of the First World War looms closer, John Henry McClintock, a Northern Irish Protestant by upbringing, meets Rose Flanagan, a Catholic, at a gospel tent mission – and falls in love with her.

When Johnny enlists and sets off to fight in the War he finds himself surrounded by death and tragedy, which pushes his trust in God to the limit.

After more than five years absence he returns home to a bitter, war torn Ireland, where both he and Rose are seen as traitors to their own sides.

John Henry and Rose overcome all opposition and, finally, marry. But a few years later comes the hardest blow of all. Can John Henry still hang on to his faith in God?

"brilliant .. this book had me captured from the start ..
moves at a fair pace throughout"
Tom Elder, *Amazon.com*

"characters you will truly care about ..

a gut-wrenching emotional ride .. a must read"

Tom Winton, author, USA

"Gerry McCullough's best book yet ..
a powerful tribute to those who died for their countries and what they believed"
Juliet B Madison, author, UK

"an emotional roller coaster ride .. an epiphany .. highly recommended
.. a book that will make you think about how wonderful life truly is"
Thomas Baker, Amazon.com, Santiago, Chile

"will hold you spellbound until the very last sentence
.. I love this book"
Sheila Mary Belshaw, author, UK, Menorca, Cape Town

Johnny McClintock's War

*One man's struggle against
the hammer blows of life*

Gerry McCullough

Published by

Precious Oil
PUBLICATIONS
www.preciousoil.com/publications

Chapter One

John Henry McClintock met Rose Flanagan when she was sixteen, and he a year or so older.

They met at a tent mission, which is a gospel meeting in a large tent. It was in a field miles from anywhere, in County Down, in the depths of Ireland.

It was a soft, warm summer night. Music poured from the lighted tent as John Henry drew nearer to it. He was one of a large crowd of people, stepping cautiously through the long grass at the field's edge – soon to be trampled flat by the hordes of visitors – and trying, not always success-fully, to avoid the still wet sticky cow pats laid down that day, and the big purple thistles which grew everywhere.

The huge dirty beige tent, which looked dull by daylight but now, in the gathering darkness, shone out as a bright focus of warmth and good fellowship, had no ribbons or other decorations. There was only a card-board placard set up at the entrance giving the times and the dates of other meetings, in bright red against a whitey-yellow background, with the name of the speaker in a bold dark green. There was a similar placard attached to the gate at the entrance to the field, where a blossoming hawthorn hedge spread its white, sweet-smelling flowers close enough almost, but not quite, to obliterate the writing.

John Henry hadn't seen Rose yet. He had gone along to the tent with friends of his own age, just as she had done a few minutes earlier. A tent mission was one of the free entertainments on offer in Ireland, in these days just before the First World War. You could be sure of meeting a large crowd of young people, who would seldom be gathered together in one place otherwise.

1

They pushed into the tent, nudging each other and whispering.

'There's Annie Kilpatrick! She's a whizzer!'

'Get off my toe, you great lump!'

'Aw – sorry, Tommy! Hey, there's Sadie Wilson with Geordie Milligan! Didn't know they were walking out!'

'Pity – she's a lovely girl!'

John Henry listened in amusement, but didn't contribute much. He liked his friends, Tommy, Willie and wee Artie, but he sometimes wondered how much he had in common with them. They had all left school early and had shown no reluctance to do so. John Henry himself had done the same, but not by his own choice.

When John Henry had left school at the age of fourteen, a few years before, it had been at his father's insistence, in spite of his evident ability. And in spite of the desire of his teacher that he should stay on, even try for teacher training eventually (the idea of university an impossible dream in the minds of most).

The master of the local Church of Ireland school in the village, Michael Patrick Fyfe, was a descendent of the French Huguenots who had come to those parts a couple of centuries ago, driven out from their homeland by persecution, and had brought their linen making skills with them. Fyfe was a clever man who deserved to be doing more than teaching in a village school. He felt this particularly when a pupil who should have achieved much more was forced to leave by his family's desire that he should go out and earn his living.

In John Henry's case he had felt it so strongly that he'd called round with the boy's father to make his protest.

Fyfe rehearsed in his mind what he would say as he knocked on the door of the three storied house beside the church grounds. He could see that the house had once been an impressive building. Tall, built in grey stone, it was covered nearly up to its second story in sweet smelling rambling roses. And the garden spread around it on all sides, neglected and overgrown with nettles and thistles now, had clearly at one time been a pleasure to see. The owners had obviously gone downhill, and the house with them. He knew that Douglas McClintock, John Henry's father, was a widower, and had heard that he drank. Maybe that was where the money for house repairs went to.

Fyfe, who was a small, thin man, still young and unsure of himself, wondered again if he was doing the right thing. Would his intervention make any difference? He took in the scent of the pink roses growing beside the door as he waited apprehensively, listening for the sound of approaching footsteps inside.

The door opened at last in response to his repeated knocks, and a tall dark haired man with a craggy face peered out at him.

'Mr McClintock?' Fyfe said nervously. 'I'm Michael Fyfe, the village school-master. I'd like a word with you about your son John Henry.'

'What's the wee skitter been up to now?' roared McClintock. He made no effort to open the door wider or to invite Michael in.

'No, no, it's not that he's in any trouble,' the schoolmaster said hastily. 'Far from it. He's a first rate scholar. That's why I'd like to suggest that you allow him to stay on for another year or two and eventually take his teaching certificate. I know you've said you want him to leave at the end of the school year, next month, but I really think it'd be a crying shame. A waste of the boy's ability. He could do so much more with his life.'

McClintock's face, which had been growing red with anger as he listened to his visitor, began to swell up alarmingly. Fyfe noticed in apprehension that he carried a strong blackthorn stick in his right hand. As he stopped leaning on this stick and raised it threateningly, Fyfe took a hasty step back. McClintock advanced on him.

'I'll be the one who says what my son should do with his life!' McClintock roared. He pushed his red swollen face so close to Fyfe that the schoolmaster could smell his rotten breath, an unpleasant reek of onions and alcohol. 'Don't come round here again telling me what to do with my own! I say it's time the lad got out and earned his living, and that's the end of it!'

The young schoolmaster jumped back out of reach of the blackthorn stick, just managing not to trip over the crumbling front doorstep, and the heavy wooden door slammed in his face. He tottered away down the village street, thankful to have escaped unmolested. He was very sorry for John Henry. But he was quite clear that there was nothing more he could do for him.

So John Henry had taken a low-skilled, and low paid, job in a linen factory, and was now contributing to the family income, like his older brother and sister, and helping to support his younger sister. To his father's great satisfaction.

John Henry was philosophical about it, but he wanted quite fiercely to get out of the linen factory, to do something that mattered with his life. He knew his abilities – his quickness to learn and to understand. He had been top of his class by a mile every year since he first started in the small local school. He wanted to make use of the intelligence he had been given.

Rose Flanagan was also working, as nearly everybody of their age and social class was; helping, mainly in the kitchen, at a nearby farm, fortunate in that she had been able to find work near her home and could return to her father's cottage most nights.

She'd got the job through the good offices of her parish priest, Father Donnelly, who knew her father well and who still thought of Rose as a sweet, innocent child, one he was glad to help. Her new employers, the Reillys, owned a small farm and were currently looking for more assistance, since their former kitchen girl had moved away to the other side of County Down when she married recently. By recommending Rose, Father Donnelly knew he was helping the Reillys, also parishioners of his, as well as helping Rose's father who could do with the extra income Rose would bring in. And, of course, he was earning the gratitude of the pretty wee girl herself. All good, Father Donnelly told himself.

'You'll work hard for these good people, won't you, my dear?' he said to Rose, giving her a toothy smile.

Chapter 1

'Oh, certainly, Father,' Rose answered. She wished Father Donnelly would stop stroking her arm. However, her father was there, so it was safe enough. Rose wouldn't have liked to be on her own with Father Donnelly. She'd heard stories.

Annie Reilly was a kind, motherly woman, and although the work was hard, Rose enjoyed it well enough. She was used to working hard. Her mother had been a bit of an invalid in the years before she died, and since her death Rose had carried the burden of the household work at home. The work at the Reillys' farm wasn't much worse.

It was her friend Mary McCartney who'd suggested going to the tent meeting.

'There'll be lots of talent, Rose. I heard Frankie Murphy and his pals are going. They think it'll be a laugh, see? I really fancy Frankie, Rose! And you know rightly that his pal Peter O'Rouke fancies you, girl! Peter was asking me if you and me might be going. Let's tell them we'll join in and go with them!'

'I don't think we should go just for a laugh, Mary. And what if we get into trouble? They might not like people from our church going.'

'Not at all! The poster says, "All Welcome!" So they want us, see?'

'I think it might be interesting, Rose,' put in Maggie Kilmore. 'I've never been to a Protestant meeting. I'd like to know what they say that's so different. And I heard the preacher was a Jesuit before he left it. I was wondering if he'd tell us why he left. That would be interesting, too.'

And Peggy McCracken, a schoolmate of Rose's since early childhood, had also been eager to go, and said, shaking back her red hair, 'Ach, come on, Rose! It won't be any fun without you!'

'Oh, all right, then,' Rose agreed at last. But not without a lingering worry.

The girls met up with Frankie Murphy and a few other boys by arrangement at the field gate, and made their way across the rough grass, avoiding the cow pats and the stinging nettles until they reached the tent door.

They and the boys went in together, greeted at the flapping door-way of the tent by a beaming, friendly man, with a red, wrinkled face, who had lost most of his hair. This man was holding out sheets with the words of the choruses, and the huge crowd had already begun to sing, as a warm-up to the meeting proper.

A group of boys whom Rose had never seen before were entering at the same time as Rose and her friends. As the two groups stood near to each other at the door of the tent, taking the sheets in turn from the friendly man, John Henry and Rose each noticed the other. Rose saw a tall, well built boy with dark hair falling over his pale face, and a sweet smile which switched on, as if instinctively, as he caught her eye.

John Henry saw a small, slim, and very pretty girl, with light brown hair, blue grey eyes, and a perfect complexion. Roses and cream, he thought, thinking of one of his favourite songs, *The Mountains of Mourne*. There was a bright intelligence in her eye as she glanced in his direction which attracted him even more than her looks. They were strangers, but through the mind of each went the fleeting thought, *Perhaps – not for long?*

Chapter Two

They went on in, and found places with their own friends, in different parts of the tent.

'This is daft, Johnny!' hissed John Henry's closest friend Tommy Maguire. Tommy was tall for his age with an attractive boyish face, smooth sandy hair and very bright blue eyes. He never had any problem getting off with girls. 'What the heck are we doing here?'

'Well, it wasn't my idea!' said Willie Morgan on Tommy's other side. His freckled face was one large grin at the idea, as he wriggled his fat, overweight body in the hard seat, trying to get more comfortable.

'Or mine!' retorted John Henry.

'It must have been yours, then, Artie!' said Tommy, nudging the small, dark haired boy beside him. Artie, the usual butt of the group, flushed bright red.

'I just thought it might be fun, Tommy!' he protested. ' See, just look round you. What about that for talent?'

Tommy looked round. Yeah, there were lots of girls, some of them quite pretty.

'Got a point there, Artie,' he admitted grudgingly, sweeping his hand back over his smooth, sandy coloured hair, as always held down by hair pomade. 'Not a bad idea, old man.'

Artie flushed again, but this time in delight at being praised by Tommy and addressed as 'old man'. The youngest of the group, he was constantly running to catch up with the others, and trying hard to seem as sophisticated as his idol Tommy.

Gradually the singing drew to a close, and the meeting opened.

The speaker was a gifted orator.

'Friends,' he began, in a soft, gentle voice, 'you all know that there's someone out there. Someone who made you. Someone who loves you.'

A collective sigh went round the tent. John Henry stirred uncomfortably. He didn't much want to be moved by this man, to respond. He was only here for a bit of fun, for company.

The speaker went on, 'Yes, friends, it was St Patrick who first opened our eyes, as Irishmen and women, to the presence of God in all nature. But St Paul said it before him, and David said it in his psalms, the songs he wrote from his shepherd's heart, "The Heavens declare the glory of God!" '

The speaker's voice grew louder, more emphatic. John Henry's attention wandered.

For a few moments he was back in his very early teens, experiencing again the wonder of the beauty of the earth in springtime. The freshness of early morning. The pink and white of the apple blossom all around. The still nights. The feeling of something – something. A presence that was trying to speak to him – which he longed, but was afraid, to listen to.

When he came back to the here and now, the speaker was quoting the Irish poet Joseph Plunkett, the young Christian Brother who had recently joined the republican movement.

> *'I see his blood upon the rose*
> *And in the stars the glory of his eyes.*
> *His body gleams amid eternal snows,*
> *His tears fall from the skies.*
>
> *I see his face in every flower;*
> *The thunder and the singing of the birds*
> *Are but his voice – and carven by his power*
> *Rocks are his written words.'*

The speaker dropped his voice, which had been soaring to the skies a moment before, and went on, speaking quietly.

> *'All pathways by his feet are worn,*
> *His strong heart stirs the ever-beating sea.*
> *His crown of thorns is twined with every thorn.*
> *His cross is every tree.'*

Something caught at John Henry's heart, stirring and exalting him. He no longer wanted to resist; to fight whatever it was that was drawing him, reaching out to take him captive.

The speaker went on. He was quoting from the Bible now, referring with all his eloquence to the death of Christ, to the need for surrender to him. All at once, John Henry knew what he was going to do.

In another part of the tent, tears streamed down Rose's face as she listened with her whole heart to the speaker's emotional words. She was miles away from that place, wandering in a bright garden, hand in hand with someone who loved her so much. The pain and the joy were intermixed to an unbearable extent. The need for action, for response, overwhelmed her.

The speaker, dropping his voice to its initial softness, drew to the end of his message.

For a moment there was silence.

Then came the final prayer, and the appeal.

At its close, when the speaker called for people to come forward, as a sign that they wanted to give their lives to the Lord, Rose Flanagan stood up and walked to the front.

While she was waiting afterwards for her turn to pray with one of the counsellors, she noticed someone standing next to her, also waiting. It was the young man she remembered seeing as she came into the tent before the meeting started. It was John Henry McClintock, although as yet she didn't know his name.

Coming out of the tent, John Henry spoke to her. 'Marvellous evening, isn't it?'

'Yes, it's lovely,' Rose agreed. The clear starry night of early May, with its dark navy blue sky studded with distant silver stones, was very beautiful.

'Come from round these parts?'

'Dromore,' she said. This was a village some five or six miles away.

'A fair distance,' said John Henry. 'If you'd like some company for the walk home, I'd be glad to go along with you.'

Rose had plenty of friends who had come with her and would have kept her company on the way back.

But for all that, she accepted the offer.

Over the next months, they saw each other regularly. John Henry made a point on the first Sunday of going to the church that had organised the tent mission where they had met. But he found that Rose, like himself, didn't belong there, and had come only for the mission. The following week, having found out which was Rose's own church, he went there.

It was then that he realised that Rose was a Catholic by upbringing.

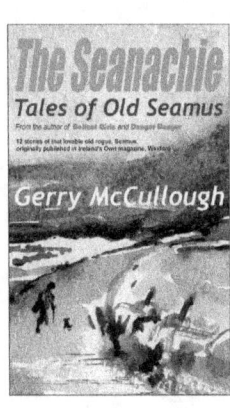

The Seanachie:
Tales of Old Seamus

Gerry McCullough

A humorous series of Irish stories, set in the fictional Donegal village of Ardnakil and featuring that lovable rogue, *'Old Seamus'* – the Séanachie.

All of these stories have previously been published in the popular Irish weekly magazine, *Ireland's Own*, based in Wexford, Ireland.

"heart warming tales ... beautifully told with subtle Irish humour"

Babs Morton (author)

"an irresistible old rogue, but he's the kind people love to sit and listen to for hours on end whenever the opportunity presents itself"

G. Polley (author and blogger – Sapporo, Japan)

"This magnificent storyteller has done it again. Each individual story has it's own Gaelic charm"

Teresa Geering (author – UK)

"evocative characterisation brings these stories to life in a delightful, absorbing way"

Elinor Carlisle (author – Reading, UK)

The Seanachie 2:

Norah on the Beach *and other stories*

Gerry McCullough

Another series of twelve humorous Irish stories, set in the fictional Donegal village of Ardnakil and once again featuring that lovable rogue, *'Old Seamus'* – the Séanachie.

All of these stories have previously been published in the popular Irish weekly magazine, *Ireland's Own*, based in Wexford, Ireland.

"gentle stories laced with Irish humour ...
Like the first collection ... very well written and an effortless read"

Bookworm

"so well written that you find yourself flying through the stories"

Tom Elder

Lady Molly & The Snapper

A young adult time travel adventure, set in Ireland and on the high seas

Gerry McCullough

Brother and sister Jik and Nora are bored and angry. Why does their Dad spend so much time since their mother's death drinking and ignoring them? Why must he come home at all hours and fall downstairs like a fool?

Nora goes to church and lights a candle. The cross-looking sailor saint she particularly likes seems to grow enormous and come to life. Nora is too frightened to stay.

Nora and Jik go down secretly to their father's boat, the *Lady Molly*, at Howth Marina. There they meet The Snapper, the same cross-looking saint in a sailor's cap, who takes them back in time on the yacht, *Lady Molly,* to meet Cuchulain, the legendary Irish warrior, and others.

Jik and Nora plan to use their travels to find some way of stopping their father from drinking – but it's fun, too! Or is it? When they meet the Druid priest who follows them into modern times, teams up with school bully Marty Flanagan, and threatens them, things start getting out of hand.

Meanwhile, Nora is more than interested in Sean, the boy they keep bumping into in the past ...

"the story ... flows in authentic Irish lilt and dialogue, captures the imagination"

Book Review Buzz, USA

"excellent prose to suit the intended audience and has enough antics to keep any young mind turning the page"
J.D., USA

Other (non-fiction) books from

A Wee Taste a' Craic:

All the Irish craic from the popular
Celtic Roots Radio *shows, 2-25*

Raymond McCullough

I absolutely loved this! I found it to be very informative about Irish life culture,
language and traditions.
Elinor Carlisle (author, Reading, UK)

a unique insight into the Northern Irish people
& their self deprecating sense of humour
Strawberry

Ireland – now the <u>good</u> news!

The best of *'Bread'* Vols. 1 & 2 –

personal testimonies and church/fellowship
profiles from around Ireland

Edited by: Raymond & Gerry McCullough

"... fresh Bread – deals with the real issues facing the church in Ireland today"
Ken Newell, minster of Fitzroy Presbyterian Church, Belfast

The Whore and her Mother:

9/11, Babylon and the Return of the King

Raymond McCullough

Could the writings of the ancient Hebrew prophets be relevant to events taking place in the world today?

These Hebrew prophets – Isaiah, Jeremiah, Habbakuk and the apostle John, in *The Revelation* – wrote extensively about a latter day city and empire which would dominate, exploit and corrupt all the nations of the world. They referred to it as Babylon the Great, or Mega-Babylon, and they foretold that its fall – 'in one day' – would devastate the economies of the whole world. Have these prophecies been fulfilled already?

Is Mega-Babylon the Roman Catholic Church?
A world super-church?
Rebuilt ancient Babylon?
Brussels, Jerusalem, or somewhere entirely different?
Should this city/nation have a large Jewish population?
Why all the talk about merchants, cargoes, commodities, trade?
Can we rely on the words of these ancient prophets?
If so, what else did they foretell that is still to be fulfilled?
Do they refer to other major nations – USA, Russia, China, Europe?
What about militant Islam?

"AMAZED when I read this book ... in awe of your extensive knowledge on so many levels: Christian, Jewish, and Muslim culture; the Jewish diaspora ... Greek & Hebrew; ... thought-provoking and troublesome ... many will be offended, but you consistently build your case instead of being sensationalistic."
James Revoir, author of *Priceless Stones*

Oh What Rapture!

Is a *'Secret Rapture'* going to spare believers from the tribulation to come?

Raymond McCullough

Many are convinced that very soon a secret event known as *'The Rapture'* will take place, where bible believers all over the world will suddenly disappear, leaving society at a loss to explain the disappearance of so many. Many non-fiction books, fiction thrillers and movies have capitalised on this theme, earning a fat revenue for their authors/producers.

But is this really what the bible teaches?
Is *'The Rapture'* genuine, or a false hope?
Are those who trust in it being duped, so that they do not get ready for what is coming?
And are they being disobedient to the clear command of the Lord?

Written by the author of Amazon best-selling book, *The Whore and her Mother*, also on the topic of bible prophecy, this volume focusses on the false teaching of a *'secret and separate Rapture'* – an event which is NOT supported by scripture!

This book investigates the scriptures used to back up the *'secret Rapture'* theory and clearly compares them to the other scriptures concerning the return of the Messiah, Jesus (Yeshua). The evident truth is revealed and the origins of the false *'secret Rapture'* doctrine are exposed.

Believers around the world are taught to expect persecution, sometimes even death, for their faith. More have been killed in the past century than in previous centuries combined – in China, Cambodia, Nigeria, Iran, Egypt, Indonesia, Vietnam, etc. Yet many believers in the west confidently expect to avoid any persecution and be *'beamed up'* out of any coming tribulation!

If you thought believers were soon going to be lifted out of a worsening world situation, be prepared to meet the exciting challenge of scripture head on!

More info from: *www.preciousoil.com/publications*